The WOLF PRINCE

Claire M. Banschbach

CAMPITOR
PRESS

ISBN 978-0-9992203-3-7

10 9 8 7 6 5 4 3 2 1

Interior formatting by Rachael Ritchey rachaelritchey.com
Cover by Magpie Designs, Ltd, 2018
magpie-designs.weebly.com
Images courtesy of Pixabay
Textures by Sascha Duensing

Other Books by Claire M. Banschbach

The Rise of Aredor Series
The Rise of Aredor
The Wildcat of Braeton

The Faeries of Myrnius Series
Adela's Curse
The Wolf Prince

To Elinore Rose
Thanks for sitting on the kitchen floor with me and
brainstorming this story.

Prologue

The cool chill of winter crept through the stone halls of Roskalde Castle. Killian pulled his hands further into the overlong sleeves of his tunic, eager to reach the fire in the great hall to finish thawing from the snowball fight. He'd held victory over Lars for a few glorious seconds before his older brother had thrown him into a drift.

His grin faded as the sight of the group of small children about his age clustered around the fire. They sat, entranced, by a young squire standing before the fire.

"It was a winter's night, colder than this one by far, when a witch came knocking at the castle gate." The squire leaned close, and the children's eyes widened.

Killian's feet took him into the shadows of a pillar. He'd heard bits and pieces of the story before. But the young man's face held a smirk that he didn't like.

"She offered to heal the old king's daughter, who was so sick the faeries couldn't even help."

"What 'appened?" A small boy wriggled forward.

The squire held a finger to his lips. "The old king let her in."

Collective gasps rippled through his small audience.

"She healed the girl, but the king refused to pay her as they'd agreed. Instead, he turned her out into the cold and snow."

"That wasn't very nice." A young girl frowned.

"No, it wasn't. The wolves were lean and hungry that year."

Killian curled deeper into the shadow. *Not the wolves again.*

"The witch cursed the king, saying wolf's blood would run through his line until they repaid the debt."

"And?" another boy prompted, leaning forward on his knees.

"And it has. He should have known the dark ways were not to be tampered with. They didn't call old Prince Hugo the Mad Wolf for nothing. He could understand the wolves. He was always going on about it until the king locked him up."

Killian's breath caught in his chest. *Uncle could understand them, too! I thought it was only me...*

"And." The young man's voice reclaimed his attention. "They say Prince Killian is cursed, too."

Killian stumbled a step back, narrowly avoiding a passing servant.

"The wolves howled like crazy the night he was born. He's got the Mad Wolf's curse, you wait and see."

Killian froze. How did the squire know? He'd never told anyone he could understand the wolves. Sometimes he thought he could hear them when no one else could.

"Killi!" A hand descended on his shoulder and jerked him around to stare up into Lars's blue eyes. "What are you doing over here?"

"I—" Killian half-turned back to where the squire had finished. The young man caught sight of him and smirked again. Lars followed his stare and frowned, his cheeks beginning to flush in anger.

Killian slid out of Lars's grip and darted away before his brother could catch him. This time he noticed the glances thrown his way, how a few of the older servants or courtiers edged out of his path with surreptitious signs against evil.

His heart pounded so loud that surely the entire castle could hear it. He turned at a corner to make sure Lars hadn't followed and saw two women standing close together, whispering to one another and glancing his direction.

He forced his feet to a run and didn't stop until he reached the safety of his room. A wolf howled in the distance, bits of words just out of reach of his understanding. Tears pricked his eyes. He hadn't even reached his seventh year yet.

Am I cursed?

He curled under his blankets, stifling tears until a gentle knock sounded. The door clicked open and then closed. The bed tipped under the weight of someone, and the blankets pulled back to reveal his father's bearded features.

"Killian, what are you doing in here? You're missing dinner."

Killian sniffed, scrubbing a sleeve across his eyes. "Am I cursed?"

His father's eyes narrowed in anger. "Who said that?"

Killian shrugged his shoulders. Everyone, apparently.

❧

3

The king sighed, and his shoulders bowed as if under a heavy weight. Killian sat up and scooted closer. His father pulled him into his arms, ruffling his brown hair with a gentle hand.

"Lars said you overheard someone telling that story earlier."

"Is it true?"

"The legend about the witch cursing our line is true. But the part about wolf's blood?" His father's chest rumbled against his ear, but his scorn didn't quite convince Killian.

"What about Uncle Hugo? They said he was mad."

He didn't remember Hugo. His uncle had died in the year following his birth.

"Your uncle's mind became sick. But it wasn't because of some curse."

"Did you lock him up?"

"Me?" His father pulled back to look at him. "No. But my father did. Your grandfather didn't really understand your uncle and didn't do anything to help him."

"Do people think I'll be like him?" Killian blurted, unable to keep the fear a secret.

"You'll learn soon enough how foolish people can be." His father tightened his hold. "But I looked after my brother as best I could, just like an older brother should. And just like the way Lars looks after you. He'll always be there for you."

Killian nodded. Except Lars didn't like anyone talking about wolves.

"Do you hear the wolves, Father?"

The king shook his head. "Killi, I want you to tell me immediately if you think you can hear or understand the wolves."

4

"Yes, sir." Killian said. But his heart clenched at the fear lurking behind his father's stern expression. *No one's ever going to know. Not even Lars. Especially not Lars.*

"Now come on. Dinner's waiting." His father prodded his side. Killian slid away with a laugh and tried to wriggle out of reach.

Their laughter died as two wolves called to each other across the frozen lake beyond the castle walls. Killian hadn't ever minded the sound before, sometimes enjoying trying to figure out what they were saying. But now fear clenched his heart, wrapping around him and threatening to strangle him.

"Can—can I just stay in here? I'm not really hungry."

"You sure?" His father fixed him with a concerned gaze.

Killian nodded, trying not to burrow deeper into the bed to escape the lonely howling.

"All right. I'm sure your mother will be around in a while to check on you." The king ruffled Killian's hair again and stood.

He paused at the door. "Remember what I said, Killian."

"Yes, sir."

Alone once again, Killian hugged his pillow tight. His father's words hadn't done much to ease his mind.

Cursed.

A thread of hope teased his mind. *But all curses are meant to be broken. That's what old Tanja says. Maybe when I'm older I can find a faery. They're supposed to know everything about magic.* He nodded firmly to himself, determined to ignore for the moment that faeries were rarely to be seen, or of very much help to humans.

But no one will know I'm actually cursed. I won't tell anyone. And I won't go mad. They won't ever know.

Chapter 1

"Killian!"

He ignored the summons, but footsteps announced he'd been found anyway. The wall of the castle and the tower joined together in the northeast corner. The wide battlements afforded a seat to anyone brave enough to perch atop the dizzyingly high wall and lean against the tower behind them.

"Finally! I've been looking all over for you!" Lars pretended to shove him off the wall and Killian swatted his hand away. "What are you doing up here?"

"I wanted some peace and quiet." Killian flung his older brother a pointed glance.

"Who disappears for some peace and quiet on their birthday?"

"Why did Father have to throw a party? I told him I didn't want one." Killian picked at a thread of embroidery that had come unraveled from his sleeve.

He never wanted a party. The wolves would howl, and a party just mean more people to hear and more whispered speculation on whether the royal curse—or worse, his uncle's sickness—had passed to him.

"Killi, you're seventeen. It's your coming-of-age party!" Lars raised an eyebrow.

"Why does it matter?" Killian shrugged. "I'm not the heir. No one cares about my age."

"You'd be a better heir than me." Lars kicked at the battlement.

"Maybe if you stuck around and listened to Father, instead of running off hunting and drinking whenever you want..."

Lars sighed. "It's better than sitting around all day listening to the old councilors drone on and signing your name on long, boring documents."

"Wait, you know how to sign your name?" Killian widened his eyes in mock surprise. Lars punched his arm and they both laughed.

Lars crossed his arms on the battlement and rested his chin atop them.

"How did you know I was here?" Killian tilted his head to glance down at his brother.

"I know all your hiding spots."

Killian hid a wince. The constant whispers and rumors drove him to keep mostly to himself.

It was easier to avoid people than face the obvious suspicion in their eyes. He'd learned early on that pretending not to be cursed didn't mean everyone else thought he was normal. Lars, and the very few people he counted as friends, were the only reason he ventured beyond his room.

He tried to be friendly, but most days were harder than others.

"Only this one is not in danger of being overrun by guests."

I'd be perfectly happy if they left.

Lars glanced over at him and smirked. "And it's a better view than cousin Dorete."

Killian couldn't hold back his snicker, considering the comparison. Definitely better than cousin Dorete. The view was the reason he often came up to this perch.

The castle sat atop a ridge overlooking a wide lake that stretched out for miles, inlets reaching out into the low hills like grasping fingers. A forest bordered the western side, sweeping down over the eastern hills in rippling waves. A wide river threaded through the hills to pour its crystalline waters into Lagarah Lake, its origin a tall mountain in the eastern reaches of the kingdom, from which flowed an endless waterfall.

Legend had long claimed that the waterfall was the seat of the faeries of Calvyrn, who inhabited the waterways of the kingdom. But faeries were rarely seen, the last notable sighting during the dark war over fifty years ago.

Killian pulled one knee up to his chest, his gaze falling to the rugged stone of the battlement. "If you could be anyone or anything else, what would you be?"

"A travelling knight. Or a highwayman." Lars knocked his boot against the wall.

Killian snickered. "Interesting choices."

"Shut up. Just anyone who doesn't have to follow stupid rules." Lars glanced sideways. "What about you?"

Killian tipped his head back against the wall and stared out over the forest. He thought about changing his answer, but it slipped out anyway.

"I'd be a—a wolf."

"A wolf?" Lars tilted an amused grin. "Have you been thinking about those ridiculous tales again?"

"Do you ever wonder if they're true?" Killian watched Lars out of the corner of his eye.

"The one about the witch? Hogwash." Lars snorted. "It's just stories for children and superstitious people."

"But what about uncle?" Killian pressed.

"He was a brilliant fighter and probably took too many hits to the head in the tilting yard."

Killian wished he shared his brother's confidence. Anyone could look at them and know they were brothers. He and Lars shared the same brown hair and broad-shouldered build, but Lars's eyes were the same light blue as the lake, and Killian's were amber and flecked with gold.

"Wolf's eyes," an old huntsman had once said and spat meaningfully.

Lars nudged him. "You can't listen to what people say. They don't know you like I do. You're not cursed."

If only you knew. Killian kept the thought to himself. Lars wouldn't listen if he tried to explain.

"Why did you come looking for me anyway?"

"Oh! Father has your present."

"Why didn't you tell me in the first place?" Killian scrambled down from his perch.

"Well, you seemed set on ignoring that it was your birthday..." Lars shrugged.

Killian shoved him and ran down the stairs.

"He's out in the courtyard!" Lars shouted, leaping down the stairs after him.

Taking the stairs two at a time and ignoring the startled glances as he ran through the great hall, Killian skidded to a halt in the wide courtyard of the castle. His father waited in the company of another knight, Killian's uncle.

"Killian, finally! I hope you weren't hiding somewhere." King Jonas half-smiled.

"Who? Him? Never!" Lars smirked, coming to a standstill behind Killian.

Their uncle chuckled. "Happy Birthday, lad."

"Thanks, Uncle Einar." Killian flashed a smile. He'd always been a little in awe of Einar, whose scarred face and limp were hard won in battles with the Baedons of the southern plains.

"I think he has waited long enough."

Jonas signaled the head groomsman, who led forward a magnificent black-and-white spotted charger outfitted with Killian's own saddle and bridle. Killian gaped at the stallion, strong enough to bear a knight in full armor and brave enough to charge a Wyvern. The horse blew out through his nostrils, taking in Killian's scent, and lowered his head as Killian rubbed the stallion's broad forehead.

"Well, son, what do you think of your first warhorse?"

"He's amazing, Father. Thank you!" Killian ran his hand over the stallion's rippling muscles in awe.

"Thank your uncle, too. I picked out the sire, but Einar trained him."

Einar only smiled and nodded to the horse. Killian grinned and stuck his foot in the stirrup, mounting and gathering up the reins as the horse arched his neck and stamped an enormous hoof against the cobbles.

Killian urged the stallion to a walk around the courtyard. Every step of the horse's smooth gait held raw power waiting for him to signal its release. The stallion pulled at the bit as they passed the open gates, and Killian almost gave into the urge to run him down the path. Stifling a sigh, he turned back to the group.

"Can I take him out?"

"I'd say yes, but the guest of honor should stay in the castle, don't you think?" Jonas raised an eyebrow.

Killian's shoulders slumped, and he dismounted. "Tomorrow, then. Want to come?" He glanced at Lars.

"Sure, want to see if you can finally keep up with me and Jeppe?" Lars smirked.

Killian rolled his eyes and the stallion snorted, as if offended at the challenge.

"You're sitting in court with me tomorrow, young man, and you will be there." King Jonas frowned at his oldest son. Lars's shoulders slumped.

"Early morning, then," Killian said.

"Morning?" Lars's voice held his distaste for the time he didn't often see. "I suppose."

Killian turned to Einar. "What's his name?"

"Leifr." Einar reached to rub the stallion's broad neck.

Killian clasped his uncle's hand and thanked him again. Einar only smiled and clapped his shoulder.

"I want a full report after your ride tomorrow," he said.

"Yes, sir." Killian grinned.

"Now." Jonas cleared his throat. "I do believe your aunt wanted to see you."

Killian muffled a groan for his father and uncle's sake. *Is seventeen finally old enough for me to avoid the cheek pinching?*

"Yes, come on, Killian." Lars draped an arm around him with a smirk, steering him towards the castle before he could escape.

Killian rolled his eyes, but his retort died as he noticed a groom looking at him and whispering to a visiting squire. His prior mood vanished faster than smoke on a windy day. "Killian," Lars grumbled a warning as his shoulders slumped.

"I know," he muttered, still grateful for the arm Lars kept around him.

*

Einar watched Killian surrender Leifr's reins back to the groom and accompany Lars back inside. His shoulders slumped even under Lars's friendly arm. Einar frowned. The change had come so quickly. The culprits scattered at the glare Lars threw their way.

"Do you think that this is wise?" Einar crossed his arms. "Continuing to throw parties?"

Jonas's friendly face creased into a frown. "What do you mean?"

Einar recognized the warning in his brother-in-law's voice, but continued the argument they'd had in the past. "Exposing him to the rumors like this?"

Jonas crossed his arms across his burly chest. "My father tried to lock Hugo away and it wasn't good for anyone. I'll not do the same to my son."

The people didn't whisper as much about Killian as they did about Hugo, but Einar had still heard plenty of wild speculation. Speculation he hated for its small-mindedness. He loved both his nephews—even stubborn, irresponsible Lars—and he didn't want to see Killian close himself off completely. Then he would lose his mind.

"Jonas, you can tell he hates these. He listens more than he should. You can tell he wonders if it's all true—"

"There's no curse," Jonas said sharply.

Einar spread his hands in apology. Neither of them truly believed that, but today he wished he could. Something about this year had him on edge. There had been disconcerting reports from the Rangers of late.

A faint howl echoed across the lake. Jonas muttered a curse and turned inside.

Chapter 2

Noak the sorcerer growled under his breath, kicking up extra puffs of dust as he trudged along the road winding through the farmlands that sprawled along the eastern side of Lagarah Lake. His brilliant plan he'd been cultivating for years had stalled. He needed the blood of a magical creature, but once the faeries of Myrnius discovered his plan earlier in the year, they'd sent all the animals into hiding.

Unfortunate, since his plan involved getting rid of all the faeries.

Since Myrnius was closed against him, he'd turned to Calvyrn. However, he'd hit another stumbling block. His options in Calvyrn were slim.

The Baedons were too fast and savage to make capture even a possibility. Even if he could get hold of a Wyvern, transport back to Myrnius would be problematic. They were bigger even than Myrnian Griffins and could spit poison. Trolls were also out of the question, for the obvious reasons.

Noak scowled. *Why can't magical animals co*ɪ *rabbit-sized shapes? Midsummer's day is in less than a the blood has to be fresh!*

Since early spring, Noak had kept his ears open for local legends, unexpected curses, faery blessings or the like. It was only a matter of time before he found one.

The waters of Lagarah Lake glistened before him, hiding a sizeable colony of faeries under its depths. *Surely there has to be some sort of magical working here.*

Noak studied the castle on the cliffs above the lake. A steady stream of traffic was coming and going up and down the road that wound up to the gates. A rumbling cough drew his attention to his left, where a grizzled old farmer watched him.

"Good afternoon." Noak nodded. "The castle seems busy today."

The farmer continued his slow study, scrutinizing Noak's travel-stained robe up to his eyes.

"Aye, there is." The farmer spat, giving Noak a wary look. "It's t' youngest prince's birthday today. Come of age, he 'as."

An extra grumble deepened the man's voice when he mentioned the prince. A young farm hand joined them, then another, curious about the patriarch's conversation.

"A great cause for celebration," Noak said. *I could really care less about some insignificant prince.*

The old man spat again. "Aye, 'cept he's a cursed one."

"Father!" A young woman shook her water pail in sharp reprimand.

"I'm not t' only one as says it." The farmer wagged a finger.

"Cursed?" Noak leaned forward, his previous disinterest forgotten.

"Only t' superstitious believe that," the woman said, with another glance at her father.

"T' whole family is cursed," the farmer said. "'Ave been for years, since a witch turned on 'em."

"How did she curse them?" Noak spoke causally, but nervous excitement tangled in his gut.

"T' story says wolf's blood runs through their line. But it's just a story t' scare t' children. Prince Killian's a fine young man." Another farm hand shot a nervous glance at the old man.

"Unlike that brother of 'is." This grumbled comment earned a disapproving glare from the woman, but a few murmurs of agreement from the other workers.

"Aye, but you all heard t' wolves when he was born and every year since. I wager this crop we'll hear them t'night," the old farmer said meaningfully. "Calling t' their own, they are."

"Father, that's bordering on treason. You know t' king has forbidden that kind of talk!" The young woman looked helplessly at Noak.

"Ah, I'm not interested in curses." Noak waved his hand with a smile. "I'm only passing through. I might stop in at the castle and pay my respects."

"Aye, what is it you do?" The farmer, having told his story, reverted to his suspicious manner.

"Merely a travelling scholar, minor historian, and sometime singer and entertainer." Noak gave a little flourish of the hand.

"Oh, then I'm sure you'd be welcome up at t' castle," the woman said brightly. "If you're any good as a singer, I'm sure t' king'd give you some coin and a meal for a song."

"Well, I'll not delay my introduction then." Noak smiled. The woman's answering smile faded and her forehead puckered in something like unease. He had that effect on most people.

The old farmer tapped his ear knowingly. "Listen tonight. You'll hear 'em."

I think I'll do that. But first to find Finn and the twins.

*

After yet another speech, Killian set his wine glass back on the table. Lars didn't share his restraint and gestured to a servant to refill his goblet. Killian rolled his eyes.

He won't listen to me and deserves the hangover he'll have tomorrow.

The tables still creaked under the weight of the bountiful food, but Killian couldn't eat another bite. He forced another bite of sugar-encrusted apple cake the servants had piled on his plate and willed himself not to listen as another lord launched into yet another long-winded speech.

He hated his birthday.

Every year for seventeen years the wolves would begin to howl at the eleventh hour and not stop until midnight. The whispers would start again, and it would take him several days to work up the courage to step outside the castle.

"Your Majesty!" A new voice cut through the merrymaking.

Killian looked up at the figure that stood in front of the main table. Silver embroidery swirled among the folds of his blue robe. Something about the way the man's grey eyes settled on Killian sent a shiver of unease down his spine. The sensation fled the moment the man looked away.

"And who are you?" Jonas spread his arms wide in a welcoming gesture.

"Noak, a humble entertainer, and self-professed master of illusion." The man smiled. "I had hoped to bring my talents before the prince in honor of his celebration."

"Ah! What say you, Killian?" Jonas turned a beaming smile on him.

He couldn't refuse when his father was in such a good mood. His mother smiled as well, so he nodded. The entertainer bowed deeply to Killian and the royal family.

"Allow me to introduce my assistant!" Noak gestured with a flourish. A thin man in a bright yellow jerkin stepped up beside him and bowed to everyone in the hall, unfazed by the curious stares of the crowd.

Noak and his assistant began with a juggling act, tossing balls, plates, wine bottles, and even knives to wild applause. Then Noak began his illusions. He draped a spare tablecloth over his assistant, rapped him over the head, and the cloth crumpled to the ground.

A collective gasp of surprise and even horror rushed through the audience until he pointed to the end of the hall, where the assistant stood upon the tables. The act garnered massive applause, several of the nobles even standing to better show their admiration. Noak bowed and turned to the dais.

"I have been gifted with a small ability to see into the future. Might I take the liberty of seeing what greatness lies inside you?" Noak smiled at Killian.

A sudden urge to run away filled him. *What if there's nothing great about me? What if he says something else for people to whisper about?*

"Killian?" His father's voice broke through his sudden panicked thoughts.

His parents still smiled, even with a hint of eagerness, as if they believed the man could see his future.

There seemed to be no objection from Lars either and the hall had hushed once more. He had little choice but to agree. But really, what could it hurt? The entertainer took Killian's hand and bent over it.

"Fine blood runs through your veins. You will help someone achieve great things. Your brother, perhaps?" He smiled.

The sight sent a tug of unease at Killian's stomach, and he again resisted the urge to back away and check over his shoulders for something...*Someone?*

"You are courageous yourself! I see you walking among wolves. Yes, you share their blood."

Killian jerked his hand away. "What?"

No one had ever spoken so boldly about the curse.

Lars's chair clattered behind him as he jerked to his feet, a knife in hand. "How dare you! Who put you up to this?"

As if that was a signal, the hall erupted in shouts. Noak's gaze darted between Killian's face and the enraged features of his brother as King Jonas added his voice to the noise, ordering a guard to seize Noak.

"Please, my King, I meant no harm!" he whined. "I don't know what you're talking about!"

Lars's eyes were wide in fury, his hands clenching and unclenching. His father's face had calmed, only the tenseness of his jaw announcing his hidden anger as he ordered the entertainer taken away.

"Wait!" Killian broke his stunned silence. Everyone paused. "Just let him go. He said he didn't know." The night was already horrible enough without a man getting punished. His father acknowledged Killian's decision with a nod, and the guard released Noak.

"Thank you, Prince Killian, thank you!" The man's voice whined as he crashed to his knees.

"Just go." Killian pointed him away with a sharp wave.

Noak bowed and scraped his way off the dais.

"He should still be punished!" Lars's face twisted in anger.

Killian glanced around the hall. The whispers had started.

"If you'll excuse me." He bowed to his family and their guests. He took several paces from the table before turning back. As bad as it was, he wouldn't give in this year.

"Lars, are you still joining me tomorrow morning when I take Leifr out?"

Lars gave him a smile. "Of course, little brother."

*

Noak watched from his hiding place in the shadows of the hall as the commotion gradually died down and men and women leaned closer together to whisper to one another. *Look at them, whispering and fearful. No doubt of the curse now.* He'd felt the raw power of the curse as the blood pounded through the prince's heart.

He barely managed to catch the last conversation between the prince and his brother and smiled. *I think I'll visit the stables.*

A wolf howled as he stepped outside. Another joined it and then a third bayed deeply. Noak almost laughed.

*

Killian shuddered, swinging the door shut on the safety of his room. He sank against the cool stone walls joined in the corner, pressing his back against the smooth surface. He gathered one knee to his chest and almost covered his ears. The howling died away on the night breeze and did not come again. It didn't need to. It was a warning. He knew it. But against what?

Chapter 3

Killian pounded a fist on Lars's door. An unintelligible mumble from the other side was his only reply. He rolled his eyes and continued down the stairs.

Leifr stood saddled and waiting for him in the stables. The warhorse shifted from one hind foot to the other, snorting and tossing his head.

"Easy, boy." He rubbed the stallion's broad forehead.

Leifr butted his shoulder, nearly knocking him back a step, but calmed.

"Are you sure you can't understand animals?" The head groom paused by the stall. "He hasn't stood still since we fed him this morning."

Killian flashed a quick smile, not about to tell the groom that he sometimes thought he could understand more than the wolves. The man was one of the few who didn't seem intent on whispering behind his back, and he'd hate to change that.

"Thank you for having him ready this early," he said.

The groom nodded. "Waiting on Prince Lars, sir?"

"Not for much longer." Killian shook his head and the groom chuckled.

"I'll send him after you when he comes down."

"Thank you, Mikk." Killian swung into the saddle. The groom stood aside with a respectful nod. "Enjoy yourself, sir."

Leifr tugged at the bit as they neared the gate, straining forward against Killian's firm grip on the reins. The guards saluted and let him through, murmuring admiration of the stallion as he passed.

The road wound down from the hill in a gentle curve to the lake, and once they reached the shoreline, Killian kicked Leifr up to a trot. They held it along the waterline for a few minutes before breaking into a canter and then a gallop. The wind swirled and tugged joyfully at them, amplifying the thunderous pounding of Leifr's broad hooves.

Killian chanced a glance behind him, where puffs of sand settled over giant strides. He laughed at the rush of freedom. No whispers, stares, or curses could touch him. It was just him, Leifr, and the wind. He checked the reins. Leifr pivoted effortlessly on his hind limbs and they turned into the forest. They kept a quick canter along a wide path.

A doe and her fawn darted across in front of them. Leifr tugged once, as if asking if Killian wanted to give chase, but a simple tap kept them on the path that would take them in a wide loop through the forest.

A figure stood to block their path. Leifr slid to a stop and Killian recognized the blue robes of the entertainer. The flourishing smile had vanished from Noak's face, but the strange eagerness remained. The hair on the back of Killian's neck stood up in warning.

Noak stared at Killian with an almost hungry expression. Unease tightened his stomach and Leifr shifted beneath him with a rumbling nicker. The man seemed more than an entertainer. Three more figures stepped out of the woods and surrounded Killian. He drew his sword, and waited for the challenge.

"What do you want?" Killian managed to force some authority into the words.

"You." Noak swept him with an appraising look. "Or, more specifically, your blood."

Killian tightened his grip on his sword. The man in the yellow jerkin raised a crossbow and Killian resisted the urge to look for his own crossbow hanging from the saddle. Leifr's ears flattened.

One of the men began to edge forward, but a flick from the sword warned him away. Killian tugged Leifr back a few paces, preparing to run. The archer raised his bow and loosed a bolt.

Killian ducked to the side, but the arrow cut a deep groove across his shoulder. Leifr reared and struck out with his hooves against another advance.

Noak released a column of smoke under Leifr's hooves, sending him into a panicked rear. The sudden motion, combined with the throbbing pain from the cut on his arm, sent him tumbling from the saddle. A surprised cry of pain ripped from him as he landed on his injured shoulder, breaking it open further.

He lay, dazed, as Noak approached, chanting in a low voice that made Killian's blood churn. Noak thrust his hands out with a final shout.

Killian tried to shield his eyes from the brightness that enveloped him. Burning pain ran from his scalp to his toes and he twisted with a howl of agony. Noak looked down at him in short-lived triumph as Leifr lunged forward, driving Noak back and blocking Killian from the rest of the men. Killian seized his chance and, ignoring the pain in his shoulder, scrambled to his feet and ran into the forest.

"After him!" Noak shouted.

Killian ran as he never had before. Every step burned his lungs and jarred his shoulder. He plunged through a small stream and kept running without any sense of direction. The uneven ground caused him to stumble, and he rolled down the edge of a dell, landing with a grunt in front of the welcoming mouth of a cave. He had to hope that the trailing moss and jumbled rocks at the entrance could hide him. He scrambled inside and huddled against the furthest wall.

His heart had just begun to steady when a noise set it pounding again. A faint glow came from deeper in the cave. It grew brighter as shuffling steps announced something's approach. A figure came through a fissure and Killian backed away until realization hit him.

A faery?

The faery's hair glinted as pale as his skin. His simple tunic and trousers were the color of fresh turned earth, and his drooping wings seemed to be giving off the light.

"How did you get hurt, eh?" The faery reached to touch Killian's shoulder.

Killian tried to follow where the faery's hand soothed the wound, but his body twisted in an awkward manner.

Something's not right. His heart began to thud again.

"What's happened to you?" The faery spoke as if to an anxious animal.

Killian's worry built even higher and he edged away from the faery. He opened his mouth to explain, but no words came.

The faery's eyes widened and he peered closer at Killian. "How did...? You're—Oh, you don't know, do you? Come with me." He beckoned, and Killian followed him back through the fissure.

Glowing cave worms lit up as the faery passed, their pulsing light reflecting off the scattered crystals that lodged in the wall crevices. They entered a wide chamber sheltering a pool in its center. The water rippled as droplets detached themselves from the finger-like protrusions that thrust down from the ceiling.

Killian paused, and a drip tapped him on the head. He shook the moisture off, but the gnawing feeling that something was wrong could not be so easily dislodged.

The faery sat by the pool and his light grew brighter.

"Come." He waved Killian over, and gestured to the pool. "Look."

Killian came closer, shivering, and peered over the edge of the water. He stared in shock at the wolf looking back at him. He slapped at the reflection and pulled out a damp paw. He looked again. His amber eyes gazed back, the same dark grey ringing his left iris, but he was now trapped in the body of a wolf.

What happened to me?

Killian looked around in helpless panic and a low whine escaped.

The faery reached out and his touch calmed Killian a little.

"Lie down," he said. "You are still injured."

Killian settled on the floor, his mind racing with a million questions. *It was Noak. He did this. Is it part of the curse? How did Noak know? What will my family think? Will they find me? Or will Noak find me first? What will they do when they find me?* The thought hurt worse than his wound as the faery took some water and bathed his shoulder, then bound up the wound with cave moss and spider's silk.

"I am Alfar," he said.

Killian lifted his head with a soft growl.

Alfar smiled. "Now, what can we find out about you?" He chanted softly, the smooth cadence nothing like the darkness of Noak's voice, and sat back as he gazed into Killian's eyes.

"A powerful curse does indeed run in your family, Prince Killian. But this." He indicated Killian's new form. "I've not seen this in many years. Not since I exiled myself to this little cave."

Alfar washed his hands in the pool. "I've heard through the waterways that there's a sorcerer on the loose looking for blood. It seems he hasn't been lucky until now."

Killian pricked his ears. It made sense. Noak had said he wanted his blood. He looked up at Alfar, tilting his head to the side.

"Can you help me?"

"I'm sorry, young prince; I can do nothing against this spell. We of Calvyrn are strongest with creatures of water. Our kin in Myrnius may be able to help. Their care is for the forest and its creatures. They might have answers."

The question Killian wanted to ask came out as a whine and he looked at the entrance.

"The sorcerer will never stop looking for you. I can give you some small protection against him once you leave this cave." He again chanted softly over Killian, his voice soothing.

"You should go to Myrnius and seek out the faeries. It's a small chance, but the best you have. My spell will hide you from him only while you are in Calvyrn. Once you cross into Myrnius he will be able to find you. But rest now and stay close to the cave. I will return once I have spoken with my people."

Alfar touched Killian's shoulder and slipped from the cave.

The light from the glow worms remained after the faery vanished. Killian curled up by the pool's edge and let himself drift asleep.

*

Killian awoke to something tickling his nose.

Lars! The rumbling growl in his chest startled him and he jerked up. The sight of his tail brought home his new reality. He whisked it away and nosed at his paws, trying to reconcile himself to the fact that they now replaced his hands.

I'd really hoped this had all been a very realistic dream.

He twisted, attempting to take in the rest of his new form, only succeeding in rolling dangerously close to the water. He grumbled in frustration and wriggled to his feet, snapping at his tail as it brushed back and forth. He let his head droop with a huff.

'I'd be a wolf.' I'm an idiot. That is the last time I wish for anything.

He took an experimental step, easier than he thought to move on four paws instead of two. He moved to the pool to lap up water. Easy enough if he didn't think about it. It was odd how natural it felt to be a wolf. Killian tested his weight on his shoulder. It didn't burn as badly, but he still limped.

Killian padded back to the entrance. Night was falling outside. He'd slept through the day. He paused for a long moment, his ears picking up sounds he'd never thought it possible to hear. His nose twitched as a light breeze carried the musty scent of a nearby badger, and the sweeter smell of two does. He watched the woods around him with the eyes of a cautious hunter.

He stepped out of the cave and padded in a wide loop around the dell, exploring with his new senses. He paused in a clearing and looked back to see the lights of the castle winking on top of the high hills.

What do they think happened to me after I didn't come back from my ride?

He hesitated, ears straining to hear anything from the walls. A prick of loneliness and desperation stung his heart. He sat back on his haunches and howled.

*

Lars stood at the window of a chamber, staring out into falling darkness. *This isn't happening.*

The castle had been thrown into an uproar when Killian's horse had returned, sweating and wild-eyed. Soldiers and huntsmen had been dispatched immediately, but they returned with the worst news. His brother's remains. Slashed and bloody clothes surrounded by the prints of wolves.

The huntsmen could not explain it. The castle was silent in grief at the unexpected news and its members whispered in corners.

King Jonas sat with his head in his hands, and Queen Aina clutched a damp handkerchief as she stared into the fire. Lars stared in stony silence out the window.

"Hasn't it taken enough?" his father whispered. "First Hugo and now Killian. How much more..."

"Jonas, please don't..." His mother refolded her handkerchief. His father flinched as a wolf howled in the forest and his mother stifled a sob.

Lars clenched his hands as the last echoes of the howl faded. *Are we being mocked?*

His father moved to comfort his mother. A knock sounded at the door and Einar and a huntsman entered. The king looked up, all hope battered from his weathered face.

"We've found nothing else, your majesty." The huntsman barely met the king's eyes before gazing back down at the tiled floor.

His mother bit back another sob. "Why?" She gasped, gripping Jonas' hand.

His uncle cleared his throat before speaking. "We've had rumors of a sorcerer travelling through Calvyrn searching for creatures of magic..."

"And you think this sorcerer attacked my son?" His father demanded. Einar shrugged. "Do you have any proof that this is more than a wild rumor?"

"No, other than one of the Rangers sent out has been missing for weeks," Einar said. "Something is not right..."

"We have the proof we need," his father whispered. "Wolves attacked our son. The curse has killed him."

Lars whirled from the window and strode to the door. His uncle stopped him with a hand to his arm.

"Don't do anything rash, Lars. Your family needs you."

Lars only brushed past him and out of the room. He didn't believe in the curse, but something had to be done. *I've heard enough of wolves. I'll hunt down and kill every one of them.*

"Lars?" A gentle voice stopped him as he rounded the corner.

He turned his face away, for once not wanting to see the speaker.

"What?" He growled.

Pauline didn't flinch. Her usual look of frustrated disappointment had been replaced with sorrow.

"I—wanted to see how you were," she said.

"How do you think?" He moved to go, but she caught at his arm.

"Lars, I know it appears that we don't get along, but—I think I know you well enough to tell you not to do anything stupid. Killian wouldn't want you to."

She matched him for height and her green eyes looked straight into his. Eyes in which he'd do anything to see something other than frequent disappointment. Eyes Killian was smart enough not to tease him about too mercilessly.

Killian. Lars tugged his arm away. "What would you know about him? You probably think he's cursed along with everyone else!"

Pauline's eyes narrowed. "Don't make me slap you again, Lars."

Lars leaned up against the wall. "Sorry," he mumbled.

She rested her shoulder against the stone beside him, squeezing his hand. "You know I'm right."

He looked away, his throat tightening again. "I know. I just—I should have—he wanted me to go with him..."

A small sigh escaped Pauline and they stood in silence for a long minute, hands still clasped. He didn't dare move, afraid he'd drive her away. Again.

"You can't blame yourself," she finally said.

Too late for that.

He dragged his gaze up to meet hers. "You want me to do something worthwhile?"

"Because I know you can."

"Then I need to go."

She didn't release his hand. "To do what, Lars?"

He knew she wouldn't like it, but it had to be done. "Something for Killian."

She surprised him by brushing his cheek with a kiss. "Just be careful, Lars. Don't do something you'll regret."

It was already too late for regrets. Killian would hate what he planned to do, but Killian was dead. Lars left Pauline without another word.

Chapter 4

Killian watched the forest around him from the shelter of the cave. Alfar had not yet reappeared. The forest hummed with fresh industry in the early morning light. His nose twitched, and he gracefully rose to his feet as his stomach declared its hunger.

He hesitated in the mouth of the cave. His nose told him exactly where he could find a meal, and a new instinct began to take over.

He'd always been a naturally good hunter, better even than some seasoned hunters. But for all those kills he'd used a crossbow or knife instead of his teeth. He ran his tongue over the sharp appendages, trying to imagine sinking them into an animal's throat.

He shuddered, in disgust or excitement, he couldn't quite tell. His stomach pinched again, and his paws moved forward, the wolf part catapulting him onto the hunt. A short time later he settled down with an unfortunate rabbit that had ventured out too early. He stared at it for a long moment before gingerly nibbling at the carcass, the taste of raw rabbit less repulsive than he thought it would be.

As he finished, he felt a little more at home in the wolf's body. Almost more than he had in his human body. His hunger appeased for the moment, he padded off, following the scent of water.

A wide river rushed by from the lake as it searched for lower ground. Killian halted in the tree line before edging forward to drink. He stared at his reflection, twitching his ears occasionally to remind himself it wasn't an illusion.

Amber eyes stared back, repeating the questions in his mind. How was he supposed to make it to Myrnius? Finding a faery sounded easy enough, but the woodland folk of Myrnius were not known to reveal themselves to many, even though two held old King Stefan's favor.

Alfar had given him protection from Noak only until the borders of Calvyrn. After that how was he to avoid a sorcerer?

A new scent jerked him from his reverie. *Human.*

The forest had fallen quiet, but he picked up the faint rustle of footsteps. Instincts warred within him. He retreated a few steps and turned to watch the figure that came to the river.

A young woman knelt at the river to refill a canteen, pulling her knee-length green dress and slitted leather tunic away from the mud. Her fitted trousers and tall boots were not given the same consideration. She splashed water over her face and patted damp hands over curly auburn hair tied at the nape of her neck with a leather cord.

Killian watched in silent curiosity. Her clothes and the light bow and quiver across her back reminded him of the

Rangers who served his father. She looked older than his seventeen years, but younger than Lars's twenty.

She glanced up and caught sight of him. Her blue eyes widened, and her hand fell to the hunting knife on her belt. They stared at one another for a few seconds and she tilted her head, confused. Killian knew he wasn't acting very wolf-like as he took one step and sat back on his haunches.

Maybe there's some way to tell her who I am.

He edged closer and experimented with a small bark.

"What're you doing, eh?" she whispered.

Her hand relaxed on the knife's hilt, and Killian nudged his paws into another step. She extended a hand. He flattened his ears in minor annoyance at the gesture.

A warning ripple spread through the forest. *Hunter!* His wolf instincts overrode his plans. Killian splashed through the river and darted into the undergrowth on the other side, breaking into a run.

*

Lars's quiver was two bolts lighter and the world was freer of two wolves when he picked up new tracks. He found the remains of a kill and tethered his horse a safe distance away before following the tracks towards the river. He held his crossbow at the ready as he stalked along the trail to the water's edge. He almost lowered the bow at the sight of a girl instead of the wolf he'd expected.

She whirled to face him. "Who're you?" The girl drew an arrow on him before he could answer.

They faced each other across their weapons.

"Who are you?" He wasn't about to let some ridiculous-looking girl impede his search.

"I'm Rose."

"Well, Rose, these tracks are fresh." He nudged the sandy bank with his toe. "Have you seen a wolf since you've been here?"

"One just crossed t' river. Why?"

"Why do you think?" He curled his lip in a sneer. "I'm going to rid the earth of it and all its kind!" He lowered his crossbow and splashed across the river without a backward glance.

"Wait!" She called after him.

He ignored her. *No. I've waited long enough to do this.*

*

Killian's shoulder began to ache, and he slowed to a trot. He didn't recognize this part of the forest. The wind brought him a familiar scent and he flinched as a twig snapped behind him. He glanced behind him and froze.

Lars!

But he almost didn't recognize his brother, blind hate so twisted his features. Killian leaped away as a crossbow bolt tore into a trunk beside him. Lars cursed, and another bolt locked into place on the crossbow as his brother took up the pursuit again.

Killian limped through the tangled ferns, Lars's footsteps gaining on him. He could barely think over his pounding heart. *He's chasing me? What's he doing this far out?*

The ground tumbled away from him into a ravine and he jerked to a halt. He turned to face Lars. Terror froze his tongue and a whine built in his chest. He never imagined his life would end this way.

Lars! What are you doing?

Lars raised his crossbow, triumphant, and pressed his finger to the trigger.

"Stop!" The girl from the river slammed into Lars, knocking his aim away from Killian's heart.

Lars whirled around, and they faced each other across drawn weapons.

"What are you doing?" He snarled.

She edged between Killian and Lars. "You can't kill it!"

"Don't tell me what I can't do! My brother was killed by their kind!" Lars jerked his chin at Killian.

Killian's heart plummeted. *They think I'm dead!* He had to find some way to let Lars know...

"*Lars!*" His cry came out as a bark.

"Move!" Lars ordered.

"No!" she retorted, readjusting her grip on her bow.

"I will shoot you!" Lars lifted the bow higher, but her chin jutted and her eyes narrowed as she widened her stance.

This is going nowhere. Killian barked again to try and gain their attention.

"You ever seen a wolf act like this? It tried t' approach me at t' river." She glanced down at Killian, who pricked his ears hopefully.

You understood! Please keep talking! He's an idiot on his good days.

Lars lowered his bow a fraction and she did the same. Killian barked again.

"Shut up!" Lars turned on him.

Fine. You'd better be grateful I can't talk right now, Lars. Killian eased his weight off his aching shoulder.

"Are you doing this?" Lars scowled at the girl, his voice laden with suspicion.

"What do you mean?"

"Are you using magic?"

"Why would I use magic?" The girl lifted her shoulders, not quite easing off the bowstring.

"You don't want me to kill it and it's not attacking you!" Lars accused.

"It's not attacking you either!"

"It might if you let it!"

"That's ridiculous!" She rolled her eyes.

"Is it? Someone told my brother two nights ago that he had wolf's blood and then yesterday wolves killed him. Curse or not, something is going on—"

"*I'm not dead!*"

"And you're out here protecting a wolf!" Lars punctuated the accusation with a jab of the crossbow.

"Killing wolves isn't going t' bring your brother back!" She stepped back a pace and tossed her head.

"*Lars, it's me!*" Killian whined in frustration and took a half-step forward.

Lars lowered his crossbow, his eyes bright with tears. "What else am I supposed to do?"

Killian growled in frustration and jumped at Lars, hitting him in the chest and sending them both tumbling to the ground. The girl gasped, drawing her bow in an instant, but Killian kept his paws on Lars's chest. The terror in his brother's gaze faded to confusion as Killian berated him in short growls.

"*Lars, you stupid, idiotic, irritating excuse for a brother —* "

Killian stilled as Lars settled a cautious hand into his fur.

"What're you doing?" The girl hissed, her bow creaking as she shifted her grip.

"His eyes," Lars muttered. "It has the same eyes as my brother."

Finally. Killian swished his tail back and forth in triumph.

"Killian?" Lars's voice gathered strength.

Climbing off his brother, Killian gave a small hop on his forepaws, looking at his brother expectantly. *Come on, Lars. Don't make me keep questioning your intelligence.*

Lars rolled to his knees. The girl lowered her bow, brow furrowed in confusion.

"You're Killian?" Lars repeated.

Killian sighed and reared up, putting his forepaws on Lars's shoulders and looking at him.

A slow smile spread over Lars's face. "Killi, you're alive?"

Killian rested his head on Lars's shoulder as Lars wrapped an arm around him. "How? What happened?"

Killian growled his frustration. *"If I could talk, wouldn't I have told you already?"*

"Killian, I can't understand you," Lars interrupted.

Killian huffed. *I noticed.*

The girl returned the arrow to the quiver and sank to her knees. "Are you mad? You think this is your brother?"

Lars glanced at her. "Yes, I suppose—this is Killian." He ran a hand over his face, shaking his head in disbelief.

Killian pushed up on all fours. *This is awkward. How is a wolf supposed to politely greet a human?* He settled for lowering his head and brushing her hand with his nose.

A slow smile crept over her face. "Nice t' meet you, Killian. I'm Rose."

He whined softly. *"Nice to meet you. Thanks for not letting my brother kill me."*

Rose laughed again, breaking off abruptly as she noticed the bandage on his right shoulder. "You're hurt?"

Killian glanced back at the faery's dressing. Spots of blood leaked through the bandage, no doubt caused by his flight. Lars knelt beside him, inspecting the bandage.

"I've some medical supplies at my camp," Rose said. "We can put a fresh dressing on it."

Killian touched her hand with his nose in thanks.

"How far is your camp?" Lars glanced down at Killian, then back at Rose.

"Not far. Just back across t' river."

Lars looked down at Killian, frowning. "Should I carry you?"

No thanks. Killian dodged his brother's grab. *Last time you tried to carry me, you dropped me.*

Chapter 5

Killian wove through the forest ahead of Lars, blending with the shadows, and occasionally glancing back at them as if to ask, "Are you coming or not?"

His little brother could be a bit pushy. *Apparently not that much really changed.*

"I'm sorry about..." He glanced at the girl. "I'm Lars, by the way."

"Nice t' meet you — Oh my! You're t' prince!" Rose's eyes widened in horror as she realized she had threatened the heir to Calvyrn. "And so are you!"

She pointed at Killian, who paused and gave an impatient flick of his tail.

Lars rolled his eyes and shouldered his crossbow. "Of course we are. Don't bother curtseying now."

Rose straightened, a frown tugging at the corner of her mouth. "But —"

"He still needs your help, if that's what you're asking."

Killian growled under his breath, canine eyes watching them, and then disappeared into the undergrowth.

She jerked her head in a nod, mouth tightening in a quick line, before following Killian.

They splashed back across the river and a few yards into the forest before reaching Rose's camp. A thick tree had come loose from its roots and leaned against a short rocky outcropping, where Rose settled into its shelter.

She pulled out some bandages from her pack. Killian lay down gingerly, favoring his wounded shoulder, and Rose sat beside him and inspected the strange bandage.

Lars sat across the fire from them, watching. *If I had gone out with Killian like I promised, I could have prevented this. It's my fault.* He'd always been so protective of his little brother and he hadn't protected him the one time it really mattered. Killian would never blame him and that made it worse.

"What are you doing out here?" He glanced at Rose, shoving his guilt to the back of his mind.

"Looking for my father." She splashed some water over the rent in Killian's fur. "He's a Ranger and he's been missing for two weeks."

"If he's a Ranger, I'm sure he's fine."

"You don't understand. He was sent off on some important mission and he hasn't come back. I know when he was supposed t' report back and come home. Head Rangers won't tell me anything. I don't even know if they're looking for him."

"So, you came after him yourself?" Lars smirked. *Now I've seen everything.*

"He trained me. Says I'm as good as any of t' Ranger recruits, and he's t' only family I have left. So yes, I came after him myself." She tossed her head in an impatient gesture.

"So, you're as good as a *recruit*. What happens if he's really in trouble?"

Killian growled low in his throat as she tied off the bandage.

"Don't know. I'll figure it out. I want t' be a real Ranger one day."

Lars laughed outright. "You're a girl!"

"So? Not an actual rule against it, is there? Not that you would know anyway."

"Excuse me?"

She turned a bright shade of red. "Nothing."

"Was I not supposed to hear that? You said I wouldn't know about the Rangers. Do explain." Never mind that he didn't even know the current Ranger commander's name.

"Well, I'd thought since I was in t' area, I would go to t' castle and try and see t' prince — you — and ask if he could do something about my father since the head Rangers won't. But everyone knows you don't care. You've never done anything with t' Rangers and you're in command of t' Company! Sire!"

Killian glanced between the two of them, ears pricked, body tensed in alertness.

She's right. The nagging thought killed Lars's protest, and he turned his glare to the ashes of her campfire.

When he turned eighteen he had been given command of the Rangers Company and the brigade of knights that investigated reports of magical animal attacks, such as baedons, trolls, wyverns and the like.

But since none of those reports actually involved wyverns, he never cared to look at them. Or attend meetings. Or anything really. Same with the Ranger Company. It was just dull reports on what the various Rangers had seen on their trips through the kingdom.

Rose bit her lip, obviously waiting for his outburst.

Lars glanced at Killian, who watched them with solemn amber eyes. Rose had voiced what Killian and Pauline had been telling him for the past two years. Longer really.

He cleared his throat.

"My uncle mentioned a Ranger missing, so they might be looking for him after all."

Wait! Uncle said something else about the Ranger! "He also said that there were reports of a sorcerer in Calvyrn searching for creatures of magic."

Killian's head flew up and he barked. They both turned to stare at him.

"Is that what happened to you?" Lars scowled. "The sorcerer?"

Killian barked again, scratching at the ground.

"But how…?" Lars's eyes widened as a rough letter took shape under Killian's clumsy paw. "N? Noak! He disappeared that night. It was him, wasn't it?"

Rose gasped. "Father mentioned someone named Noak. Said his mission was t' find him. My father went after a *sorcerer?* He could be injured or—or…"

The three of them sat in somber silence. Lars began to fidget with his hands after a few seconds.

"Why'd a sorcerer go after your brother?" Rose curled her arms across her stomach.

"Haven't you heard the legend?" Lars curled his lip in a faint sneer. "Many years ago, a witch cursed a king, telling him that wolf's blood would run through his line until we repaid the debt for turning her away. Everyone thinks

Killian's cursed because wolves happen to howl on his birthday."

"Wolves howl all t' time. They're just talking."

"Well, if you're superstitious, you believe the opposite. They thought that about my uncle, too."

It'd long been a bitter point for him. He had few memories of his Uncle Hugo, none of which included the supposed madness people whispered about in corners or behind closed doors.

"There must be some sort of truth in it, though, if Prince Killian was turned t' a wolf by a sorcerer."

Lars narrowed his eyes in anger and she hastily continued. "But why would he need a creature of magic anyway?"

"I don't know. Let's find him and ask. He can change Killian back while we're at it."

"You want t' go after a sorcerer?"

"Why not?" Lars challenged.

"Sorcerers are dangerous!"

"So?"

"She's right."

They both whirled to face the speaker, knives drawn, but Killian pricked his ears and whined a greeting. The stranger wasn't tall, and an unfortunate cowlick sent his pale hair sticking out from behind an ear. A faint shimmer like rippling water flashed around his figure and vanished.

"Who are you?" Lars gripped the knife in his hand, half-hoping the man would confirm his suspicion.

"I am Alfar of the water faeries."

Rose's jaw dropped in surprise and Lars barely managed to snap his mouth shut. The oldest chroniclers had been young when the last faery sighting was recorded.

"A friendly dragonfly told me when you crossed the river and I came as quick as I could. I helped your brother shortly after his transformation, Prince Lars." The stranger bobbed his head, eyeing the girl curiously.

"I'm Rose," she said.

"I came to find you." Alfar glanced down at Killian. "I have a warning for you, and now for your new companions."

Apparently, this whole mess can get worse. Lars sheathed his knife.

Killian whined and stood, favoring his injured shoulder.

"Noak, the sorcerer, is pursuing you, Prince Killian. I have spoken with my people. We've had news through the waterways." The faery glanced at Lars and Rose. "The sorcerer began in Myrnius. He is trying to make a spell that will destroy the magic of our Myrnian kin. But the disease will spread to the rest of faery races and kill us all. The last piece of his spell is the blood of a magical animal."

"Killian?"

"Indeed." Alfar nodded. "I have given your brother some protection. He is hidden from Noak's sight in this country. Once he steps across the border, the sorcerer will be able to find him. We believe that Noak will attempt to enact this spell on the summer solstice when the world's magic is at its strongest. He will have to find Killian before then. This must not happen."

"Well, then, it's simple," Lars said. "He doesn't leave Calvyrn."

Killian growled, obviously annoyed at being left out of the discussion.

"Maybe," Alfar said. "But my people have no way to turn him back to a human. We believe that our kin in

Myrnius may have some answers. Even if Noak himself cannot see Killian, he has spies. If the solstice passes, he can always wait until the winter festival or the year after. He'll never stop hunting you."

Killian sat back on his haunches, staring up at Lars with those familiar eyes.

"Sounds like we don't have much of a choice, do we?" Lars frowned and rested a hand on his sword. Killian huffed and Lars half-smiled. He could almost hear his brother's sarcastic retort. "We'll go to Myrnius, then."

"I'm going, too," Rose said.

"No, you're—"

"I'm going." Rose scowled, crossing her arms. "It might be a chance for me t' find my father."

And, of course, I can't deny that chance, even if she's the last person I want along.

Alfar's head tilted and he regarded her intently. "The Rangers know of this sorcerer. One has gone west towards Myrnius. We sent word down the water, but don't know what he's found." He shifted his gaze to Lars. "Rose should go with you. Blood will be spilled before the end of your journey. The three of you will need each other."

Lars tilted a glance up at the sky. *This just keeps getting better and better. Fine.*

Killian shook himself and yipped up at Rose. Of course, his brother would take Rose's side.

"When should we leave?" Rose gripped the quiver strap across her chest.

"The solstice is in three weeks," Lars said. "We should leave now." He half-turned to Rose. "I left my horse just down the path. I'm already packed for a journey."

"I'll start packing my things," Rose said.

Alfar nodded, moving past them to kneel beside Killian. "How is your wound?"

Killian growled and twisted his neck to nose at it.

"And a fine job she did, too." Alfar smiled.

"You can understand him?" Lars jolted forward in surprise.

"For the most part."

"How did he get hurt?" Lars wanted, *needed*, to know.

"A crossbow bolt struck him."

The words struck him like a punch in the gut. "It wasn't...?"

"No, not yours, Prince Lars. He wants you to know this is not your fault." Alfar cast knowing eyes at him.

"Of course he does!" Lars muttered, scrubbing his eyes. Killian barked at him.

"I'll be back."

Lars trudged along the path to where he left his horse. Perhaps he could get one of his companions to join them. Dagmar would come if Lars could promise him he'd find his true love on the journey. Gustav might come, but only if he brought at least two squires and his ceremonial armor. Lukas would be useful, but Killian disliked him.

Lars sighed and kicked at a protruding root. Most of his friends, acquaintances really, would be less than useful on this quest.

Jeppe, his stallion, waited for him. He'd torn furrows in the ground with his massive hooves and chunks of bark were missing from the tree. He whinnied loudly when he saw his master and pawed another chunk of dirt from the path.

"Jeppe!" Lars fixed him with a stern look. The stallion snorted but settled.

Lars untethered him and paused. He couldn't ride back to the castle and tell his parents. They would likely forbid him to go. But Killian would want them to know he still lived. Lars drew out paper and charcoal from his saddle bags and scrawled a short message.

Killian's alive. We have to get help.

He hesitated, tempted to add something for Pauline. His shoulders slumped. She'd surprised him last night with her comforting words, but he didn't know if his actions would change her frustration to pride. *She deserves better than you,* a painfully honest voice nagged.

He shoved the voice away and pinned the missive to the tree with a crossbow bolt. Hopefully someone would find it — hopefully not the sorcerer still on the loose.

Lars pulled Jeppe around and headed back to Rose and his brother.

*

Killian heard Lars coming long before they arrived, Jeppe stamping and snorting his irritation. Rose had packed up the campsite and sat on a log, waiting. Alfar had vanished after one last warning to avoid attracting attention.

The sorcerer would be watching.

"Will we be able t' bring him?" Rose nodded to the horse as Lars re-entered the small camp.

"I don't want to set him loose. And I'm not about to let another rider-less horse show up at the castle and make everything worse. Besides, we might need him." Lars shot a glance at his brother. "I left a note saying you were alive."

Killian released his breath in a relieved sigh. They couldn't return to the castle. Once his parents found out, the whole army would be looking for them. They didn't need that complication. Their best chance lay in making it across the border without attracting undue attention.

"Leifr knew you were alive," a voice boomed.

Killian flinched at the sudden noise and glanced at the others. They didn't seem to notice.

He gingerly approached Jeppe, slowly wagging his tail in cautious greeting.

"I can understand you."

Jeppe lowered his head to snuff at Killian's ears. *"You now speak our language."*

Killian flicked his ears away. *"Leifr is all right?"*

"Yes, and furious that he couldn't better protect you." Jeppe stomped a hind foot. *"He tried to tell the humans, but they would not listen."*

"I'll have to thank him, then."

Jeppe bent his head before Killian. *"I'll do my best to serve in his place. A rather flighty sparrow told me much of what has happened."* He lifted his head with a trumpeting neigh, earning confused looks from Lars and Rose. *"We are finally questing!"*

Killian hid a wolf grin. He'd always thought Jeppe and his brother shared some of the same characteristics, and now he knew for certain.

He joined Lars and Rose, barked to interrupt their inane argument, and set off into the afternoon sun. Commotion broke out as his companions hurried to collect their gear and catch up.

They were finally setting off on their own quest. He and Lars had always talked of sneaking off on their own journey.

I just never imagined it including a sorcerer lurking around every turn.

Chapter 6

Killian slowed his pace and fell back between his now-silent companions. Dusk had begun to encroach on the evening's light as they drew near the edge of the forest. Beyond the trees lay open plains, and then the western hills.

He shook himself, panting. Too many open spaces before they reached the border and the forest of Celedon in Myrnius.

"We can't go much further tonight." Lars frowned.

"Aye," Rose said. "There's not many places t' camp out in t' plains. We could find a good enough place here."

Lars rolled his eyes and Rose's hand clenched about the strap of her quiver. Killian prepared to jump on Lars again if he decided to argue the point. They'd be safe in the forest. Search parties wouldn't penetrate that far yet, and hopefully the sorcerer wouldn't suspect them of actually heading for Myrnius.

"Here it is." Lars nodded.

He ground-tied Jeppe and loosened the girth. Rose watched for a moment.

"I'll go get some firewood," she said.

Lars barely spared her a glance. Killian grumbled in irritation and pushed up next to her, offering her a cheerful wag of his tail.

"Thanks." She smiled down at him and led the way into the forest.

Rose added a branch to the pile in her arms as Killian nosed the ground around her, exploring the scents that crossed their path. He dragged another branch over to her. She crouched to add it to her collection.

"You all right?"

She must have noticed him limping again. He tilted his head up to her, then bounded toward a suitable branch for their collection.

"You seem t' be taking all of this well."

Killian cocked his head to the side. *I already knew I was cursed, so it's not exactly shocking.*

"I know we don't know each other, but I'm sorry this happened t' you. Nobody deserves t' be cursed like this."

Killian released the kindling he'd dragged over to nose at her arm. Maybe she believed it to be a curse, but with every passing hour he felt more at home in his new form than he ever had in his human skin.

Perhaps it was true. Perhaps he really did have wolf blood in his veins. A scent tickled his nose and he rose and followed it. Dinner.

"See you in camp," Rose said, and he bounded off as she stood and left to deliver the firewood.

*

"Where's Killian?" Lars said sharply when Rose returned alone.

"Hunting." She set down the wood, pausing as she noticed he'd set out both their packs and blankets. He stacked the firewood neatly as she nursed the fire to life.

He caught her sideways glance and rolled his eyes. "I might be a prince, but I'm not entirely useless, you know."

She pressed her lips firmly together and gave a slight shake of her head. He narrowed his eyes. *It's almost more insulting that she's obviously trying not to say something.*

She settled across the fire from him and they both dug into their packs and pulled out dinner.

"So, um—you ever travelled much before?" She might be a commoner, but she clearly didn't have any problem speaking to him.

"Never more than five miles from my house until I decided t' go look for my father." She bit into a piece of dried meat. "You?"

"A few times a year for routine visits and inspections." *Which were boring.* "I just never imagined my first adventure would be like this."

He and Killian had long planned for the day when they would travel to the Black Hills in the north and take on a Wyvern. *We would have too if he hadn't been attacked!*

"The faery seemed t' think we'd find answers in Myrnius."

"We'd better," he growled, half to himself.

*

Killian watched them from the trees surrounding the sheltered dell where they'd camped. He'd eaten his catch in private. No need to upset his brother.

At least Lars and Rose weren't arguing at the moment. They had one thing in common; they all needed answers in Myrnius.

He licked the last traces of blood from his muzzle and trotted down to join them at the fire, curling up a short distance from the flames.

The human part of him knew it was safe, but the wolf didn't trust the flickering light. Rose had the first watch and he swiveled his ear, effortlessly tracking her circuit around camp. Killian rested his nose on paws and lifted his gaze upward to the stars.

He knew them now by human and animal name. Erik the Mighty, first king of Calvyrn, or Wyvern's Bane. He was a hero to the animals as well, but only for driving the Wyverns into the Black Hills in the north. The dread serpent circled Erik, and the white wolf held up the moon.

He yawned and shifted onto his side, tucking into a protected ball, and fell asleep.

Sometime later, he woke with a growl in his throat. Rose looked over in alarm as he crouched low and bristled. Lars came awake and sat up, scrabbling for a knife when he saw Killian's bared teeth.

Rose moved to their side, eyes wide in fear.

"Show yourself!" Killian barked.

Jeppe shifted, snorting threats as he tried to put up brave front, but his nickers were too high-pitched for comfort.

"You are young yet and not quite one of us, so I will forgive you." A low growl rumbled, and a grey wolf stepped out of the shadows.

Killian let his hackles fall and he investigated the new scents in the midnight air. The pack filed around to join their alpha, eyes bright with friendly interest and tails waving high in greeting. Killian glanced back at Lars and Rose, wagging reassurance, and approached the grey wolf. He lowered his tail in deference to the pack leader. *"Forgive my rudeness?"*

The alpha circled around him, taking in his scent. *"The magic one was right. You do not smell right."*

"Magic one?" An image of Noak and his terrible light flashed through Killian's mind.

"The water dweller sent us to find you."

Relief washed through Killian. For a moment he'd thought the "magic one" might be the sorcerer.

"Why?"

The alpha eyed him. *"Our blood has run in your pack for many years. All wolves know this. We can sense it."*

So, people really were right. The wolves were calling to their own.

"We've come to offer you a place in our pack."

Killian started, his head flying up with pricked ears. The grey wolf cocked his head, amused.

"You are one of us. Wolves do not travel alone."

Killian's heart pounded. He could be accepted into the pack. He kneaded his paws in the ground in anticipation of joining the hunt. Acceptance leapt to the tip of his tongue, but a breeze tickled his nose with the scent of human. Killian looked back over his shoulder at Lars and Rose, who crouched by the dying fire, knives close at hand.

"I'm not sure." It slipped out.

The alpha's growl silenced the rumble that ran through the pack. His mate pushed forward and circled Killian.

"Run with us before you decide."

The pack yipped and barked as they vanished into the forest. Killian hesitated only a moment before his wolf instincts took over and he tore after them, not heeding Lars's shout.

He caught up to the pack and they allowed him into their midst. They ran with no destination, occasionally stopping to pounce on one another and scuffle playfully in the moonlight.

Eventually they padded to a stop. The other wolves threaded around him, taking time to meet him, tussling sporadically when nips became too playful. The alpha stood apart, joining in only when he thought the wrestling turned too serious.

Killian flopped to the ground, tongue lolling as he tried to catch his breath. His shoulder twinged, all but forgotten since he had bolted after the pack. He nuzzled at the bandage and it came free. A brawny male nosed at it with some interest before wandering away out of deference to the approaching alpha.

"Now that you have run with us, would you join the pack?" The grey wolf stared into his eyes.

"But I'm not really a wolf."

"You are more like us than like the humans."

Killian's throat closed, and he flattened his ears. Was he really just a wolf that had been living in human skin?

An owl hooted, and he swiveled an ear. Lars had always wanted a tame owl. *Lars.* Killian pushed to his feet. His brother would be furious at him for running off. The alpha's offer lingered in his mind.

Every wolf needed a pack. He knew that. *What about my family?* They'd be worried sick. And Rose was looking for family, too.

"I can't. I already have a pack."

The alpha growled deep in his throat. *"The humans."*

"The man is my brother."

The alpha shook himself. He understood family. *"Very well. But it will not be safe for you. Is your pack strong enough to defend you?"*

Killian didn't know Rose very well, but he did know Lars.

"Yes."

"Very well. May your pack stay strong."

"And may the white wolf guide you." Killian nuzzled the alpha respectfully.

"There are strange scents in the wind. Tread carefully. If you need more teeth and claws, my pack and I will come."

Killian bowed his thanks. He loped away, pausing to join his voice to the howls of farewell.

Dawn's blush teased the sky when he limped into the camp. Rose and Lars sat by the fire in silence. Lars's shoulders drooped, and Killian's heart twinged with guilt. *He must have thought I wouldn't come back.*

Rose glanced up and her cry of relief jerked Lars's gaze in Killian's direction.

"What were you thinking, just running off like that?" Lars's voice rose in anger, but Killian heard the fear behind it. "It's been hours!"

Killian cleared the distance between them in two bounds, knocking Lars onto his back.

"Stop doing that!" Lars grumbled.

Killian lay on his chest in response. Lars rolled his eyes and shoved him off.

"I was starting to think you wouldn't come back," he admitted.

"You're my pack." Killian nudged his arm, growling. *"Of course I came back."*

"I hope that was something sweet and endearing." Lars rubbed the fur on Killian's head the wrong way—as irritating in Killian's wolf form as it had been when he was human.

Well, more human. Killian huffed and shrugged away, nipping at his brother's hand.

"I see you went and tore off your bandage." Rose frowned at him.

Killian ducked his head sheepishly and offered a wolfish grin.

She rolled her eyes. "I have another."

After she re-bandaged Killian's shoulder, Rose and Lars packed the camp in silence and stepped out into the wide plains of Calvyrn. Killian lingered for a moment longer, hesitant to leave the safety of the forest. He could find places to hide within the familiar trees, but out on the open plains, discovery lurked over every rise.

Chapter 7

Rose adjusted the quiver over her back and dragged a sleeve across her sweaty brow. She stifled another grumble of irritation. *Prince* Lars walked ahead of her, leading the stallion. He'd walked at least two steps ahead since they'd left the forest the morning before.

Maybe he did it purposefully, maybe she unconsciously let him. They hadn't exchanged more than a few words, which was probably for the best. It kept them from arguing.

Or rather, kept him from contradicting and arguing anything she said.

No, I should be more respectful, no matter how hard that might be. At least Prince Lars had grudgingly allowed her to come. She just needed to prove herself useful enough to convince him to let her join the Rangers.

Her aching feet and growling stomach, contrasted with his self-confident walk, made it difficult.

And I'll have to be dying before I ask to ride that horse.

Rose kept a watchful eye on her surroundings as her father had taught her, looking for anything out of the ordinary. Anything that might give away the fact that he was about to ambush her during their training sessions.

She allowed a quick smile. It was getting harder for him to surprise her.

The plains rippled with uneven hills topped with scrawny sage and sweet-smelling grete bushes. Grouse and gophers darted away when they sensed Killian and the occasional buzzard hovering overhead.

She glanced back at Killian. He'd followed close to Lars all morning, but had since fallen behind, hobbling gamely after them. He caught her gaze and tried to hurry, only succeeding in limping worse. Lars didn't seem to notice.

She pursed her lips in irritation.

"Lars!" She was probably supposed to address him with his title, but technically he hadn't specified.

He kept walking. *Absolutely insufferable.*

She clenched her teeth. "Prince Lars!" This time he stopped.

"What?" His growl was almost as impressive as Killian's. She jerked her head at Killian who kept on walking, ignoring them both.

"Killi." Lars used his prince voice and Killian growled at him.

Rose left them to snarl at each other, opting to look for a decent spot to rest off the narrow, worn track someone considered a road.

Just over a low hill she found a hollow wide enough to fit all of them. She clambered back over to the road.

"We can rest over here," she said, breaking into their conversation.

Killian stalked over and eased a breath of relief as he settled down at the bottom of the hollow. Lars must have heard it too, because he said nothing, moving to Jeppe to loosen his girth.

Rose checked the bandage on Killian's shoulder. She didn't know much beyond basic aid, but she could see the journey was not helping the gash heal.

Trouble was, Killian would refuse to be carried. He seemed a shade more considerate than his brother, but just as stubborn.

Father always said I'm too stubborn for anyone's good, and if I'll ever agree with Prince Lars about anything, it'll be on Killian.

Killian slept for over an hour as Lars and Rose ate a light meal in silence. The dry grass crackled under her boots as she shifted her feet.

Is there anything we can possibly talk about without arguing?

A bead of sweat trickled down her collar under the touch of the warm afternoon sun. Or from the realization that she couldn't think of one neutral topic. Her stomach flipped in relief as Killian woke. He yawned twice and stretched, staring at them with amber eyes full of reproach.

Rose didn't feel any guilt whatsoever as he walked more easily back to the road.

I'll have a word with Prince Lars tonight when Killian's off hunting, then.

*

The sun sank in a haze of brilliant red. Killian watched the light cast across the empty plains, highlighting their wild and lonely vastness. He focused on the sight to ignore the emptiness remaining after a less-than-filling meal of gopher. He licked the last traces of the meal away and trotted back to camp.

Rose and Lars had agreed for the first time that it might be better not to light a fire, since the whereabouts of the sorcerer remained unknown. He paused on the outskirts of their camp. They hastily finished a conversation when they noticed him in the fading light. It clearly wasn't an argument, since Rose looked pleased.

That's suspicious.

Rose stood and grabbed the medical supplies out of her pack, crossing to his side in two quick steps.

"Have a good hunt?" She settled by his side.

He flicked his ears back, but she eyed his bandage with determination. He sighed and sank back on his haunches.

She's a little fussy. Honestly, it's barely a scratch. Killian didn't care to remember how tender his shoulder had been earlier that day. Rose finished re-wrapping the bandage and stationed herself beside him as he laid down.

Lars took up a sentry position on the opposite side of camp, turning away from both of them. Killian marked an unfamiliar tenseness in the set of his brother's shoulders. He huffed a sigh.

Rose shot Killian a sideways glance. "He always act like this?"

Killian's usual defenses of his brother leapt to his tongue, but he paused, and not just because Rose wouldn't be able to understand him. Guilt pricked his conscience. He'd always stood up for Lars—he was his brother after all—but he'd never been able to get Lars to realize that the way he acted gained him no favors with his subjects.

"Sorry, I probably shouldn't have asked." Rose broke into his thoughts. He nudged her hand to tell her he didn't mind.

"Wish you could talk." Rose sighed. "You could tell me how t' get along with him."

Killian rested his nose on his paws and rumbled agreement. *I couldn't even get him to stop acting like an idiot when I could talk, so we might both be out of luck.*

Chapter 8

Killian lashed his tail in impatience as Rose took longer than usual to change his bandage. Lars had saddled Jeppe already but was fiddling with the packs.

I could be in Myrnius by now if it weren't for these two.

Rose frowned and shook her head, releasing the bandage and beginning again. Killian twisted his head to gently nip at her fingers. She flicked at his nose and he flattened his ears.

"I'm almost done," she said.

He swiveled his ears back up and tipped his head to the side to apologize. She tied off the bandage and tapped his nose again with a slight smile.

"Sorry." Her gaze flicked past him.

What – ?

Lars's strong arms encircled him, hefting him off the ground.

"Put me down!" He barked and twisted. But the one thing Lars had never neglected was training, and his grip couldn't

be broken. Lars walked over to Jeppe, staggering a little as Killian continued to thrash.

Killian grabbed at his sleeve, wrestling the fabric in his teeth. Lars shook him.

"Don't even think about it, Killian!"

"*Then put me down.*" He growled and managed to kick at Lars with one of his hind legs. "*I'll put a carcass in your bed roll. I can make your life miserable!*" He noticed a blanket arranged as a sling around Jeppe's saddle. "*Don't even think about it!*"

Lars grunted and hoisted him higher in his arms. Jeppe nickered in amusement and bent his forelegs a little, bringing the sling closer to Lars.

"*Traitor,*" Killian growled, but the stallion only rumbled another chuckle.

Rose appeared at Lars's side and helped wrangle Killian into the sling. He ended up propped up against the saddle itself, the blanket supporting his hindquarters. He glared balefully down at them both, letting his fangs show for a brief moment with another growl.

Lars ignored him and checked the bindings on the sling.

"Sorry," Rose mouthed again and scooped up her pack.

Killian scrabbled for a grip as Jeppe stepped out in response to Lars's tug on the reins. He precariously rocked back and forth for a few steps until he found his balance and settled more securely in his new seat.

How humiliating.

Killian frostily ignored the stallion's chuckles and tried to figure out a way down. There was no alternative that didn't involve landing on his injured shoulder, so he spent the better part of the morning in an irritated sulk.

The sun had begun its midday arc when Killian noticed Rose over ten paces behind them. *At least she's paying attention.*

Lars stared at the ground in front of his boots as he led Jeppe. A growl tickled Killian's throat. Maybe he couldn't talk, but he'd make sure Lars extended some basic courtesy to their traveling companion.

I swear some days he acts like he's younger than me!

He waited until Lars dropped back a pace before swiping at his brother's head with a heavy paw.

"Killian!" Lars exclaimed as he dodged a second swipe. "How old are you?"

Killian stared at him balefully. *"I could ask the same!"*

"What do you want?"

"You to stop making this the worst adventure ever." Killian looked pointedly at Rose trailing behind them.

"What do you want me to do? She seems perfectly fine back there."

"So help me, Lars!" Killian growled and flattened his ears.

"She doesn't like me, and I don't care for her either, so why bother?"

"Because I have to put up with both of you."

"I'm not going to walk around with a girl who wants to play Ranger dress up," Lars hissed.

"Oh, so when we did it as children, it was fine?" Killian growled again, deeper and more menacing. *"Just tell her she can walk with us!"*

"I don't know what you're saying, but it's not happening."

We'll see about that.

Killian had always been adept at manipulating his brother, even before he had an irresistible canine charm.

Killian dropped his ears and let his head droop, staring up at Lars from under hooded lids.

"Killian, don't you dare!"

A low whine escaped.

"That is not fair!"

Killian dropped his head to rest atop his paws.

"Fine!" Lars scowled. "But I'll get my revenge when you're least expecting it."

Killian huffed and resettled himself on Jeppe, who helpfully stopped before Lars tugged on the reins.

Lars frowned. "You're turning my horse against me now?"

"*Anything to help,*" Jeppe said, and Killian let out a triumphant bark of laughter.

Lars glared at Rose, who had paused to watch their exchange.

"We're not waiting if you fall behind." Lars dodged Killian's paw. "My *dear* brother would love someone else to pick on up here."

Rose's head ducked to hide a smile as she hurried to Jeppe's other side. Killian twisted around, tongue flopping, and grinned down at her. She shot him a grateful wink and stepped out smartly to match Lars's new pace.

Lars lifted him down when they stopped for lunch, whereupon Killian promptly raced away. He wasn't hungry, but he was full of restless energy after being trapped on Jeppe for hours.

A sharp twinge in his shoulder cut short the run. He clawed at the ground in frustration before reluctantly turning back to camp. Killian padded cautiously forward, keeping one eye on Rose, while searching for Lars.

Warning sparked in Killian's chest at Rose's triumphant grin. He had seconds to brace before Lars tackled him from behind, securing him once again. Killian managed a few nips before Lars bundled him back onto the saddle.

They glared at one another and Killian took a moment to finish planning his revenge. Lars rolled his eyes, as if he could read Killian's mind, and tugged Jeppe on.

*

So much for an early start. Lars crossed his arms.

"One more day, Killi. That's all we're asking. You have to rest your shoulder."

Killian crouched near to the ground and snarled, clearly not taken with the idea.

"Killian!" Lars snapped.

Killian barked back, an incomprehensible insult. He probably could understand if he tried, but he couldn't bring himself to admit the shaggy animal growling at his feet could be his brother.

His brother whose stubbornness and sense of adventure was only heightened by the rambunctious nature of a young wolf. His brother who would never hurt anyone had been singled out by a stupid, pointless, petty curse. *And it's all my fault.*

He moved towards Killian, who backed up. Lars clenched his jaw.

The only reason I'm not jumping on you again is because I don't want to hurt you. But I'm about past caring.

Rose cleared her throat and Lars whirled. "What?"

She gave him an even stare. "Can I try?"

He threw his hands up. "Fine!"

Lars stalked over to Jeppe, uncomfortably aware that he acted childish around Rose. She deserved to be treated better. He had once declared that he didn't care about a person's station as long as they could handle themselves. That fact prodded him like a thorn in his foot.

She certainly acted like she could use her weapons.

But she's a commoner! He could practically hear his friends' mocking laughter. *And a girl!* He frowned and crossed his arms.

Is it because she's exposed the truth about yourself you've tried to ignore? Pauline's nagging internal voice surfaced.

Lars glanced over his shoulder, watching Rose as she knelt before his brother.

"Killian, please ride Jeppe again today. Your brother is right. You need to rest your shoulder."

She bit a quivering bottom lip. Judging from Killian's startled posture, he'd noticed it, too. *About time he gets a taste of his own medicine.*

"I just want t' make sure the wound will finally close properly," Rose coaxed, smoothing the hackles on the back of Killian's neck. "You can probably walk tomorrow."

Killian darted a glance between Lars and Rose and growled in defeat, finally padding over to Lars. He didn't look up, just waited to be lifted up onto Jeppe.

Lars bit back a chuckle as he scooped Killian up, but it still escaped. Killian shook his head and went limp. Blood rushed to Lars's face and he clutched his brother, struggling to adjust to the sudden dead weight in his arms. Killian hung for a moment before graciously helping Lars place him in the sling.

Rose stepped forward, taking Jeppe's reins. "May I, Prince Lars?"

He couldn't miss the faint sarcasm in his title, but Lars wordlessly nodded, following as she led the way back onto the road. This time, Lars lagged a pace behind.

Fresh guilt swept over him at Killian's bark. He slowed under the weight of the shame that accompanied the sensation, hating himself a little more at the sight of Rose holding a one-sided conversation with Killian as they walked.

She's trying. Unlike me.

He'd let the talk of the curse affect him more than he'd like to admit. Some days it was easier to leave Killian behind than face the whispers that dogged his brother. He had purposefully drunk too much at the feast so he wouldn't be woken by the howling wolves that night and, as a result, hadn't woken to go ride with Killian. He hadn't been there to protect him from the sorcerer.

A growl jerked him from his thoughts and he looked up. He'd fallen further behind than he'd realized. Killian and Rose had stopped to look back at him, expressions puzzled and a little concerned. Lars touched the sword at his waist and jogged to catch them.

He didn't look at Killian. Maybe he'd explain if they ever broke the spell.

If? When did it become if and not when?

"Let's go," he said gruffly, and brushed past them.

Chapter 9

"So, Miss Ranger, where are we?"

"Is t' prince lost?"

"I'm not lost. I'm just not entirely sure where I am."

Killian watched them both try to interpret the faded markings on the weathered post at the crossroads. The narrow dirt track they'd travelled on since yesterday did not appear on Lars's map, and consequently, neither did the crossroads.

Lars frowned down at Rose. "I thought *Rangers* were supposed to know the roads of the kingdom."

"T' roads on a map, maybe. Obviously, it hasn't been updated in a while, *your highness.*"

"And where do you think we get that information?" Lars lifted an eyebrow.

Killian sighed, twitching his nose and sampling the breeze. There were humans close by, and not just his pungent travelling companions. Humans, and running water. It stood to reason that there would be a town or village around the river.

Clearly the village wasn't marked either or they would be headed there now. They needed information and supplies. He should know, since he'd sat on their sad, flat packs for two days.

"Jeppe, I don't think these two will move any time soon." The stallion snorted. *"My master can be quite headstrong."*

"That's one word for it. What do you say we head east?" Jeppe stamped a hind foot. *"It might look odd for a wolf to ride a horse into town."*

"Then let's hope they follow." Killian allowed a canine smirk. *"Onward!"*

Rose and Lars broke off their argument, chasing after Jeppe as Killian looked over his shoulder. *Serves them right for being so stubborn.*

"Where do you think you're going?" Lars stumbled in a gopher hole but kept running. "Woah there, Jeppe!"

Killian steadied himself against the saddle. *"Keep going."*

Jeppe blew out a breath of laughter and quickened his trot. *"I'm blaming you if he cuts my feed, sir."*

"Leave him to me." Killian grabbed a mouthful of mane as Jeppe overstepped to avoid another hole. *"Just don't dump me off before we get there."*

For the sake of self-preservation, Killian told Jeppe to halt when they were in sight of the town. Even Rose didn't look too pleased.

"Couldn't have told us about this?" Lars gestured at the cluster of buildings.

"You weren't listening." Killian twitched his nose. Now that they were closer, something else tickled the air. Some scent that made his stomach churn.

"You smell it too?" Jeppe shifted his forelegs and tossed his head to look around.

Killian almost told Jeppe to head in the opposite direction.

"Might as well go down." Lars wiped at the sweat beading his forehead.

"We need some supplies." Rose nodded.

"They might know something about the sorcerer, or at least if anyone's looking for us."

"No one's looking for me, so you don't have t' worry," Rose said, and Lars's expression softened ever so slightly.

Killian shifted, rising to scramble down from Jeppe. Lars caught him just in time and set him safely on the ground.

What is that scent? He nosed the ground, searching his memory, and came up with nothing. Even his wolf's instincts could tell him nothing, except that something dangerous waited nearby.

"You should probably change your name," Rose was saying.

Lars opened his mouth to object, but wisdom won out. They were trying to minimize the chance of discovery after all.

"Ivar for me, then. Killian, you're Ulfr."

"Wolf. How original." Killian injected as much sarcasm as possible into his growl, shaking his head.

Lars scowled at him. "Shut up."

Apparently, sarcasm still translated.

The closer they came to the village the more uneasy Killian became. He kept pausing to sniff the wind or flick his ears to hear anything besides the silence that covered the town. Something lurked out there beyond the tall stalks of corn swaying gently in the light wind.

The main street stood empty and the house and shop doors were shut tight. Nothing stirred in the fields. Rose placed an arrow on her bow and Lars unsheathed his sword, the same unease tightening their movements.

"Where is everyone?" Rose whispered as they tiptoed along the sparsely-paved street. The wide center square opened up before them.

"There." Lars pointed to a double-story inn that took up a whole side of the square, cobbled together from weathered boards and smoothed river stones. A young boy spotted them, and then darted inside the broad doors.

He returned in a moment, followed by dozens of men and women in homespun clothes. Their eyes were wide in fear and surprise as they stared back at Lars and Rose. Killian caught sight of children clustering behind the doors and windows of the inn, curiosity gleaming in their bright eyes.

"How'd you get here?" A man demanded as he crossed his arms.

"Walked right in." Lars lifted his chin.

"How'd y' get past them?" A shrill voice cried.

"Who?" Lars returned, his knuckles whitening in a new grip as his shoulders tensed again.

"Baedons!"

Lars and Rose blanched, and a growl broke from Killian. He'd never seen a full baedon, only a head drug back to the castle by a battered knight. *That explains the smell.*

Lars cleared his throat. "How many?"

"Two," the first man said. "They've kept us trapped here for weeks. Crops need tending, and those foolish enough t' go out don't come back."

"Have you reported it?"

"What's t' point? A messenger on foot would never get through and we don't 'ave a fancy horse like yours. Besides, we all know t' prince wouldn't do anything about it."

"Adam!" Another woman slapped his shoulder.

A flush tinged Lars's face but Killian couldn't tell if it was anger or embarrassment. Lars cleared his throat again.

"He's right." He stumbled over the words. "Can we help?"

Adam gave a bitter laugh. "I've heard tell that it takes a score o' knights t' take down one baedon. What are you going t' do about it?"

"Look at 'im. He at least 'as training." Another man shouldered forward. "Ever fought a baedon, lad?"

Anxious and curious faces studied Lars, traces of fresh hope evident.

"No, but I've heard stories," Lars said.

This sparked a heated debate among the townsfolk who each had heard variations of tales on the best way to take down the creatures.

The smell Killian had first noticed outside the village grew stronger and he tried to still his quivering paws. Rose tapped Lars's arm and pointed at the figure of a young girl sprinting towards them.

The girl fell into Adam's arms, tears streaming down her pale face. "Ernst insisted on going out! They're 'ere!"

Lars whirled and pulled the packs from the saddle, loosening the bindings on his heavy hunting spear.

"What're you doing?" Rose grabbed his arm, her eyes wide.

"I have a responsibility to these people, don't I? It's my fault they're trapped here. It's probably my fault those baedons are so far from the eastern caves. That boy might be alive out there." Lars gritted his teeth.

Rose hesitated only a moment. "I'm coming with you. There are two out there. You can't take on both."

"*I'm coming, too,*" Killian growled.

"All right." Lars glanced at both of them. "Rose, your light bow won't pierce their hide. Take this." He handed her the loaded crossbow and quiver of bolts. "You know how to use it?"

She nodded, buckling the quiver around her waist. Arguments stilled around them and murmurs rippled through the townsfolk.

Adam rushed forward. "You can't go out there!"

"Someone has to." Lars freed the spear and tightened Jeppe's girth.

They ran for the edge of town. When they broke past the last house, Killian got his first look at a live Baedon.

Built like a man and taller than most knights, its long limbs were covered in dull grey-green scales. Curved claws and the sharpened fangs protruding from its narrow muzzle glinted in the sunlight as it paced through the fields, searching for its prey. Even from this distance, he could see its most dangerous weapon; beady red eyes that conjured up its prey's worst fears when caught in their stare.

It was said that baedons preferred their meat sweetened by fear. Even being in their presence brought on a paralyzing terror.

Every instinct urged Killian to tuck tail and run, but he willed himself to stand firm. Lars and Rose held their weapons in a white-knuckled grip.

Rose swallowed hard. "There's — there's only one."

"That we can see." Killian's heart slowed a beat at Lars's steady voice. "Rose, you and Killian stay here and watch for the second."

Killian dug his trembling paws into the ground, more than happy to obey as Lars swung into the saddle, spear at the ready. Jeppe threw his head high and snorted fearfully.

"Jeppe, take care of him!"

Killian's words seemed to calm the stallion and he lunged forward at Lars's command. The baedon saw them coming and ceased his hunt through the corn. It pushed stalks from its path as it began to stride towards them. Jeppe swiveled on his hindquarters and passed behind it. Lars's fear showed in his quick jerk of the reins.

"Steady, Jeppe!"

The baedon lunged and Lars jabbed with the spear as Jeppe reared. A human figure broke from the cover of the field and bolted towards them. Rose waved him on with a shout, raising the crossbow to cover his flight. When the boy was safely inside the town, they turned their attention back to Lars, only to see he'd been unhorsed and faced the baedon on foot.

Lars dodged a swipe from curved claws and retaliated with the spear. Killian didn't need to see his pale face to sense his fear. Lars wouldn't last much longer alone. *This is what we've trained for, isn't it? To battle monsters together?*

He took a trembling step, even as his pounding heart told him to go in any other direction.

Lars tumbled with a cry and staggered to his feet. Killian growled. His brother needed help. He couldn't let Lars get hurt. He looked to Rose.

"I'm fine," she said. "Go!"

The words barely left her mouth when Killian bolted, racing toward the baedon.

Lars's eyes widened. "Killian, no!"

Killian ignored him, baring his fangs in a savage snarl. He launched into the air, sinking his teeth into the baedon's thigh. The bitter, oily taste of its scales filled his mouth, but he hung on, dimly hearing Lars's war cry.

Killian released its leg and attacked again, darting between its legs, snapping and growling. Lars used the distraction to thrust at its chest. The baedon batted the spear away and lunged at Lars with a high-pitched wail. Killian leapt up and latched onto its arm.

The baedon's other paw swung at Killian, and he could only wait to be torn apart.

But it never came.

Only a wild cry from Lars and a *crunch* as his spear embedded itself in the baedon's scaled chest. Killian leaped back as it fell to the ground, watching in grim satisfaction as Lars drew his sword and plunged it through the baedon's neck.

They both stood in silence for a long moment over the fallen beast. Killian ran his tongue over his teeth, gagging at the rancid taste. He glanced up at Lars. Color slowly returned to his brother's face, but a scream cut off his words.

They whirled to see the second baedon advancing on Rose, and Lars cursed.

He wrenched his sword free from the dead baedon, but the spear stuck.

Killian laid his ears back and whined. "*Hurry!*"

The spear budged a fraction. Lars cursed again. The Baedon was closing in.

"Killian, go!"

But he was already gone, tearing back to help Rose.

*

Rose watched, her breath frozen in her throat as the brothers fought the baedon. Her cry of triumph died as a nightmare rose out of the cornstalks before her. Scarlet eyes glimmered as she tried to raise the crossbow, its fangs dripping as it stalked forward.

Her terror won out and she screamed.

Some corner of her mind fought back. *Do something! Buy time for help to come.*

She stepped back and raised the crossbow but fired too hastily and the bolt flew just wide.

The Baedon's lips curled back in a fanged smile of triumph. They both knew she didn't have time to reload. Rose yanked a knife from her belt as a brown streak slammed into the baedon. Killian's momentum brought it to the ground, where they tussled with enraged snarls.

Rose set the nose of the crossbow on the ground and jammed her foot into the stirrup. She pulled a bolt free, set it on the string, and hauled back with all her might until it clicked into place.

The baedon swatted Killian away and leapt to its feet. Killian scrambled up, barking furiously, keeping its attention away from her. Rose took a steadying breath and darted in front of Killian, raising the bow and firing in one smooth motion. The bolt slammed into the Baedon's chest, burying itself almost up to its fletching.

The baedon staggered, but still tried to keep coming. A new cry sounded and the baedon halted as Lars's bloody sword protruded from its throat.

A sob of relief escaped her as the baedon crumpled to the ground. She fell to her knee, fading adrenaline leaving her hands trembling.

"You all right?" Lars bent over, his hands on his knees, breathless.

She nodded, concentrating on making her hands stop their frantic shaking. Killian pawed at her knee, concern evident in his amber eyes.

"I'm fine." Her hands sunk into his fur as she hugged him. "Thank you."

He nudged her shoulder and barked, then went to Lars.

"Killian, don't ever do that again." Lars dropped to one knee as Killian bulled into his arms.

Rose laughed, breaking the tension.

"I thought I told you to stay put." Lars cuffed the back of Killian's head.

"You could have gotten hurt." Rose prodded at Killian's bandage.

Killian nipped at both of their hands and retreated with a growl. Lars ruffled Killian's fur and offered her a hand to rise to her feet.

"That was a good shot." He looked genuinely impressed.

She retrieved the crossbow from the ground, offering a tentative smile. "Told you my father trained me."

A grin touched the corner of his mouth. "So you did."

"Although it was my first time in any sort of fight."

"Mine too." He pulled his sword free of the baedon.

"Really?" Rose frowned. "I thought you would have been in plenty."

"Killian and I hoped to go after a Wyvern together. Clearly we underestimated Baedon fights."

"Right, because what's not t' love about this?" She gestured to the carcasses with a smirk.

Lars's chuckle died as Jeppe limped up to them. Rose caught the reins and ran a soothing hand down Jeppe's sweat-streaked neck as Lars gingerly touched the bleeding gashes on Jeppe's hindquarters. Jeppe edged away until Killian wove around his shaggy fetlocks, whining reassurances to the stallion.

"Will he be all right?"

Lars wiped bloody hands on his trousers. "We need to close these wounds."

"Allow us t' help." Adam and a few other townsfolk edged closer to them, casting fearful glances at the dead baedon. "If I hadn't seen you two do it, I'd never believe it." He shook his head. "Who are you?"

"I'm Ivar," Lars said. "This is..." He stared at Rose. They hadn't discussed that question.

"His sister. I'm Rose." She smiled. Hopefully, it would prevent any further questions.

"Where'd you come from?"

Obviously not.

"Our village isn't too far from Lagarah Lake. Do you have someone who might be able to help my horse?" Lars rubbed Jeppe's nose.

"Aye, Marten can." Adam jerked a thumb over his shoulder.

Rose led Jeppe as they entered the town where cheering villagers engulfed them, pushing each other to get closer to them. Rose's shoulders began to ache from slaps and wild embraces. Killian obtained a following of his own as the youngsters discovered he wasn't as fierce as he looked, and he tried to dodge tiny hands.

Lars hovered like an anxious hen as Marten cared for Jeppe. Rose waited beside him, and Killian crept as close as Marten would allow to nudge at Jeppe's foreleg with his nose. Marten stepped back and wiped his hands on a tattered cloth.

"That's all I can do for now," he said.

Killian returned to nudge at Lars's legs. Concern showed in Lars's eyes as he rubbed Jeppe's nose, crooning softly as the stallion settled.

Don't make me feel sorry for you now. Rose couldn't quite stop her heart from softening at the sight.

"Come on back t' the inn and we'll get you a meal." Adam beckoned them from the stable.

The innkeeper, a middle-aged man of impressive girth, practically shoved them into chairs.

"You'll 'ave the best of everything, and stay 'ere of course," he declared. "You'll just 'ave to wait until some of these folk that've been trapped 'ere leave, and we can get rooms ready for you."

Rose prepared to contest the price of the rooms at least, but her stomach growled audibly and the innkeeper chuckled. A smile touched the corner of Lars's mouth.

"I'll take that as a yes, then." He hurried back to the kitchen, returning a few minutes later with steaming plates.

Lars raised an eyebrow at the beef hash and brown bread, but tentatively dug in.

Probably not up to castle standards. Rose scooped a large spoonful, still trying to avoid liking him after the events of the last few hours.

But he graciously scraped the plate clean, as grateful as she was for a hot, cooked meal.

Killian finished his portion and curled up by the fire. He tipped his nose up in a definite air of satisfied smugness before closing his eyes to nap while she and Lars were besieged by a thousand and one questions from the grateful villagers. For once, she actually envied him.

Chapter 10

Lars took a seat on one of the worn benches that lined the outskirts of the town square. It wobbled as he shifted his weight to lean against the wall behind him. The party had been in full swing for several hours, yet the bonfire in the center of the square still blazed, and the tables boasted plenty of food.

It was certainly different from any celebration he'd attended, and not just because of the water in his mug. *I wonder if they would still treat me with the same friendship if they knew who I really am?*

Killian nudged his leg and settled on the ground at Lars's feet, escaping the sticky-fingered attention of the youngsters for the moment.

"Where'd you get him?" Adam sat on the bench beside Lars, sending it rocking again. "Wolf, isn't he?"

"Not full." Lars scowled defensively. "He's been following me around since he was a pup."

That, at least, was true.

"Have t' admit, most people were a bit wary at first."

"Most are." Lars nodded. "He'd never hurt anyone."

"Suppose we should be grateful he took exception t' those baedons, then."

Lars laughed and nudged Killian. "Scared me to death, though. Don't know what I'd do without him."

A rumbling growl came from Killian and Lars could picture his brother rolling his eyes.

Adam only chuckled. "Can I get you another drink?"

Lars glanced at the clear liquid sloshing in his cup. It was so tempting.

"No." He shook his head.

"Sure? I heard you've only had water all night. We celebrating or not?"

"I — uh — last time I had too much, I wasn't there when my brother needed me." His gaze fell to Killian's amber eyes.

Adam regarded him for a moment. "I see. What happened t' him?"

"Ran away from home. He's the reason for our journey."

"Well, I wish you luck, lad." Adam raised his mug.

Lars simply nodded his thanks.

"But in t' meantime, I'd look t' your sister." Adam chuckled, heading back to the brew master.

Lars looked for Rose and laughed. She'd been surrounded by the young men of the village, looking more and more like a trapped animal. She saw him and gave a quick, pleading look. He waved, and she practically sprinted across the square.

"Some 'brother' you are." She collapsed onto the bench beside him.

"How am I supposed to know? I've never had a sister." He grinned, enjoying the easy camaraderie. "Unless you count Killian."

He was rewarded with a sharp nip to his shin.

Rose laughed. "You're lucky, though. It's just my father and me." Her smile faded and she blinked suspiciously fast. "Sorry."

She sheepishly glanced at him. "I know I shouldn't worry, but…"

All-too-familiar guilt twinged in Lars's chest. It was easy to forget he wasn't the only one who had lost a loved one to Noak's power.

"I'm sure he's all right." It wasn't much, but it was more effort than he'd ever put forth. Rose offered a small smile, appearing at least to appreciate it.

The vibrant notes of a fiddle broke their somber mood. Rose took a quick breath and smiled, a sudden gleam in her eye.

"We should dance. It'd be rude not t' at our celebration."

Lars glanced at the lines of dancers forming. "I don't know how to do this one."

It was rapidly turning into something rowdier than the stately affairs at the castle.

Rose stood. "I'll teach you. That's what sisters are for, right?"

She raised her eyebrows, both uncertainty and a challenge in her voice.

The highborn pride he'd carefully fostered urged him to refuse. His rebellious streak won out, and he stood. Maybe it was time to learn something about his people.

If nothing else, it would be a story to make Pauline laugh when they got back.

Rose's eyes widened in mock surprise.

"Don't fall over. I might not catch you," he warned. His wry grin was rewarded by a genuine laugh. She took his hand.

"Come on. And you're next." She pointed to Killian who responded with a bark and a toothy grin.

Lars thought he could hear a bit of Killian's laugh in the noise.

*

"'Ere you go, boy." The innkeeper placed a bowl full of meat and bread chunks in front of Killian and ruffled his ears.

Killian twitched his nose in mild annoyance at the gesture. But it wasn't the man's fault. He thought Killian was just another dog. He pushed to his feet to eat as the innkeeper coaxed a fire back to the hearth.

Killian licked the bowl clean as Lars stumbled down the stairs. Killian watched in amusement. His brother had never been one for mornings, much to their father's dismay. Lars took a seat at the table closest to Killian and the fire, resting his head on a hand.

"Why?" he groaned.

Because you both wanted an early start and asked to be woken up. Just as well he couldn't actually say it out loud.

"Here, lad." The innkeeper's wife set a steaming mug by Lars. The potent scent wafting through the room elicited a sneeze from Killian. Lars lifted a questioning eyebrow.

She smiled and nudged it closer. "Kaffe. My husband can't function without it in t' mornings."

Lars took an experimental sip. "Where have you been all my life?"

The woman laughed. "I'll make sure he includes some in your packs."

"You'd hate it," Lars told Killian as he took another sip.

Judging from the smell, Lars was probably right. A creak on the stairs announced Rose as she joined them. She'd done away with the overdress and wore trousers and a tunic. She hesitated for a brief moment as they both stared at her new outfit. Lars pushed out the chair across from him with a foot.

"Morning." She took the offered seat.

Lars nodded and took another sip. The kaffe had not yet restored his ability to speak more than a few words.

"Is that kaffe?"

"You've had it?"

"Once. I love the smell, hate the taste." She smiled. "My father drinks it. I think almost all Rangers do."

The innkeeper's wife returned with plates of breakfast. Even though Killian had already eaten, he perked up at the smell of spiced sausage.

"I'm not sharing." Lars nudged Killian's ribs with the toe of his boot.

Killian nipped at his foot. *"Jerk."*

Breakfast and the kaffe resurrected Lars to something almost coherent by the time Adam and Marten walked through the swinging doors.

"I've some bad news," Marten said. Worried frowns creased their weathered faces. "Adam's saying you want t' leave today? Well, that horse of yours ain't fit t' travel."

"What?" Lars straightened, and his eyes narrowed in anger.

"Aye, I closed t' wounds, but he's going t' need a good bit before trekking t' wherever it is you're headed. And he's sure not going t' be well enough t' ride."

"How long?"

"Three or four days at t' least."

Rose bit her lip and cast an anxious glance down at Killian. He looked from her to Lars, knowing they were thinking the same thing. They couldn't afford to wait that long.

The solstice was coming, like it or not, and the sorcerer was still out there. They needed to get to Myrnius.

"You're welcome t' stay as long as you need," Adam said. "You won't lack for food or lodging. Take some time t' think about it."

The men left, and Killian hopped up onto Adam's vacated chair.

"What do we do?" Rose picked at the cuff of her sleeve.

Lars spun his empty cup between his hands until Killian growled at him.

"We can leave Jeppe here." Lars settled the cup on the table. It obviously tore at him to leave the stallion behind. "I have some silver coins. Maybe it will be enough to lodge him until we come back."

Warmth pooled in Killian's chest. *He really thinks we'll make it back.*

"But what if something happens?" Rose frowned. "Just ask them t' kindly return him t' the castle? They're farmers. They can't just trek across the country for a horse."

"Then they could keep him or turn him loose." Lars spun the cup again, staring down as it tracked circles on the table. *"He could find his way back."*

"He's just a horse," Lars said. "We have to get to Myrnius."

"I'm all right, I have two legs t' walk on. He's your horse, so you make t' decision." Rose rested her arms on the table.

"I'll go talk to Adam, then." Lars pushed away from the table. "Will you make sure we have the provisions we need?"

Lars asked instead of ordered. Perhaps more good had come out of the battle with the baedons than Killian had realized.

Rose left to seek out the innkeeper's wife. Killian brushed against Lars's leg, following him outside, and his brother bent down to ruffle his ears.

*

Adam and Marten agreed to look after Jeppe until Lars, Killian, and Rose could return. At first, they offered to do it for free, since Jeppe had helped Lars take down the baedons, but Lars insisted on paying them. As they discussed a price, Killian slipped away to tell Jeppe.

The stallion wasn't exactly happy to be left behind.

"He thinks he can leave me? I've been with him since I was a yearling! I practically raised him!" Jeppe smashed a hoof into the side of the stall.

Killian shook his head to clear his ears of the thundering reverberations. Technically, Lars had been seventeen when he'd been given Jeppe, but perhaps horses measured age differently.

"Keep it down." Killian poked a nose into the stall. *"We don't need to attract attention."*

"I will not!" Jeppe trumpeted. *"Just let him come in here and tell me himself!"*

Killian backed up a step, huffing a breath in frustration. *"Jeppe."*

"No. I don't see why I have to stay."

Killian leveled a pointed stare at the hind limb Jeppe kept hovering above the ground. Jeppe snorted and swished his hindquarters around to face him. Killian blinked. It still startled him to hear animals' opinions so strongly.

Still, a chuckle wiggled in his chest, *it's rather amusing to see how much he and Lars are alike.*

"What did you do?" Lars stared down at him over crossed arms.

"Had a conversation." Killian twitched his ears to flop along his head. Lars wasn't taken with the look.

Jeppe hobbled around to face them.

"Careful. He might bite."

"Jeppe!" Lars snatched an arm away from clacking teeth. Jeppe eyed Lars balefully.

"Killi." Lars turned narrowed eyes at him.

Killian gave his brother his most innocent eyes. Lars shook his head and reached a tentative hand out to Jeppe's broad neck. Jeppe turned his head away.

"I'm assuming that somehow you know you have to stay here." Lars rubbed the stallion's neck, making his way down to the withers. "It's for your own good. They'll take care of you."

Lars slid a treat from his pocket and held it out. Jeppe snorted before grudgingly lipping it from his hand. He butted Lars's chest, almost knocking him back a step.

"Don't think I'm going to forgive you. I'll show you how upset I am when you climb back up there." Jeppe crunched the sugar.

A chuckle teased Killian's chest. *As entertaining as that would be, I don't need Lars breaking his head. I'll have to warn him when I get my voice back.*

*

Killian swished his tail impatiently against the rough floorboards. It had taken two hours to obtain supplies and say farewells to the townspeople, and Killian itched to be away. Lars and Rose finally shouldered bulging packs.

Lars frowned at the spear in his hand. "I don't really want to carry this all the way to Myrnius."

"I'll take it off your 'ands, lad." The innkeeper rushed over, a gleam in his eyes. "It'll look good above that fireplace."

Hands on hips, he turned to study the soot stained bricks, already planning the placement of the weapon. Lars's mouth twitched in a pleased grin and he surrendered the weapon. The innkeeper beamed and struck the spear butt against the ground in what was probably meant to be a martial stance.

"Maybe we should've kept one of those 'eads t' put up there with it." He chuckled.

"I would not 'ave one of those filthy things staring at me day in an' out." His wife swatted his arm.

"They're better off burned," Lars agreed.

The townspeople flooded the square to wave them off. Rose and Killian were ready to strike out on the path that ran parallel to the river, but Lars hesitated a moment, turning to Adam.

"I—I know the prince." Lars shifted uncomfortably. "When we get back, I'll talk to him. He'll send a Ranger or one of the Brigade out."

"How is it you know t' prince, lad?" Adam narrowed his eyes in suspicious disbelief.

"Ulfr and I have helped on a few hunts."

Killian swished his tail in relief that Lars had a plausible answer. His mind had gone impressively blank at the question.

"You really think he'd listen t' you?" The innkeeper frowned. "No offense, lad, but we've all heard about Prince Lars, and you don't seem like much."

Lars's shoulders tensed, and he looked down at the ground, but Rose spoke up before he could respond.

"Prince Lars isn't all that bad." She nudged his arm. "Ivar here can do it."

A few tentative smiles were exchanged, and Adam nodded, a faint bit of hope flickering in his eyes.

"Well, thank you, lad. Though we won't blame you if nothing happens." Adam shook Lars's hand.

Lars said nothing, just headed down the road. Killian's heart twisted at the sight, though he couldn't help but be a little grateful that the villagers' bluntness had opened Lars's eyes. Rose finished her last goodbyes and they both ran after Lars. The trio walked in silence until the village was out of sight.

"Did you really mean it?" Rose sent Lars a sideways glance.

Lars nodded and readjusted his pack. "Did you?"

A faint blush touched her nose. "Maybe."

Killian snorted and darted between Lars's legs, nearly tripping him.

"Your vote doesn't count, Killi," he grumbled. "And I'll still beat you up."

Killian barked and darted up the road, followed by Rose's laughter. He glanced back and saw Lars nudge her shoulder in a brotherly fashion. She hesitated, eyes wide, then nudged him back.

*

Three days of endless trudging along the river road brought them into hills that reached a little higher than their predecessors, with occasional patches of scrub forest littering their sides. Herds of small gazelles became more frequent, and Lars would have sworn to seeing a Wyvern in the distance. His heart had leapt in excitement, but when the winged shape did not reappear, he was forced to continue walking.

The river gradually carved deeper into the ground until they walked alongside a sizeable gorge. As they made camp for the night in a protected rock outcropping, Lars consulted the map Adam had helped them update in the village. The path they were on was not exactly marked on the map.

No surprise there. It had, on more than one occasion, disappeared among the grass. But they just continued along the river until it picked back up again.

I swear this might be the most useless map ever made, except it's one of the newer ones Father commissioned.

Fortunately, large landmarks were on the map, such as the ruins of some old watchtower that stood guard across the river from their camp. He'd even been able to match a town they'd passed that afternoon to a small scribble.

"Maybe another day until we make it to the ford," Lars reasoned.

Rose looked up from kindling a small fire. "How far t' Myrnius after that?"

"Two, maybe three days. Good news is, there looks to be a few more places we can stop." Lars refolded the map and stowed it back in his pack, glancing around for Killian, but his brother hadn't returned yet from his hunt.

"Assuming, of course, your map is accurate."

The tease was obvious in her voice, but he still frowned a little. He was getting used to her forthright ways, tolerating most like a brother. *Even if she still manages to irritate me at least twice a day. Probably a sign she's growing on me.*

"More accurate than your memory, *Ranger*." He smirked.

"Apprentice."

"*Aspiring* apprentice."

"All right." She flicked a rock at him.

He caught it and tossed it into the darkness. "That's not very nice, you know, trying to murder someone with a rock."

"Your exaggerations will probably kill me one day." She rolled her eyes.

He grinned as he handed her a pack. They sat in silence as she poured a bit of oil into the small pan, adding several bread slices as the oil began to pop and sprinkling a bit of pouched seasoning as she turned them. It would make a welcome addition to the near flavorless jerky.

"Can I ask you a question?" She glanced up from her task.

"If I say no, will that stop you?"

Rose smiled. "It'll probably offend you."

"Do go on."

"You're a prince."

"That's my general impression."

She frowned. "You have people t' cook and start fires even when you're on t' road, so how..."

"Have I survived this trip without being a complete dead weight?"

"I wasn't going t' say it like that!" She fished the fried bread out onto the plates he held out for her.

Lars settled back against the rough stone and smirked.

"My great-grandfather, King Adolf, went to war against the Wyverns. One day, two great male Wyverns fell out of the sky in a surprise attack, leaving all but Adolf and one of his men dead. The other soldier was wounded and therefore of not much help to Adolf. So, he was alone in the wilderness with a wounded companion and a crown that wasn't going to do much to help him survive."

"What happened?" She crunched into her bread.

"He was on his own for almost a week before they found a division of his army. After that he declared no son of his would be helpless like he had been, so my grandfather trained with the Rangers for two years, as did my father, and Killian and I."

Rose licked oil from her fingers. "When?"

"Fourteen to sixteen, spread over those two years, spending at least a season at a time with a Ranger. We never went far from Lagarah. You can learn enough to survive around there." Lars set his plate aside. "Killian was better at it than me. I never really thought I'd have to put it to use."

"What about hunting wyverns together?"

"Two princes would never be allowed to go off on their own." Lars shrugged. "Unless one of them gets turned into a wolf and the other, in his infinite wisdom, goes off to hunt revenge and ends up on a quest with his wolf brother."

Rose's giggle built into a full laugh. "Well, when you put it that way..."

Lars's chuckle joined hers as he splashed some water from the canteens to rinse the plates.

"Still, probably just as well we have an apprentice Ranger with us."

"Aspiring," she reminded him as she stirred the fire, adding more fuel of packed grass and gazelle dung. "You know, I really hope you washed your hands before touching that bread."

Her eyes widened in the firelight and she rubbed her hands on her trousers. Obviously, she hadn't really thought about it.

"What's the matter, *Prince* Lars? Afraid of a little extra nutrition?"

"Not at all. I thought it added nicely to the flavor." He managed to keep a straight face.

Rose gave another snort of laughter. "You're disgusting."

When Killian returned from his hunt, the western sky held the remnant of sunset in a canvas of dark purple and pink. Lars knew Killian ate in private so he didn't have to see. More than a little part of him was relieved. Sometimes it was hard enough just watching him lick his paws clean like any other dog.

Killian growled as if he sensed Lars's thoughts. Lars offered a half-smile by way of an apology. Killian stared back, amber eyes glinting in the firelight, finally laying his head on his paws.

Chapter 11

Einar shielded his eyes from the bright sunlight, sighing in relief at the thatched roofs coming into sight along the river's gentle curve. They needed more provisions if they were to make it back to the king's main encampment. And cold gazelle jerky sounded highly unappetizing at the moment.

His retinue spurred up to a trot behind him. The horses' hooves clattered against the road paved with smoothed river stones. Villagers stepped out of their way, most following them into the main square to stare curiously.

The gathering crowd parted to allow a well-built man to come forward.

The man in charge, then. Good. I won't have to search him out.

"What can we do for you, sir?" He addressed Einar with a bow.

Einar had to cough once to clear his parched throat of dust. "Water for the horses and provisions if you can spare."

"O' course, sir. My name's Adam."

"Einar Regnak."

Adam offered another bow and most of the villagers turned to each other with wide eyes and nods. Einar inclined his head in response. He usually did not attempt to capitalize on his well-known name, but he was short on time and patience. He dismounted and handed the reins to his young squire.

Now for the part I hate. But we need news, if this out-of-the way village might have any.

"I doubt you would have heard. Prince Killian was killed near a week ago." His voice tightened over the words and he took a deep breath as the people murmured in shock. Not even the cryptic note signed in Lars's hand had convinced the family otherwise.

"How?" One woman held her own son close.

"Wolves."

The murmurs grew louder and the people made signs against evil as whispers of the curse slid through the crowd.

"Prince Lars has disappeared as well, and we search for him," Einar said.

'We have to get help'. *Of course, Lars couldn't have given any other indication of what that meant.* Einar shoved the recurring thought away again.

"We wouldn't 'ave seen him, not with being trapped by t' Baedons." Adam shook his head, regret creasing his weathered features.

"Baedons?" Einar laid a hand to his sword. Every man in his retinue did the same as they heard the word.

"No worry," Adam hastened to reassure him. "They were taken care of."

"How? By you?" Einar didn't attempt to hide his disbelief as he looked over the less-than-warlike villagers.

"Bless me! No. We didn't 'ave the weapons. We were trapped in 'ere and giving up hope when two days ago, in come some travelers. Young man by t' name of Ivar and his sister. They and their wolf took on both, if you can believe it." Adam shook his head, as if amazed at the bravery, or foolishness, of their storied saviors.

Einar narrowed his eyes. *Could be nothing. But I also think I might know a certain young man who would be reckless enough to try…* "I'd like to hear this tale."

Adam was ready to oblige and embellished the tale only a little as Einar shifted in impatience.

Einar rubbed at his chin. *It sounds like it could be Lars, but I can't read too much into this tale – if even half of it's true.*

"Sir?" His captain stepped closer to him, one eyebrow raised, his thoughts apparently running similar to Einar's. "You think…?"

"You said they left their horse?" Einar glanced back at Adam.

Adam nodded, one corner of his mouth pursing, some comprehension beginning to spark in his eyes.

"Captain Oskar, check the stable," Einar ordered.

The murmurs started again as the captain hurried away, but this time the soldiers joined in. Oskar wasn't gone long, sprinting back to Einar.

"It's Jeppe. I checked the tack. It's his."

"Thank the Creator!" Einar closed his eyes for a moment. Lars. *But what else did he say? A young woman and – a wolf?*

"There was a wolf with him?" He grabbed at Adam's shoulder in sudden desperation.

"Aye, sir, but not like any I'd seen. I swear it knew what we were saying. Wouldn't 'ave been surprised if he started talkin'."

"They say how they came by it?" Einar resisted the urge to shake the man.

"Ivar said it'd been following him around since it was a pup."

Blood drained from Einar's face and Oskar muttered something closer to a curse than a prayer.

"That's..." Einar stammered. *Exactly what Killian's been doing since he could crawl.*

"There wasn't technically a body. Just scraps of clothes," Oskar murmured, still loud enough for some to hear.

Einar snapped his head up, sickening realization hitting him in a rush.

"The sorcerer!" he spat.

Adam lifted his hand to ward against evil for the second time.

"Who's the girl?" Oskar asked.

Einar responded with a shrug. "I don't think Lars knows any young women who'd join him on such a journey, let alone fight a Baedon."

Oskar chuckled, and Adam described Rose upon request, but no recognition stirred in Einar's mind.

"Sounds like Ranger gear, though." Einar looked to Oskar.

Oskar nodded as he rubbed his chin. "I think I remember something about that missing Ranger having a daughter."

Even if that's so, my first duty is to those boys. Einar squared his shoulders. "Send a rider to the king, informing him that both of his sons are alive and well."

"Both?" Adam raised both eyebrows.

"Aye, the young man who killed the Baedon was Prince Lars," Einar said. "And you all know the curse on the king's family?"

Uneasy nods were passed among the villagers—with good reason, as the king discouraged any talk of it.

"It seems it's true. That wolf was Prince Killian, cursed by a sorcerer that the Rangers have been hunting."

The talk hadn't died down in the hour it took for Adam to marshal supplies for the troop and the horses to be watered to Einar's satisfaction. He noted a few villagers taking to the river in small boats, determined looks on their faces as they paddled away.

So much for keeping a low profile. This tale is going to be told in every corner of Calvyrn by morning. I suppose it might be too much to hope that the sorcerer won't hear of it.

He patted his stallion's nose, checking the girth again. They would follow the messenger's path back to the king. Adam had told him the trio planned to head to Myrnius. He had a destination. Now they just had to catch up.

Chapter 12

Only a few hours of daylight remained when they reached a bridge spanning the river. The river fell out of the gorge it had carved, plunging down a slope onto the plain below. It meandered into the distant line of forest and the Myrnian mountain range that had become visible in the last day.

At least we found the bridge. Killian scrambled down the steep slope alongside his companions, his claws giving him a little more purchase than their boot soles. *Even if it's not where Lars expected it to be.*

"That's it?" Rose brushed a lank curl from her face and surveyed the rickety bridge that stretched across the river. Killian worried for the aged pylons that challenged the churning river.

"No, the ford is further downriver." Lars shook his head, frowning at the map. "I've travelled this way before with Father, but I don't recognize this area at all."

"But why build a bridge here?" Rose stared at the rushing waterfall.

"There used to be trouble with trolls further downriver. But that was probably a hundred years ago."

"About when this bridge looks like it was built." Rose crossed her arms.

"Oh, not quite a hundred," a voice laughed.

Rose and Lars whirled and drew knives in unison, Killian growling around their legs.

"Oh, my! I should have said something sooner!" The speaker held the skirts of her dress, the same green as the churning river, and dipped a curtsey. "I'm Kaja."

A pair of translucent wings, beaded with glistening droplets, unfolded from her back. The shimmering membrane swirled with faint colors between the bony framework stretching it tight—a shape reminiscent of a fish's fin.

"I'm not going to hurt you." The faery spread her hands wider. "Word has been spreading through the waterways to look out for you."

"Why?" Lars lowered his knife.

"I know we're not generally helpful," Kaja said. "But there's a sorcerer out there with a spell to wipe us out."

"That's why he needs me?" Killian growled.

Kaja nodded, reaching down to smooth a hand over Killian's laid-back ears.

"We've sent messages to Myrnius. They'll be watching out for you."

Lars echoed Killian's growl of thanks.

"Thank me by getting rid of that sorcerer if you see him." A wild and ferocious expression twisted Kaja's face.

"Do you know anything about a missing Ranger?" Rose leaned forward in undisguised eagerness.

Her eyes widened as Kaja flung her arms around her in a hug.

"Alfar said you were looking for your father."

"Have you seen him or heard anything?" Hope trickled into Rose's voice.

"I don't know where he is now, but a Ranger crossed weeks ago heading west," Kaja said. "Rangers haven't been around this bridge in years, so maybe it was him."

Rose's smile was too small to be real. Killian nudged her leg and she brushed his ear.

"Oh, but there's someone looking for you!" Kaja perked up. "A knight came to that village the three of you helped — a rather attractive one, too, rumor has it." She giggled. "He figured out it was you, Prince Lars, and that you were alive, Prince Killian, but—you know…" She gestured to Killian's wolf form.

"What knight?"

"Oh, I didn't quite get his name. I heard it all secondhand from a trout who overheard the villagers on the river. But I did catch a glimpse when I went upriver, and they were watering their horses. The sigil was a two-headed Wyvern, which doesn't exist—"

"Uncle Einar!" Lars's face brightened in excitement. "He'll make sure Father knows you're not dead!" He grinned down at Killian, who thumped his tail on the ground.

"Should we find your uncle and tell him what's goin' on?" Rose glanced up at Lars.

Lars's smile faded. "We could…"

Killian shook his head. He didn't want any more of his family to see him under the curse and travelling in a large company of soldiers would also draw unwanted attention.

Assuming Uncle Einar would even allow us to continue our journey.

Lars met his gaze, his thoughts apparently running parallel to Killian's own.

"He might let us keep going, but I don't know about Father..."

"I'd be sent home?" Rose frowned.

Lars scuffed the ground with his boot. "Most likely."

Kaja clasped her hands behind her back and twirled slowly.

"Then forget it." Rose stammered as she watched the faery.

"We should probably put more distance between us and them," Lars said.

Rose glanced down at her feet with a frown. Killian didn't blame her. His paws ached and his shoulder still twinged.

Kaja stopped twirling and clapped her hands. "Oh, let me help! I'll take you to the next village by boat."

"Boat?" Lars's eyebrows pulled together as he scanned the bank—and its lack of vessel.

Kaja waltzed to the river and plunged her hand beneath the swirling water. Foam whisked away, and the water piled atop itself before smoothing into a high-prowed vessel. Kaja wiped her hand on her skirt and winked at them.

"That will hold us?" Killian's companions seemed to share his doubts. Though large enough for all of them, he just didn't quite trust the building material.

Kaja laughed and Killian couldn't help but open his mouth in a wolfish smile.

"Magic!" She wiggled her fingers. "You won't even get wet. Though all of you could use a wash."

Rose flushed and tugged at her hair.

Lars took the lead, stepping into the boat as it obligingly drifted closer to the shore. Rose accepted his help into the boat. Killian waited until they settled on the bench before hopping in. The watery craft did not even rock in response, and he lay down in the wide prow.

Kaja clambered aboard and sent her creation out into midstream with a wave of her hand.

Once they passed under the bridge, they picked up speed. From the wild grin on Kaja's face, Killian suspected they outpaced the river. Rose's hand clamped the side of the boat, but Lars's grin almost matched Kaja's. Killian sat up to better enjoy the wind tousling his thick fur.

The next village was over an hour's ride downriver. Kilian didn't even want to think about how long it would have taken them on foot.

Kaja stopped the boat a good distance upstream. "I'd rather not be seen by any more humans. They tend to get overly excited when they see a faery."

She took their thanks with a beaming smile.

"Good luck to you." Kaja hugged all three of them. As she stepped back, her smile faded. "I don't have to warn you about how dangerous sorcerers are. Sometimes you can't trust your eyes or ears, so always trust your instincts."

She sounded like the Ranger who had trained Killian. There was a hard edge to her now, nothing like the twirling water faery of that afternoon.

"Be careful. Blood will be spilled before your task is complete."

An uneasy feeling tugged at Killian's paws. Alfar had said something similar. Lars and Rose nodded, hands tightening on their weapons.

Kaja assessed them as a commander would his troops.

"Creator bless and guide you." And then she was gone, whirling back to the boat and sending it back upstream.

They watched until her shimmering wings disappeared into the gathering dusk before turning to the village lights twinkling in the distance.

"Is it just me, or did she seem a little..." Rose hesitated. "Crazy?"

Lars glanced back upriver. "A little. But my experience has been limited to one other faery."

Rose hitched her pack higher and shrugged. "Still. Think she was right about one thing. You both need a bath."

Lars shoved her, and she stumbled sideways with a laugh.

"Speak for yourself! Not quite living up to your name."

"So clever!"

Killian ignored their banter as the fresh evening breeze swept across the village fields, carrying the scent of corn and furred animals. He veered off the path, now focused on dinner.

"Killi!" He paused, looking over his shoulder at Lars's call. "We'll meet you outside the village."

Killian barked once, then loped away.

*

As Killian disappeared into the low hills, Lars began to head downriver to the village.

Rose caught at his arm. "Do you smell that?"

The evening air carried the scent of the river and earth. It took another moment before he caught the sickly-sweet stench floating by on the light breeze.

They both paused, unease prickling along Lars's shoulders. *I should know what this is.*

A growl came from the dim light to his left and Killian slunk forward, hackles raised as he peered at the boulders that rested in their path.

Lars's heart stuttered a beat as the rock shifted.

Rose beat him to the realization.

"Troll!" she hissed.

"Go!"

They backed away, hoping they could vanish into the hills without the trolls noticing. No such luck.

"Where are you going?" A deep voice spoke, smooth as the flowing river. Pinpricks of green flared in the dusk as the boulder grew and shifted to a figure taller than Lars by a foot.

"Run!" Lars shoved Rose's arm and they took off in a sprint, Killian running beside them.

Lars gained only a few yards before a thick tendril erupted from the earth, wrapping around his leg and bringing him crashing to the ground.

"Lars!" Rose skidded to a halt.

Killian bounded to his side in a second. Lars tried to jerk his leg free, but the root anchored into the ground.

Lars waved at them. "Keep going!"

Rose hesitated, drawing her knife and hacking at the root.

"Rose, you and Killian get out of here!" He tried to shove her away. The root tightened against her efforts, and he fought a grunt of pain.

"Yes, run. It makes it so much more fun for us." The voice spoke again.

Rose dropped a curse and instinctively moved away, but not fast enough. The earth leapt in a new tendril, grabbing her knife hand and dragging her to the ground. She fell with a cry, twisting and trying to yank free.

A feral growl ripped from Killian. His ears flattened against his head and he dropped to a crouch.

"Killi, don't!"

The troll chuckled. "You'd think you'd have more sense than your human companions."

Killian dodged with a yip as the earth shifted beneath him. He squirmed away from another tendril with a growl, and Lars heard more irritation than threat in the noise. Killian barked, an impressively deep sound, lunging forward.

Lars drew his own knife and stabbed into the earth holding him prisoner.

Killian is going to get himself killed.

A grumble broke from the troll and the ground shuddered as a dark shape landed in front of Killian, releasing an ear-shattering roar. Killian flinched, turned tail, and disappeared into the dark hills.

The troll straightened with a laugh. Lars sawed frantically at the strange binding around his leg. The earth grabbed his hand and slammed it to the ground, breaking his grip on the knife.

"I'd hold still, little man," a feminine voice spoke, and Lars twisted his head enough to see the shape of a second troll looming above him.

The troll reached down, freeing his hand into a crushing grip. She forced his wrists together and bound them in the same earthen bonds. The first troll hauled Rose to her feet after similar treatment.

"Come along, humans," the male said. "You'll walk, but I think you know what happens if you try to run."

The female shoved Lars between the shoulders and he lurched forward. Rose stumbled against him, her hair hitting his face as she whirled to glare at the troll.

The trolls only laughed and prodded them forward. The faint lights of the town faded into the night as they were forced away from the river and into the empty hills.

Lars tripped on an uneven hillock in the darkness and, aided by the troll, he tumbled down into a depression ringed by hills. Rose managed the descent with a bit more grace, still hitting her knees beside him.

"Now, let's see what we caught."

A fire flared to life, its sudden light blinding Lars. He finally dared to open his eyes to look at their captors.

The trolls crouched in the center of the dell, the fire casting shadows around their bulky forms. Their light brown skin, as craggy as the dried earth they sprang from, was spotted with small green growths—the source of the sweet scent.

The female's dark hair, woven with pale yellow flowers, reached to her hips, and the male's was spiked in matted tufts. They weren't ugly; they actually had the same lonely beauty as the hills that rolled for miles.

Lars pushed himself upright, Rose helping as much as possible with bound hands, as the male narrowed his eyes at them.

Don't let a troll touch you, his ranger training screamed in his mind. The troll's green eyes glistened mockingly in the firelight as Lars tried to back away. Tendrils jumped from the earth, wrapping around his chest and yanking him to the ground.

"Lars!" Rose struggled against the new bonds that circled her legs.

Lars cursed as the troll pressed a smooth hand against his forehead. Pain lanced between his eyes, but he couldn't shake off the troll.

"Well, well, looks like we have a prince on our hands." The troll chuckled. "Not a very good one either."

"Get off me!" Lars futilely ordered as the troll invaded his mind. His vision spun as memories surfaced and darted away without his consent.

"That's interesting. Your little dog isn't so common after all."

The female came up behind him and peered down at Lars. "What?"

"That wolf is this one's brother under an enchantment. Oh, the cause of some bitterness, I see. A sorcerer!" The troll spat.

"I thought I smelled magic on the three of them," the female said.

Lars's head pounded against the troll's touch and the coppery tang of blood coated his tongue.

"What else can we find in here? Green eyes. Hmm—she's lovely. What does she see in you?"

"She doesn't," Lars gritted, driving a knee up into the troll's side. The male growled in mild irritation, but he removed his hand after a few more seconds.

A relieved gasp broke from Lars as the pain faded. But the bonds tightened against his struggle as the troll turned to Rose.

Rose spat in the troll's face as he loomed over her. The troll flinched away, hastily wiping the spit from his face.

"You're in his mind too. You want to know what he thinks of you?"

"Not really interested." Rose twisted her head away, only to have the troll wrench her back around with a large hand.

"This one's trying to prove herself to the world, even though she thinks she's not good enough."

The female clucked her tongue in mock sympathy. Her companion laughed and turned back to Rose who paled under his touch. But the troll frowned.

"There's a different magic around you. Just as old." The troll fixed green eyes on Lars. "Wolves and sorcery here too."

Rose sagged back with a soft cry as he released her. The troll straightened.

"The earth whispers of the passing of a sorcerer," he said. "A powerful one. It fears for the faeries."

"If he's going after the faeries, is that a bad thing?" The female's face cracked in a trollish smile.

"Perhaps not. But I think he needs that wolf."

"We have them. Do we turn them over to the sorcerer? He's not far." The female twisted strands of her hair into a braid.

Lars's heart lurched painfully hard. *How far? Killian!*

"The wolf maybe. We'll keep these two. We came this way looking for blood, did we not?"

"But a prince?" Doubt creased the female's face and her fingers started on another braid.

"Not sure anyone would mourn this one." The male kicked Lars's leg.

Lars couldn't ignore the sickening truth.

"Besides, royal blood would sweeten our fruit like nothing else."

"Well then!" The female clapped her hands together. "Where did that wolf go?"

A growl rumbled through the night air and the trolls turned as one. Lars's heart plummeted as he recognized the sound. He twisted to see the fire reflected in bright circles.

"Killi, no," he whispered.

But another growl broke from the right and then the left. The firelight cast far enough to illuminate the striped muzzles of two of the wild dogs that lurked in Calvyrn's hills.

"Well, well," the male sneered.

Killian growled, and rage flashed over both of the trolls' faces. Killian leapt forward, snarling with another round of insults, judging by the way the male troll's face darkened. Killian's tail lashed from side to side as the wild dogs added their barks.

"Change of plan. Kill them all!" The trolls lunged, and the dogs and Killian vanished into the darkness.

The trolls' shouts echoed behind the deep bays of the dogs as Lars and Rose were left alone.

"Is he mad?" Rose squinted into the darkness, as if she could see beyond the hills.

"Possibly." Lars tried to twist against the ropes that pinned him to the ground, but they didn't budge. "We need to get out of here."

"Don't really fancy being bled dry t' water their fruit trees?" Rose futilely tugged at the bonds around her legs.

"Not very much, no." Lars growled in frustration. *We're not getting out of here.* That annoying voice of reason nudged his mind. "Any ideas?"

"I'm trying. Trolls…" She grinned. "Water."

Lars paused his struggles. "What?"

"Water. They hate water. It kills them, washes them away like mud."

"I'm not seeing enough water around here to kill them when they get back."

"I know. But these roots are their magic. What if it works on them?"

Lars held his bound hands up for inspection. Grass, dirt, and roots had been twisted into rough fibers. Even a small blue flower sprouted from the rope. "It's worth a try."

"I think I can reach my waterskin." Rose stretched her bound hands around to the pack still slung over her back. The trolls hadn't disarmed them either.

It took some creative maneuvering, but Rose freed her waterskin from the pack and uncorked it.

"Here." She tried to lean over to him.

He shook his head. "Get yourself free first."

"Don't think I have enough for both of us." Rose frowned.

"Get your legs free, then help me up," Lars said. "If we can get back to the river, we can take care of our hands."

Rose nodded and carefully poured a trickle of water over the ropes binding her legs. Lars held his breath, but nothing happened.

"It's working." Rose looked closer. She kicked her legs free, leaving a broken cage of earth where she had lain.

She knelt beside him, soaking his tunic in her haste. He didn't complain as he ripped free.

"Remember which way we came?" They paused at the top of the hill, waiting to let their eyes adjust to the natural moonlight.

She jabbed her bound hands to their right, but a howl brought their attention to the hills on their left. A lean shadow passed over the top of the hill, leaping away from the lunging grasp of the ground.

They sprinted back to the river without another word, running in silence, their frantic breathing and the slapping of packs and weapons the only sound between them.

Are we going the right way? I don't think we're going to make it back. His quick despair lifted as he caught sight of its long silver glimmer ahead. The trolls roared behind them, and they once more quickened their steps.

"Get in the river!" Lars shoved her as they neared the bank.

But Rose slowed, hesitation showing in her expression. "I can't swim very well."

Lars barely restrained a curse. "I'll help you. It's better than staying out here."

Cold seeped through his boots as he waded in. The water rushed around their chests as they reached the center of the river. The rope disintegrated around his wrists and he pushed back against the current.

"What about Killian?" Rose wobbled with a splash.

"Let's worry about them first." Lars nodded to the shapes that thundered to a halt in a spray of earth at the river's edge.

"Clever," the male troll spat. "But the cowardly little wolf is still out there. Maybe we'll just let you freeze while we hunt him down."

"He's not a coward!" Lars splashed water toward the bank and the trolls recoiled with a hiss.

"That's right. *You* are. That's what you think, isn't it?"

"Don't listen t' him, Lars." Rose said, her words cut off by a rope snaking from the bank around her neck.

Lars shoved her under water until the coil dissolved. She re-emerged with a gasp, coughing water from her lungs. He edged in front of her, watching for the troll's next move.

It came in a blurring flash and he barely managed to get a hand up in time for the rope to wind about his forearm, instead of his neck. He prepared to plunge it under water. *Wait! He's holding it.*

He yanked back and the troll lurched forward, startled. Lars grabbed the rope in both hands, struggling to keep it above water. The troll pulled back and Lars jerked it with all his strength. Rose joined him in a swirl of water and grabbed the rope.

"I've had enough of this." She joined her strength with his.

The female hurried to help her companion, but two shapes jumped her from behind, sending her stumbling into the water. She collapsed with a wail and the water churned where it claimed her.

The male howled in anger and hauled them closer to the bank with a mighty burst of strength. Rose lost her grip on the rope, tripping, and Lars tried to dig his feet into the soft river bottom as he lost ground. But the troll dropped his end of the rope, shoved forward by an unseen force and fell into the river.

A second splash followed the troll and Killian swam into Lars's chest.

"Killian, you idiot!" Lars grabbed him in a hug. "You all right?"

Killian shook water from his ears, yipping at Rose.

"You scared me t' death!" She ruffled his soggy ears.

They waded back to the bank, Killian reaching the shore before them and shaking dry before the wild dogs pounced on him with playful growls.

I wish it was that easy for us to get dry. Lars squeezed water from his shirt.

"Now what?" Rose wrung her hair out.

"Head back to that town?" Lars sat down to empty water out of his boots.

"Sounds better than sleeping out here." Rose shivered. "What were they doing this far north anyway?"

Lars's shoulders slumped, the troll's words returning to mock him. "You're probably looking at the reason."

Killian growled, padding over to them and flopping down beside Lars.

Rose frowned. "Lars, don't believe what that thing said."

"Like you're not going to?"

"I know." She sank down with a sigh. "But at least you've started t' prove me wrong about you."

He mustered a faint smile at her teasing words. *But everyone's been right about me so far.* He shoved the thought away.

"You're not worthless either, you know. Two Baedons killed with your help, and now two trolls." He nudged her shoulder.

She chuckled as she re-tied her hair. "Aye, but if two Wyverns show up next, you boys are officially on your own."

Killian growled as Lars laughed and pulled his boots back on. He glanced at Rose.

"What did he mean about you having magic?"

Rose shrugged as she emptied her boots. "Don't know. As far as I know there's never been magic in my family."

"Strange."

"Know what else is strange? Green eyes..." Rose cast him a sly look.

Lars rolled his eyes and Killian yipped, rolling onto his back with his tongue lolling.

Rose laughed. "Who is she?"

"Someone I think you'd get along with a little too well," Lars said wryly.

"She sounds nice, then."

Lars raked a hand through his damp hair with a wry grin. "She is. Though I think I might have destroyed any chance I ever had with her."

"Don't be so hard on yourself. She sounds smart, so you might be surprised." Rose gained her feet. "You coming?"

Chapter 13

Noak swirled his thumbs around each other as his men set up camp around him. He'd been casting spells to try and find his escaped wolf, but every time a frustrating wall of nothing stared back. Faeries were probably involved. *Another reason the meddlers need to be dealt with.*

Still, maybe he should thank them before he destroyed them. Without the inaction of the faeries in his youth, he would never have discovered the power of sorcery.

A muffled curse disrupted his thumb twirling. Finn had gathered fuel for a fire, but it smoked in defiance of his best efforts.

"Let me." Noak shooed him aside and lit a fire with the snap of his fingers.

Finn wiped his hands on his yellow jerkin and put away his flint. The other two men joined them. After a week and a half scouting trying to find the prince, they had reconvened among the hills.

"What now?" Finn tore apart jerky and shoved it into his mouth with grimy fingers.

Noak ate his own meal with a little more refinement. "We wait. We have spies scattered around. Surely one of them will see something."

"When do we head back t' Myrnius?" One of the brothers spoke. Noak still couldn't tell them apart, even after months spent in their company. But then, it'd never really mattered.

"When we have our wolf," Noak said. "I need his blood for the spell, or everything has been for naught."

"Could 'e have gotten very far? Maybe 'e's still in t' forest." The other brother handed out hot corn cakes.

"We searched the forest." Finn juggled his hot corn cake for a moment before biting into it.

"There are rumors that Prince Lars also disappeared. He might have made it further than we think."

"Or been killed."

This came from the other brother. Jokum perhaps? It was true, they had found the remains of several dead wolves during their search of the forest. Noak frowned at the man. He'd been trying to avoid considering that possibility.

A warmth in his coat pocket distracted him. He frantically dug for the stone, ordering Finn to fill a bowl with water.

Finn handed it over and Noak tipped the smooth blue stone into the bowl. The water bubbled a moment before the surface smoothed and a soldier with the insignia of the king stared out at Noak from the reflection.

"You have news?" Noak gripped the bowl tight.

"Yes," the man said. "A young man Sir Einar believes was Prince Lars was at Sandnes village along the river three days ago. A girl and a brown wolf were with him."

Noak laughed in his relief. "Where is this village?"

"Ten miles southwest of Ammelby. The villager said they intended to travel to Myrnius."

"Thank you. The talisman I gave you should bring about even more luck."

"Thank you, sir." The soldier bobbed his head.

Noak fished the stone from the water and the image faded.

"Why Myrnius?" Finn inhaled a corn cake whole.

Noak returned the stone to his robe. "I'm willing to bet they are trying to find a faery. Break camp. We're heading back sooner than I thought."

The men did not argue and a few minutes later, they trudged through the hills, guided by the ball of light Noak sent bobbing ahead of them.

*

Noak and his men halted on the bank of the churning river, just downstream from a derelict bridge. After traveling for two days, they stared wearily at this new obstacle.

"Give it a try?" Finn sent a skeptical glance at the tenacious wooden structure.

Noak wrinkled his nose.

Finding the ford further downstream would take several more hours. They could chance the bridge—and the swirling depths in front of them—and save some time on their hurried march.

Noak placed a timid foot on the first plank and it creaked a warning beneath his weight. The river erupted in a geyser and a faery emerged from the water.

He scowled and retreated a step.

"You!" She pointed a trembling finger at him, her eyes flashing with rage.

"I see my reputation has preceded me." He flashed a smile, twitching his sleeves back to allow his hands freedom of movement.

"You and your ilk will not pass here."

"I've been wanting a challenge." He thrust out a hand, sending water funneling at her chest.

She raised a hand and carelessly diverted it away.

"I've fought your kind before," she sneered and extended her hand to the water. Droplets flew up to form a spear in her hand. Noak caught a breath of cold as it hardened to ice.

"Then maybe we share some of the same fond memories of the war." Eagerness leapt in his chest. *If she fought in the war, I'm going to enjoy this even more.*

She stepped forward, the water solidifying under her feet. "You know nothing of that war."

He placed one hand on the bridge's crumbling rail and laughed. "I remember plenty. I remember a village, fire, and death, and a faery who stood and watched it happen."

A madness in her gaze had shown in her gaze before, but horror caused the spear to tremble in her grip.

"Lublin."

"Very good!" he sneered. The wood creaked under his touch. "Then you understand why I have a score to settle with the Myrnian faeries. Let me pass and I'll consider sparing the water."

She heaved the spear upright to level at his chest. "I've heard plenty of lies from your kind. You'd no sooner spare us than care for those men behind you. I had a duty once to fight magic like yours. I am Kaja of the raging spear and you shall not pass."

His smile didn't quite reach his eyes. "Then let's hope you're not out of practice."

He uttered a sharp word of magic and the bridge collapsed, the jagged pieces darting toward the faery.

She threw up an arm and the attack halted. He raised both hands, chanting under his breath. Her hand quivered under the strain, but she hefted the spear, crazed eyes fixing upon his chest.

Finn's crossbow creaked behind Noak and he increased the tempo of his chant. The wood shook in midair, torn between the commands of the magic users. Kaja's gaze flicked behind him to Finn, who now stood with a bolt trained on her.

The archer pulled the trigger without hesitation.

Kaja swatted it out of the air with the spear, but Noak only needed that brief moment of distraction. A broken plank snuck around her guard and smashed into her gut. She doubled over with a cry, unable to stop the rest of the ancient bridge from crashing down upon her.

The river churned and boiled as Noak sent a wave to wash over the spot where she'd vanished. A whirlpool spun the debris for a second, its edges almost reaching the bank and then the river quieted, resuming its regular course and sweeping the wood downriver.

"She gone?" Jokum glanced at him.

Noak shrugged, sending a tendril of magic into the water to test its depths. Nothing but water and silt settling under its caress.

"Looks like it." He swept a hand over the river, collecting some of the drifting remnant of the bridge and melding it together to make a rough footbridge. "Let's go."

They had no more time to waste. Likely the faery hadn't gone very far. He wanted as much distance between them and the river as possible. *And,* he patted the stone in his pocket, *we have a wolf to find.*

Chapter 14

Sir Einar found the king and his search party a day's ride from Sandnes. King Jonas practically pulled him from his horse.

"Is it true?" He crushed Einar's arm in an iron grip.

"I don't know if I can believe it myself," Einar admitted. "But there's no other reason for Jeppe to be there."

"And a brown wolf?" Jonas' brow furrowed.

"It has to be Killi. *Has* to be."

"This curse…" Jonas bowed his head, dragging a hand through his brown hair. Einar rested a hand on his shoulder.

"Courage, brother. At least he's not dead." *I won't believe that my nephew is dead.*

"Small comfort." Jonas cleared his throat, leading Einar to his tent. Einar removed most of his armor and took a cup of wine.

"You think they're headed to Myrnius?" Jonas settled into a chair with his own goblet.

"That's what the villagers indicated."

"Faeries?"

"The most logical explanation." Einar rubbed a sore shoulder. The muscle had been in knots since the beginning of the whole nightmare.

"We've had no more reports of this sorcerer," Jonas said. Einar tapped his ring against the cup, debating on stating the likely reason the sorcerer had disappeared. "Most likely searching for Killian as well."

Jonas frowned. "So, both my sons and an innocent girl have put themselves in his path. You think they know?"

"Lars and Killian are smart. They might."

"You might have a higher opinion of my eldest than I." Jonas traced the rim of his goblet and sighed.

Einar had never given his brother-in-law his full opinion on his wayward nephew, and now seemed hardly the time. *But there might be some hope for the future yet.*

"The villagers did say he promised to see about sending the Brigade to check up on them after the baedon attacks."

A bit of hope lurked in the small smile that creased Jonas's face. "Did he? There's something."

Einar refilled both their goblets. "What do we do now?"

Jonas rubbed the stubble that coated his chin. "I don't want them out there on their own. If something happens I won't just lose sons, I'll lose heirs."

Einar nodded. His fragile daughter wouldn't ever be ready for that position if the worst happened.

"But we have to find them first, and sending an armed troop after them might attract even more unwanted attention." Jonas sighed. "I'm open to suggestions, Einar."

"You don't want to ask your council?" Einar gave his brother-in-law a slight smirk.

Jonas snorted and slouched into his chair, stretching his legs out. "If you would ever accept my invitation to join the council, I technically would be."

Einar chuckled as he set his cup aside. "If we ride hard, we could reach the border within a few days. Bring a few soldiers with us, leave the royal banner behind, maybe we find them without attracting too much unwanted attention."

"We?" Jonas raised an eyebrow.

"Your sons and my nephews," Einar said. "I didn't think you'd be interested in staying behind. You've already put everything in order with your council and the queen just to be out here. Technically, we'd just be moving the search party further west."

"You're a bad influence on me."

"My sister is more than capable of overseeing the kingdom for a few more weeks."

"Why do you think I married her?" Jonas smiled as he stood and spread a map of Calvyrn on the table. Einar joined him, placing weights on the parchment corners.

"They were here three days ago." Jonas tapped the bend in the river. "If you were looking for a Myrnian faery, you'd head for Celedon Forest."

Einar scanned the field of parchment from Jonas's finger to the legend marking Celedon. It was a fair distance, but for once the sparsely-populated southwest corner of Calvyrn worked in their favor.

"They'd be foolish not to stop for supplies," Einar said.

"Or some ale," Jonas said with a wry smile.

Einar again held his tongue concerning Lars. "There's only so many towns or villages where they could be."

Jonas leaned on the table, studying the most likely options. "You think we can catch up?"

"Creator willing." Einar shrugged.

"One of these days you'll have to share your secret to such a straightforward faith." Jonas sighed. "It seems to have eluded me."

Einar clapped his shoulder with a smile. "It might seem easier than you think. When do you want to leave?"

"When can you be ready?" Jonas countered.

Always impulsive. "We can be ready again by dawn."

Chapter 15

I *will never walk anywhere ever again.* Lars pulled his hood up higher against the rain. *And I'm about ready to swear off the outdoors altogether.*

With nothing much in the way of civilization between Halden, the river town, and Moss, the next village closest to the border, they'd elected to continue instead of waiting out the rain.

Which meant trudging through a steady drizzle and occasional enthusiastic downpour most of the day.

Whose bright idea was this? Of course, it was mine.

He and Rose at least had the protection of cloaks, but water clung to Killian's coat, gathering it in thick chunks despite his repeated attempts to shake the rain free. The twinkling lights of Moss appeared through the pattering rain and they quickened their pace, slogging through the thick mud of the main street in search of an inn.

"Finally!" Rose pointed a dripping hand at the inn's faded sign that declared itself to be *The Weary Wyvern* in chipped paint. Above the lettering, a wyvern curled on its back, a puff of smoke curling from its snout.

"I always thought they'd be more terrifying," she said.

"We should go find a real one for proper comparison." Lars scraped muck from his boots onto the stoop.

"I'll leave you boys to it." Rose shuddered, struggling to relieve her boots of the miles of countryside they'd brought with them.

Killian waited until they were under the relative shelter of the eaves before shaking water and mud from his coat in a damp spray. Lars pushed the door open to escape the flying droplets.

The room was filled with patrons and the murmurs of conversations, and the snapping fire in the expansive hearth gave off a welcome warmth.

"No dogs allowed," a voice called, and Lars followed the speaker's outstretched hand to Killian standing in the doorway.

"But it's raining out." Rose gave the young man her most pathetic look. Lars had to admit it was impressive.

The young bartender set the mug he was drying down on the high counter and slung the cloth over his shoulder. "Put it in t' stable out back."

Lars scowled. He wasn't about to let Killian spend the night in some drafty barn after the day in the rain. But he shouldn't have worried.

"Let them in, Jannik!" A burly man laughed, brushing past them with hands full of brimming tankards.

Killian let his head droop low, his ears a floppy mess. His front legs looked to be supporting most of his weight with a pathetic quiver. Soulful amber eyes stared up at Jannik.

The young man cleaned another mug with a professional twist of his cloth. He leaned on the counter, taking in the piteous sight that was currently Killian, and sighed—defeated.

"Fine!" He glared at the patrons. "And if Father hears about this tomorrow night, you're all getting charged double for your drinks!"

A chorus of "Aye, Jannik!" and laughter came from the amused onlookers, but Jannik was forced to smile as Killian perked up and trotted into the room, taking up residence under an empty table in the corner. Rose joined him as Lars moved up to the bar.

"Thank you." Lars shifted back to avoid dripping on the spotless counter.

"Some dog you've got there." Jannik filled his newly-cleaned mugs from a cask labeled Wyvern's Poison. "Wolf?"

"There was some wolf on his sire's side," Lars said. "Bit far south for wyverns, isn't it?"

"My father served in t' garrison fore I was born. Got sent up north t' fight the wyverns. Got sent back missing part of his leg. King gave him a decent compensation and he started this place."

"Looks to have done well." Lars took the drinks.

"Aye, we can't complain. Where you in from?"

"Sister and I came over from Halden day 'fore last," Lars said, attempting to model his speech more after the clipped common dialect. He and Rose had decided to keep their fictional backstory. Might as well embrace the charade.

Jannik nodded. "I'll get your food right out. Mutton tonight, if that's all right."

"Long as it's hot." Lars smiled. After days on the road, he didn't much care what he ate as long as it wasn't cold or salted.

Lars joined Rose, who'd been answering her own friendly inquisition from the interested townspeople. He unslung his pack and crossbow from his back and set them beside hers under the table. Thankfully, with his arrival their table neighbors left them to their drinks.

Lars nudged Killian with his boot. "I think you enjoy this sometimes."

Killian grinned back, sprawling on the floor.

Rose chuckled. "Does anyone ever tell you no?"

Killian shook his head, showering Lars's feet with the last few droplets. Lars rolled his eyes, drinking the thin layer of foam from the top of his cider.

Jannik wasn't long with the food, balancing plates as he emerged from the back kitchen in a cloud of steam. He slid two onto the table in front of them, a medley of tender mutton chunks, seasoned potatoes slathered in gravy, and dark bread to mop up the bits.

He placed a third plate of mutton and bread scraps on the floor for Killian, who barked his thanks, inhaling his dinner with all the enthusiasm of a starving wolf — or young boy.

Jannik frowned down at him and turned back to the table. "Need anything else?"

"Just a room for t' night, please." Lars ignored Rose's teasing eyebrow.

"Only got one open. Mind sharing with your brother?" Jannik glanced at Rose. He obviously wasn't taken in with the siblings story.

Rose gulped at her cider. "No." Her voice squeaked.

"Staying long?"

"Just t' night," Lars answered for her. "We'll be on our way in t' morning."

"You might 'ave to rethink that, lad," a man at the neighboring table piped up. "It'll still be raining tomorrow."

"Don't listen t' him," his tablemate broke in. "My bones tell me it'll be sunny tomorrow."

"Just like your bones told you t' sun would shine during that blizzard three years ago?" The first man scoffed.

Jannik smiled as the table and three of its neighbors broke into an argument about the predictive validity of the man's bones and the more trusted nose of farmer Hans.

"It'll be upstairs, third door on t' right," Jannik said, artfully dodging his way out of the rapidly escalating argument.

"What do we do if it is raining tomorrow?" Rose carved up an overlarge potato chunk with her spoon.

Lars attempted to cool a hot piece of mutton with a sip of cider. When he could finally talk again, he shrugged. "We're almost to the forest. We could find some shelter there."

She cast a forlorn look at the fire and he couldn't help but agree. He could do with a few days' rest, fresh clothes, and a bath. They all could.

But their money wouldn't last forever, and they still had to plan for the trip home. He'd been developing an annoying bit of foresight. *Pauline would laugh.*

"How long do you think —?" Rose broke off, staring at Killian. "What's wrong?"

Kilian stood on all fours, ears pricked, focused on something behind Lars. Lars twisted in his chair to see, ignoring the plump merchants at their table and the granite-featured farmer, and instead settled his gaze on the lone man at the back table.

The man ignored Lars, studying Killian with a slight tilt to his head. He nodded once and went back to his mug.

"Lars?" Rose whispered, reaching for her knife below the table.

Lars shook his head and turned back before anyone caught him staring. Killian's posture conveyed alert curiosity, but not particular aggression.

"He's leaving," Rose spoke softly.

Lars tilted his head to watch from the corner of his eye. The man stood a bit shorter than average, an impressive bulk to his arms under the short-sleeve jerkin. He carried no obvious weapon but moved with a sure grace that announced he knew how to handle himself.

As they watched, he turned to take in all three with a glance, then stepped out into the rain, devoid of a cloak.

Killian sat back on his haunches, licking his nose with a contemplative air.

"He was watching Killian."

Rose leaned closer. "One of t' sorcerer's men?"

Killian shook himself, lying back down under the table.

"I agree with Killian." Lars pushed his empty plate away. "But I think he knows something."

"Kaja did say they sent word t' Myrnius." She stared at the door.

"Not much we can do now," Lars said. "If he turns back up, we might have to talk."

"And what if he's sending word t' the sorcerer right now? We don't know who serves him." She lifted a shoulder in apology to Killian, who growled.

His brother agreed with Rose. But now that they were closer to their goal, the odds were beginning to rear their ugly heads. *If Uncle Einar found Sandnes village, then chances are the sorcerer might know too. He's not far behind, according to the troll. And how are we to find a faery?*

Faeries weren't exactly known to be very outgoing, and it wasn't like Celedon was small.

"Figure it out in t' morning?" Rose offered a smile.

Lars sighed with temporary defeat. They pushed away from the table, dragging packs and damp cloaks over their shoulders. They'd made it halfway to the stairs, exchanging friendly goodnights, when Lars glimpsed Killian lagging behind.

"He might as well," Jannik called, collecting their plates. More cheers greeted his goodwill and Killian trotted up the stairs behind them.

"Sure you're all right with sharing?" Rose opened the door to their room. Two beds stood on opposite sides of the small room, with a table tucked in between.

"It's not terribly different than camping, is it?" Lars tossed his pack by the bed closer to the door. *Except Mother would be coming after me with a vengeance for this.*

"Suppose not." She set her pack on the floor and lit the candle.

It stood to reason they were a bit past propriety by now. *And this is just like camping,* he sternly reminded himself. Funny how having walls around changed the dynamic of sharing a space to sleep.

A bucket of clean water and some towels rested on the small table. Rose washed her hands and face, then Lars had his turn. Lars dunked his towel into the water and glanced at Killian, who backed against the door and bared his teeth.

"You're still covered in mud."

Killian drooped, reluctantly allowing Lars to scrub chunks of mud from his legs and chest. Lars ruffled his ears and Killian shoved his head into Lars's shoulder, almost knocking him over.

"You're welcome," Lars grumbled, pushing Killian away with a last ruffle of his fur.

Rose laughed, taking the towel and rinsing it as Killian retreated to groom his fur back to order.

Rose shucked her boots and tunic, diving under her blanket on the second bed. Lars did the same, pausing before snuffing the candle. Killian rustled on the floor, trying to get comfortable.

"Killi, come on."

Killian cocked his head.

"There's enough room."

It would be a tight fit, but it could work. He slid closer to the wall as Killian jumped up onto the bed. As soon as he settled, Lars reached over and extinguished the candle, plunging the room into darkness.

They lay in silence for a few minutes as a pale grey light filtered in through the window. The rain kept up its patter on the peaked roof, but despite the soothing sound, Lars couldn't find sleep. Rose's breathing evened out across the room. Killian heaved a deep breath.

"You all right?" Lars whispered.

Killian placed his head on Lars's shoulder, cold nose dampening his shirt. In the faint light, Lars glimpsed an extra shine in Killian's eyes. He shifted to wrap an arm around his brother, holding him tight.

I wish there was something to say instead of the same stupid thing. What if it's not going to be all right?

He released his hold and let Killian curl up closer before they finally drifted off to sleep.

Chapter 16

Rose woke with the dawn. The dim, grey light filtering through the narrow pane grew stronger the longer she resisted the call to rise. She breathed a sigh of relief at the silence.

The rain had stopped.

She peeked over the edge of her blanket. The boys were still asleep across the room. She crawled out from her nest of blankets, sliding her feet back into her boots and grimacing at the residual dampness. She laced up her tunic and re-tied her mess of hair. Her damp curls had dried to a frizzy tangle. She gave them one last half-hearted pat and sighed. *It'll be a nightmare trying to untangle that later.*

She took the bucket on her way out the door, still full of murky water from the previous night. They'd need fresh water. Maybe she could use it to do something with her hair. She paused at the foot of the bed where Lars lay sandwiched between the wall and Killian.

"Good morning!" She inserted an extra dose of cheerfulness into her voice.

Lars pulled the blanket over his face. "Go away. Just a few more hours."

Killian burrowed his head under the pillow and growled. Rose smothered a laugh. She'd have to see if Jannik had any kaffe or they might never get Lars moving.

"I'm going t' get water."

Lars mumbled a reply through the blanket and Rose rolled her eyes, heading downstairs. Jannik was already up, stirring at the fire.

"Where can I get some water?" Rose held up the bucket.

Jannik looked up in surprise. "Your brother didn't offer?"

"Oh, I don't mind. He's not much of an early riser. Have any kaffe?"

"Aye, I'll have t' cook heat some water. Well's through there." He pointed at the door set behind the bar. Rose thanked him with a smile.

Clouds still gathered, their sober countenance reflected in the pools that filled the cobbled courtyard. She dumped the old water, picking her way across the yard by way of the stones that rose above the water like tiny islands. A hint of coolness carried through the air on a light breeze.

Rose studied the sky as she cranked the handle to haul fresh water. The clouds looked to have spent most of their fury, but she wouldn't be surprised to see a few drizzles later. Hopefully it would hold off long enough for them to get back on the road.

She filled the bucket and made her way back to the inn, water sloshing dangerously in the bucket as she tried to save her boots another soaking.

"I tell you, they said it was Prince Lars 'imself!" An excited voice halted her just outside the door.

"Prince Lars?" Jannik's voice dripped with doubt.

"Aye, an' his brother Killian, t' wolf prince," the first speaker said.

"Wolf? Just a story isn't it?" Someone else chimed in.

"Not anymore. Seems a sorcerer or somesuch changed 'im t' a wolf. Now they're wandering Calvyrn with a Ranger doing good deeds t' break the spell."

"And where'd you hear this?" A woman spoke this time.

"Heard it from Holt, who 'ad it from a merchant that came through from Fjorn."

The murmur that followed indicated this Holt was a fellow of some repute. She didn't wait to hear more but pushed through the door. The crowd by the bar didn't pay her any mind, but Jannik glanced up. She hurried up the stairs to the room.

Not surprisingly, her companions still weren't up. She scooped a handful of water and flung it over them.

"Get up!"

Lars pulled the blanket down to glare at her through sleep-filled eyes. Killian didn't even move, so she flicked more water. Lars propped himself up on his elbows as Killian slithered off the bed, warily eyeing her and the bucket.

"There had better be a good reason for this. It's probably treason to throw water at princes."

Rose almost emptied the bucket over him. "I think we're famous."

"We are princes." Lars yawned and dragged a hand through his hair.

"No!" She explained what she heard, gratified to see new alertness show through their tired faces.

"This changes things." Lars reached for his boots and frowned. His hadn't dried either.

"Any chance you'd be recognized?"

"I don't know, but we probably shouldn't stick around to see." Lars rubbed his eyes with another yawn.

How has he survived this long? "I asked for some kaffe."

"So, breakfast?" Lars looked up hopefully, Killian mirroring his brother's expression. How did anyone resist those two?

"Breakfast first."

They took turns changing behind the curtain hung in the corner opposite the beds. Adam's wife had kindly washed their clothes after the fight with the baedons. The rain had soaked through the packs, leaving them a bit damp, but at least they were still clean and didn't smell as strong.

Rose found her comb at the bottom of her pack and attempted to bring some order back to her hair. The boys finally gave up and went downstairs, leaving her to finish. She fought long enough to declare a victory — or at least a truce — and re-tied the leather cord around the bulk of her curls. She scooped up her pack and bow and trudged down to the common area, where hot breakfast awaited.

*

"We need some more supplies, don't we?" Lars gulped down the last of his kaffe.

Rose nudged her limp pack with her toe. Lars's wasn't in much better shape.

"Yes, and we should probably get them here."

She dug out her small coin purse while Lars rose and settled their bill with Jannik. She and the prince might finally be on good terms, but she wasn't going to be completely in his debt.

Killian stretched and rose from under the table. She stared down at his shaggy profile as he watched Lars. *I wonder what he really looks like. How similar are he and Lars? In looks or personality.*

Killian had always sounded like the more respected prince, even with the rumors surrounding him.

She'd never really thought how hard this must be on him. Never really asked either, even though she wouldn't understand the answer. *Some friend I'm turning out to be.*

"Ready?" Lars's voice startled her.

Rose shouldered her pack and stood, starting to call her thanks to Jannik, but his frown froze the words in her throat. He stared at them again, gaze lingering on Killian. She walked quickly to the door, frowning. *I think he might know who we are.*

"Think people believe that story about us?" Rose glanced at Lars once they'd reached the relative safety of the street.

"As flattering as it is, I'm hoping not," Lars admitted. "If it's spread this far, who knows who else has heard it."

"True. Shouldn't take long t' get supplies, and then we can be gone before we find out." She picked her way down the muddy street.

"How do you know where you're going?" Lars followed her around the edge of a particularly large puddle. Killian padded carefully around the opposite side with delicate paws.

"Most towns aren't that different. Supply shops should be close t' the inn. How're your negotiating skills?" She tossed a grin back at him.

"Better saved for important state affairs, not for buying meat and biscuits." He ducked under dripping roof water and splashed her.

She slid out of reach and scowled. "Really, *brother?*"

"Payback for this morning." He winked, flicking more droplets at her.

She wrinkled her nose at him, but grinned, scooping a handful from a water barrel under the butcher's eaves, tossing it at him. Lars dodged with a smirk, which faded into a yelp of alarm as his boots slipped precariously in the mud.

He recovered without incident and they both laughed until Killian jumped in a puddle, showering them both.

"Killi!" They yelled in unison. He retreated with a bark and a flick of his tail.

Lars brushed mud flecks from his trousers. "Remind me why I love him?"

Rose laughed. "Because he's your brother?"

Lars's smile faltered for a brief second. "Aye."

"It'll be all right."

His smile wasn't quite the same as a few minutes before and he obviously tried to force confidence into his voice. "I know."

"Come on, let's see if an aspiring, apprentice Ranger can teach you anything." She tapped his arm and led the way into the butcher's shop.

Fifteen minutes later, they emerged from the bakery with the last of their supplies. Killian stood, tail swishing slowly back and forth, in front of the short man from the inn the night before. Lars cursed and dashed toward the man kneeling in the mud. Rose's hand found her knife as she followed.

"Prince Lars, I presume?" The man spoke first, glancing up with no trace of alarm at their charge.

"What do you want?" Lars stiffened, feet sliding into a fighting stance.

"To talk to your brother." He nodded to Killian, rising to his feet in a fluid motion, no trace of mud on his trousers.

"Who are you?" Lars clenched a hand around his knife, eyes narrowing.

Killian growled, looking between Lars and the stranger. As the night before, he stood relaxed, his growl pitching higher in some sort of insistence.

"My name is Felix." The man eyed Lars with curiosity. "We've been looking out for you. We heard you'd been helped as far as Halden."

"You're a faery?" Rose's voice grew louder in her sudden surprise.

A flash of annoyance crossed Felix's face. "Don't shout. These villagers already poke around in the woods as it is."

"How do we know you're telling the truth?" Lars straightened. "You could be working with the sorcerer, for all we know."

Rose squared her shoulders, ready to back Lars if the man should turn into a threat. *Though he seems more than capable to handle the two of us.*

Disgust creased Felix's mouth into a frown. "Don't worry. The only reason I'd get close to that filth is to kill him."

Killian growled again, and Felix nodded.

"That faery's cloaking spell was clever, but we have to cross the border to get some proper aid. I'm not going to be much help reversing the sorcerer's spell."

"You can understand him?" Rose lifted her eyebrows.

So far, faeries had been the only ones able to interpret Killian, and rather poorly at that. The man didn't seem to have much trouble.

"Not well. I'm not very strong with animals. Though Damian would say I'm just not good at talking to anyone."

"Damian?" Lars had still not relaxed his stance.

"My brother. We'll need his help. Come on." Felix jerked a thumb back down the main street.

Killian looks like he trusts him. And Father says to trust an animal's instincts. Rose moved to follow, but Lars hesitated. He glanced to Killian, who gave an impatient huff.

Lars frowned at Felix, but gave in.

"Let's go."

Chapter 17

Killian loped to catch up with the smart pace Felix set out of the town. New and nervous energy swept through him. They would meet the Myrnian faeries within the next few hours, and if they had a way to help him, he could be human by sundown.

The thought almost stopped him in his tracks. He'd only been cursed for a little under two weeks, but at times it truly hadn't seemed a misfortune.

He leapt effortlessly over a pool of water barricading the path. Did he want to give this up — this sense of belonging in his own skin?

He caught a glimpse of Lars trudging beside him, shadows of hope lingering in his brother's features. Remaining a wolf meant giving up his brother. His family. He wasn't ready for that.

Pine trees began to march closer to the road, gathering in whispering clusters. Killian let the tang fill his nose as he listened to the industry of the animals that resided in the protection of the forest. A squirrel chattered boldly from its safe perch. Killian growled back, unimpressed by its remonstrance. It shrilled a final warning and threw a pinecone, wailing victory as Killian followed Felix off the path.

"I'm glad you're around to protect us from the scary animals." Lars pressed his lips together in mock seriousness.

Killian snapped at Lars's leg and his brother darted away, his laugh drowning out Rose's snicker.

Felix paused and glanced back at them. "This is the border."

Killian almost expected a physical marker, but the forest spread away uninterrupted.

"Killi, wait!" Lars knelt beside him. "What about the sorcerer?"

A flash of fear quivered through Killian's paws. It had been easy to forget the sorcerer's power when he knew the spell protected him. Discovery lay only a few feet away.

He looked to Felix, who only shrugged.

"It's your decision."

There's really no choice. We have to keep going.

He padded across the border, his fur prickling as Alfar's protective spell melted away. Killian fought the sudden urge to run. As if that would keep Noak from finding him.

He planted his paws more firmly into the rain-softened dirt and looked back at his companions.

Lars tightened his grip on his sword, looking faintly queasy. Rose had also lost some of her confident air, her shoulders drooping and a frown creasing one side of her mouth. Felix waited in studied patience. Killian knew he'd have to get them moving or Lars would start doubting himself again.

"*Come on!*" He trotted a few paces, joining Felix. Lars and Rose trailed along behind them.

Felix turned onto a faint game trail. Wolf prints scattered the mud. A pack wasn't far. Killian considered calling to them until the stronger scent of human teased the breeze, reminding him of his own pack.

"*How much longer?*" Killian trotted beside Felix.

"Soon," Felix replied.

Killian caught a strange scent—something that shouldn't belong in the forest. A slender shape flickered between shadows, its white fur stained with black spots in a strange patchwork disguise.

Cat. He snarled.

The scent faded as a man appeared in its place. Rose and Lars started at his sudden approach.

"Damian." Felix nodded.

"Felix." Damian clapped him on the shoulder.

Killian couldn't help but stare at the four parallel scars that marked the right side of Damian's face, twisting the edge of his mouth. Something about the gruesome sight seemed familiar.

He looked away, murmuring an apology, as the faery leveled hazel eyes at him.

Damian spared him a brief half smile and greeted the others.

"Now, then." He knelt before Killian, his movements eerily resembling Felix. The two were no doubt brothers, with the same hazel eyes, despite Felix's darker hair. Damian's neat appearance gave Felix's lightly-creased tunic an almost disheveled look.

"May I?" Damian lifted one hand.

"Of course." Killian closed his eyes as Damian placed his hand on Killian's head. As with the other faeries on their journey, Killian could sense the faery's power. It rolled from the faeries in waves, but his human companions didn't seem to detect it. Damian felt different, a softer, more comforting magic, and the wolf within him knew he could trust this faery.

"I've never seen the like," Damian said. "Old magic and new bound up together. All three of you have a touch of old magic about you. Interesting."

"I did tell them you'd be helpful." Felix snorted.

Damian grinned and ran a hand over Killian's left shoulder. "This healed well."

The scar twinged in faint discomfort under his prodding fingers, but Killian remained still.

"They both fussed enough."

Damian flashed another smile.

"Can you help?" Lars broke in.

"It will take some time before I know for certain." Damian gained his feet in an effortless motion. "I need to know more about both curses and speak with faeries more talented than I."

Felix's scoff indicated he thought no such faery existed. Damian shot him an exasperated glare.

Brothers.

"We don't have much time," Lars said. "The water faery said his spell would protect Killian only until he crossed the border."

"I can replace the spell," Damian said.

"Or we can use you to draw the sorcerer in." Felix shrugged, and ran his thumb along the metal rod tucked in his belt.

"Felix!" Damian glared at his brother. Felix spread his hands in a gesture that wasn't apologetic.

"We won't." Damian turned to Lars. "You two boys are royals of Calvyrn. We won't risk your life. I have been tasked with finding and dealing with the sorcerer. We'll find another way."

"*I'll do it,*" Killian barked and laid back his ears. *Though I will most definitely regret it later.*

"Killi, don't even think about it." Lars scowled down at him.

"You can understand him?" Damian raised his eyebrows in surprise.

"We're brothers. I know when he's going to do something stupid."

"Sounds familiar." Felix smirked.

Damian smiled and looked down at Killian. "No, I can't ask that of you."

"*It's my life.*" Killian stared up into Damian's eyes. "*The sorcerer cursed me. We use me to find him and break this curse.*"

"What did he say?" Lars demanded.

"He wants to do it."

"Killian, no!" A note of desperation filled Lars's voice. He dropped to a knee. "It's too dangerous."

Killian nudged underneath his brother's arm and wagged his tail. "*So is running for the rest of my life. Or never becoming human again.*"

Lars pulled him close. "What if something happens to you? What am I going to tell Mother and Father?"

"*You can't always protect me.*"

"It's my job to protect you." Lars sighed. "You're my little brother. I should have been there when the sorcerer attacked you."

Killian butted his head into Lars's chest. *Don't be stupid. He'd have killed you.*

"Killi!"

He opened his mouth in a wolfish grin. *"Calm down. We beat the sorcerer and go home."*

"How are we going to defeat a sorcerer? It's just us."

"You've got me." Rose raised her chin. "You two are like t' annoying brothers I never wanted. Besides, if we find t' sorcerer, we might find my father."

Killian squirmed out of Lars's strangle-hold and wound about her legs. She grinned down at him.

"You're welcome."

"We'll be with you as well," Damian said. "And an army of faeries if necessary."

"Fine." Lars stood and crossed his arms, sighing.

Like you wouldn't have done the same in a heartbeat if our places were switched, idiot?

"We'll keep moving." Damian rested a hand on his sword. "There are warded places for you to stay. We'll draw the sorcerer to our own battleground."

Damian turned to his brother. "Felix, take them to the oak. I'll report to King Borys and find you later."

Brown wings sprouted from Damian's back. Like Kaja, the wings looked to be made of a toughened membrane, but Damian's stretched tight over a bony framework like a bat. The wings gave a powerful flap, stirring the rich loam with the wind, and he vanished into the treetops.

"Come on." Felix kicked straying leaves from his boots. "It'll take a few hours to get to the oak."

He took the lead again, but this time Lars's hand rested on his sword and Rose carried her strung bow in her hand. Killian paused for a long moment before loping after them. *So much for being human by sundown.* His fur prickled uncomfortably at the thought of facing more magic. *I'm definitely going to regret this.* Though a small part of him was still glad to be a wolf for a little longer.

Chapter 18

Something has changed.

A persistent nagging prodded the back corner of Noak's mind. He halted his trudging feet and called up his tracking spell.

Delighted laughter burst from him when he saw a shaggy brown wolf padding through a sun-speckled forest. *No more faery spell protecting you!*

The image hovered between his outstretched hands, the blurred edges preventing him from picking out any other details.

A girl in trousers and tunic appeared in a flash of red. She walked beside the wolf for a few seconds before vanishing beyond the edge. Her green and brown clothes reminded him of the troublesome Rangers that had interfered since he had entered Calvyrn.

I didn't know those meddling idiots allowed girls. Interesting.

Noak continued to watch the wolf, taking the time to admire the effects of his spell. It was a piece of art, if he might even say so, perfected by the canvas of aged magic just waiting for a brush.

He brought his hands together, dispelling the rippling picture.

Noak let his eyes slide closed, allowing his mind to empty of all thoughts save one—the scarred face of Calvyrn's most valiant knight, Sir Einar. He'd been leading the search for the prince and, according to Noak's contact, was headed to Myrnius as well.

He murmured the words, letting them slip from his lips and scurry away to find and cling to the knight before spreading his hands wide. A new image floated—six men on horseback, clad in simple, unadorned tunics and mail coats, their bearing marking them as anything but common. Glimpses of the river flashed between the horses' flying hooves and Noak frowned. If he was not careful, paths might cross with unwanted consequences.

He snapped his hands together. "How far to Myrnius?"

"Less than a day," Finn reassured him.

Noak grimaced. They'd been journeying for two days with only necessary rest breaks. The thought of another forced march was about as appealing as facing a troll.

The brothers' stoic faces were as unchanging as ever, only the dark rings shadowing their eyes indicated their weariness. But then, Noak didn't look much better. His robe's silver embroidery had been turned a fine brown and the reek of their fires clung to the seams.

"We rest for a few hours and continue."

They nodded in silent affirmation, all four sinking wearily to the ground and sleeping despite the brightness of the afternoon sun. Noak curled into the folds of his robe, thinking of the messages to be sent to his men in Celedon Forest.

For once the afternoon heat felt good, soaking through the cloth to soothe his aching joints. His eyes slid closed against his will. Messages could wait.

Chapter 19

Einar reined his charger up at the bank of the river where the water skimmed over the shallow sands of the ford. King Jonas loosened the reins to allow his mount to drink, dismounting to refill his own waterskin. The soldiers with them followed their leader's example.

Einar pulled out the map, spreading it against his horse's flank.

"Well?" Jonas came around to join him.

"Moss is the closest town to the border and to Celedon. We should be there by tomorrow." Einar drained the last of his waterskin as the king took the map, studying it.

"Resupply there." Jonas refolded the map. "I should send word to King Stefan before the entire neighboring royal family invades his forest."

Einar chuckled as he dipped the canteen into the river. "That might be for the best."

"I would say so," a voice agreed.

Einar flinched, jumping away and tossing the waterskin down in favor of a more formidable weapon. He wasn't the only one to blink in confusion at the woman who stood in the shallows.

"Oh, I should have remembered from last time." She giggled. "Sir Einar." The river curled with her curtsey, her pale blue dress somehow escaping the damp.

"Who's asking?" He growled, sword still at the ready, confident in the men who protected his flanks.

"I am Kaja. I spoke to your nephews four days ago."

"What?" Jonas pushed forward.

Einar held out an arm to prevent his advance. "Who are you?"

She smiled, and sunlight glinted in myriad colors off glistening wings. The men immediately lowered weapons and Einar struggled to overcome his shock enough to formulate an apology.

But the faery continued as if humans meeting faeries by the river was a common occurrence.

"They seemed eager for their family to know they were safe," Kaja said.

"And are they?" Jonas demanded.

"You are?" A tiny smile teased the corner of her mouth.

Einar shook his head, trying to warn Jonas not to say anything, but the boys came by their impetuous nature honestly.

"Their father." Jonas crossed his arms, straightening into a regal posture. Einar stifled a sigh.

So much for inconspicuous.

Kaja sank into a deeper curtsey with a slight bow. "They were when I took them downriver several days ago. They should be in Myrnius by now."

"I don't know if I should be relieved or not." Jonas glanced at Einar.

"You should be. Our Myrnian kin are watching for their arrival." Kaja stepped from the river, giving Jonas's temperamental mare a pat on the nose with none of the usual consequences.

"Is Killian truly a…" Jonas's voice caught before he could say the cursed word. For a terrible moment, Einar didn't know if he wanted the answer.

Kaja's features softened and she encompassed both of them with her look. "Would you like to see?"

Einar nodded silently, Jonas still frozen. Kaja bent to the river, sliding her hand beneath the surface. Droplets rose in shining beads, twisting round each other in a quick spray until they merged into a sheet. The liquid shivered, and a brown wolf stood on the bank, ears pricked, amber eyes staring out. Two other figures emerged—one was Lars, looking slimmer, older, and dirtier than he'd ever been. The other was the red-haired girl the villagers described.

Einar ignored her, focusing on the images of his nephews. Jonas stared with something like horror at the wolf. Einar rested a hand on Jonas's shoulder, unwilling to fathom his thoughts. Bad enough it was his nephews, Einar couldn't imagine having sons suffer that fate.

And for Jonas to stare at the embodiment of the curse that had stolen his brother?

Einar tightened his grip. He hadn't known Prince Hugo well, but his death had been a blow.

Jonas gathered a breath. "How is he?" His voice came out a gruff whisper.

"You've raised a strong son." Kaja withdrew her hand and the image wavered for a few more seconds before cascading back into the river. "Two strong sons."

Einar managed a tight smile, a poor excuse for thanks.

"Where did they go from here?" Jonas said, his voice regaining strength.

"I helped them as far as Halden."

"Moss isn't that much further to the south," Einar said. "We could make it there by tomorrow night."

"And then search the whole forest?" Despair crushed Jonas's shoulders into a slump.

"No," Kaja broke in. "Our people will find them, but they won't know you're coming. I'll help them find you." She cast about the river bank, digging through the sand to unearth stones, finally coming across one that seemed to suit her fancy. She brushed it clean, cradling it in her palms and whispering.

Einar caught only a few words that didn't make much sense in isolation yet retained an air of hope and merriment. She handed the stone to Jonas.

"Cast it into standing water and it will bring friends to you."

"Thank you." Jonas graced her with a courtly bow.

She fiddled with strands of her silver-blonde hair and smiled. "Good luck to you." She glanced to Einar. "Creator bless and guide."

Einar inclined his head and the faery stepped into the river, a graceful heron taking her place and winging away. Einar stared after her in silence before Jonas spoke.

"Never thought I'd live to see a faery." He smoothed his thumb over the stone before tucking it away.

Einar turned to check his stallion's girth again before he mounted. "Aye, I just hope these friends she spoke of will know more than her."

"They will. I'm sure of it."

Einar allowed to himself to believe in Jonas's newfound hope as the company spurred their horses across the river.

Chapter 20

Long shadows flitted among the trees, daring the lingering golden beams to withstand their advance when Felix stopped under the branches of a sprawling oak tree. The trio gratefully took seats among its roots to rest aching feet and paws.

"The warding stretches as far as the roots," Felix warned. Small leaves kicked up where he pointed.

Killian noticed clusters of star-shaped flowers following the same outline, their purple petals taking on a faint glow in the fading light.

"I wouldn't leave unless one of us is with you," Felix said.

A small bunch of the flowers nestled in the crook of a root. Killian nosed at it, the bittersweet scent driving a sneeze from him. He pawed at his nose, disregarding the flora as a stray breeze betrayed a rabbit.

A deer grazed several paw-lengths beyond it, and he ignored it with an effort. He couldn't bring one down himself. Smaller prey would have to continue to satisfy him.

He stood at the boundary line before he realized it, one forepaw hovering above the flowers.

"Killian?" Rose's voice held a note of cautious curiosity.

He planted his paw inside the line, stomach rumbling in regret as the rabbit fled. He turned back to join them at the base of the tree.

"You won't go hungry." Felix gave him an understanding smile.

A new scent, more like a feeling of safety, rippled over them. Killian pricked his ears. Damian. And someone else came with him.

The others seemed unaware, so he sat back on his haunches to wait. Felix didn't react, so Rose and Lars sat in silence, exchanging an occasional puzzled glance.

Killian's ears picked up voices and finally the others heard them. Lars looked to Felix in brief alarm, but the stoic faery only shrugged.

"It's Damian."

Damian stepped into the oak's protective boundary with a young woman. She pushed wavy brown tresses from her face and smiled at them. Felix stood and gave a nod, changing to a bulky lynx in the blink of an eye and bounding away.

"This is Adela, my wife." Damian motioned to the newcomer as Lars and Rose stood to greet her.

"I'm so pleased to finally meet you." Her voice had a soft music to it, as if she'd rather sing.

Killian stepped closer as she knelt, the skirts of her blue dress settling around her.

"Don't worry about a thing." Her warm gaze reassured him. "Damian will do everything he can for you."

"*Thank you.*"

Her smile brightened her face again as she stood to clasp the others' hands.

"Wait. You're not—*the* Adela and Damian, are you?" Rose's cheeks blushed a brighter pink.

Damian and Adela exchanged a glance and a smile.

"We are." Adela tilted her head.

Killian stared. That's why the scars on Damian's face had seemed familiar. He'd heard the story often enough of the two faeries who helped the then-Count Stefan defeat a witch and her brother who'd plotted against him.

They'd both given Stefan a faery blessing and predicted his rise as Myrnius's first king and long and prosperous reign.

"*But that was years ago!*"

King Stefan had passed his eightieth year, and the faeries before Killian didn't look past their thirties.

"Aye, nearly sixty by your reckoning." Damian glanced down at Killian. "Time passes differently for us. We're both young yet. I'm just barely over one-hundred and fifty."

Adela couldn't hold back a giggle.

"You really live for six hundred years?" Rose recovered herself enough to close her mouth.

"More or less."

"You killed the witch?" Lars stared at Damian's scars with renewed interest.

The faeries' expressions grew somber as Damian nodded. According to legend, Damian and the witch battled in both human and feline form. The scars came from her claws.

"Aye, and almost lost my life," he said. "I rushed to battle last time. This sorcerer might be more powerful than the witch. I won't make the same mistake again. I trust you'll respect my caution?"

The iron in his voice left them little doubt that it wasn't their choice.

But Lars didn't even seem to think about arguing. Killian flicked his tail in amusement at the surprising sign of maturity.

"What's King Stefan like?" Rose blurted out, turning to Lars and Killian. "Have you met him?"

Killian shook himself. King Stefan might be in excellent health, but he didn't travel much. Killian had met King Stefan's son and grandson. Lars, on the other hand...

"A few years ago." Lars cleared his throat in sudden awkwardness, "I—um—didn't stick around much, so I'm not the best person to ask."

"He's a kind and generous man," Adela said, relieving the tension. "As a count they used to say, 'his hearth is always open.' That hasn't changed. Now, how about some supper?"

Damian slid a satchel from his shoulder as Adela hung small rounded lanterns from the lowest limbs, setting them alight with a quick word. Rose and Adela took over laying out the meal, Rose's movements shy and stilted next to the faery.

None of the spread looked appetizing to Killian and he sighed.

Lovely. I suppose I'm going hungry tonight.

The scent of lynx grew stronger.

Killian scanned the trees, stifling a growl when the lamplight reflected two bright orbs and the cat slunk from the darkness, morphing back into Felix holding the rabbit carcass. He winked at Killian, who took it with a grateful rumble.

Killian retreated several paces away from the others, placing the tree between them as he tore into the carcass. They gave him the dignity of eating in peace as they turned to their own meal, Adela and Damian asking after their journey.

Killian finished with rabbit and licked the remnants away, then edged closer to his companions as they lingered over the meal. Damian looked at him, then at Lars, asking further questions about the spell.

Lars recounted the story of the family curse, any old scorn he might have borne the tale long gone, but the bitterness still evident. Then Killian gave his account of the sorcerer's spell, Damian repeating some of it for the benefit of the others.

Killian nipped at Lars's arm as guilt flickered across his brother's features.

"There was nothing you could have done."

I'm actually grateful you weren't there. Noak and his men would have just killed you.

"You keep saying that. It isn't going to make me feel better." Lars scowled at his brother when Damian passed on Killian's comment.

"Fine, idiot."

Damian didn't bother to translate. "Glad I'm not the only one who has a brother who won't listen."

"You're one to talk." Felix snorted as he pulled out parchment and charcoal, ignoring them as he began to sketch.

"May I take some of your blood?" Damian turned to Killian, who blinked at the odd request.

Damian smiled. "The magic is in your blood."

Killian mustered the effort to stand still as Damian pricked his shoulder with a dagger, allowing blood to run into the blade's channel. Damian held the blade steady and pressed his hand over the stinging wound. Warmth blossomed under his touch and the pain faded to nothing.

Killian twisted to nose at the area and found it completely healed.

"Magic must be useful."

"Aye, but my healing magic is still limited. I only trained long enough to be of use in emergencies." Damian didn't look up from the blood he had drawn.

Rose leaned closer. "Train your magic?"

"Yes, we all have something our magic gravitates to." Adela glanced at her. "Damian is strongest in communicating with animals. He helps care for the forest. Plants and growing things respond best to my magic. The warding is mine."

"How did you make it? It's the flowers, isn't it?" Killian tilted his head up towards her.

"Well spotted." Adela smiled. "It is the flowers. And, I don't know, I've never tried to explain magic before."

She plucked several blades of grass from the ground, holding them in the palm of her hand. Words Killian couldn't understand danced from her tongue and the grass darted up from her hand, weaving around each other, then swirling away to form shapes of trees, wolves, and leopards.

A shiver tickled the fur between his shoulders. *Magic.* It felt nothing like Noak's. The sorcerer's magic terrified him.

It flared wild and angry. The same wildness was present in Adela's, but her words gave it a sense of calm.

Killian laid down and rested his nose on his paws.

All the same, I think I'll be happy if I never see magic again.

He looked at Felix who still hadn't joined their conversation, still absorbed in his drawing.

"What about you, Felix?"

"Metal." Felix didn't look up. "I'm a blacksmith."

"He's actually the reason we discovered what the sorcerer was up to," Adela said.

"How?" Lars glanced at Felix, who reluctantly looked up.

"Some little idiot faery bothered me until I took him on as apprentice. One day I sent him off into the forest to collect wood for arrow shafts, and the little idiot faery got himself in trouble and was hurt by the sorcerer."

"So, you're along for revenge?" Lars raised his eyebrows.

"Course not. Revenge isn't the faery way." Felix gave a snort of derision, rolling his eyes, and completely negated his statement.

"Is he all right? Your apprentice?" Rose shivered a little.

Felix's granite expression softened a fraction. "Didn't think he would be for a while, but he'll be fine. Unlike that sorcerer when I find him."

A growl ripped from Killian. The sorcerer had hurt someone else. Badly too, it sounded like. Just one more reason to stop him.

But he'd seen Noak's power.

"I don't mean to be rude, but are the three of you going to be enough to stop him?"

"That's what Borys and his council are hoping," Felix said.

"Felix!" Damian rebuked the note of sarcasm in Felix's voice.

"Fine, yes, three faeries should be enough to take care of the sorcerer." Felix shifted his attention back to his sketch. "If not, we send a message back home and get an army."

"Army?" Lars crossed his arms. "I thought you were supposed to be peaceful."

"We are. Except for Felix." Adela stifled a grin and the other faery smirked. "There are still warriors trained in our halls. As long as magic is in the world we are here to defend against those who use it for evil. As Damian said, this is not our first time to confront the misuse of this power."

She sent a soft glance to Damian, but her expression changed to concern. "What's wrong?"

Damian's brow creased down into a frown. The old injury to his face twisted his mouth further. It took him longer than Killian wanted to bring his gaze back up. Killian's inquisitive growl brought the others' attention to Damian.

"I'm not going to pretend this is simple. I need to talk to someone before I do anything." Damian took a napkin and placed it over the knife, the blood soaking through its clean surface.

Adela moved to stand by him, worry creasing faint lines around her eyes. Killian fought panic at the sight. *What if he can't help? What am I going to do?*

Damian's touched Killian's shoulder, soothing his anxiety.

"I'll be back tomorrow."

Killian turned his face up to him and whined.

"I'll do everything I can." Damian's whispered promise would have to be enough. "Felix will stay with you tonight. Tomorrow, we'll set the plan to catch the sorcerer."

Felix looked up from his work long enough to bid Damian and Adela goodnight, rising to his feet as they disappeared among the trees.

"I'll watch tonight. Get some rest." He stepped out of the oak's circle, leaving them in silence.

"Well?" Lars rubbed a hand across his eyes.

"Well." Rose sighed and grabbed her bed roll. "Sounds like we have a full day of playing bait tomorrow."

Don't remind me.

Killian found a spot among the roots smooth enough to almost be comfortable.

Lars and Rose settled down, the lanterns dimming and winking out. Killian blinked in the sudden darkness, his eyes adjusting as the moon sent beams to play among the branches. He wriggled forward until he could see the bulk of the waning moon.

Killian raised his head a wolf howled, joined one by one by the voices of the pack. He wanted to call out, to tell them another brother was nearby. He buried his muzzle between his paws, bottling up his howl until the pack moved on.

He growled and smacked a paw against the ground. He thought he knew what he wanted—thought he wanted to be human again—only to be reminded how effortless it felt to be a wolf.

He'd never prayed very much, but Uncle Einar was devout so perhaps that counted for something.

Please help us through this. Uncle Einar says there's a grand purpose to our lives we can't always see. I hope he's right and You have this planned because I'm terrified.

Killian resettled himself against the soft grass. Whether because he'd finally admitted to his fear, or because Someone was listening, the anxiety that had lurked since crossing the border faded for the moment.

A movement tickled his subconscious and Killain jerked his head up as Lars settled beside him.

"I heard the wolves. You all right?"

Killian rested his nose on his paws. Lars ruffled the thick fur between his shoulders.

"You know, that's the first time I've actually listened to a wolf howl. It's almost beautiful. Father said once that Uncle Hugo could understand them. You could too?"

Killian looked up at his brother, blinking.

"You were trying to tell me that day on the battlement, weren't you? Why didn't you?"

Killian tilted his head to fix Lars with one amber eye.

Lars's smile was filled with regret. "Not just because you didn't want me to worry?"

"That's one of the reasons."

"You should have been able to tell me, Killi." Lars sighed and looked out into the dark forest. "I should have paid attention—to a lot of things. Makes me wonder what I've missed over the years. If Rose had come to the castle asking for help, I would have found someone else to deal with it. But you would have tried to help her right away. You and Father. I'm too selfish."

He pulled his knees up and rested his arms on them.

"Lars." Killian nudged his brother's knee with his nose.

"No, I need to be hard on myself. You've always seen something in me and I want to live up to that."

Killian pushed up to sitting. *I wish I could figure out how to tell you that you don't have to live up to anything. You're my brother.*

"I remember Uncle Hugo, and after he died, how Father acted whenever he was mentioned. I thought maybe if I ignored it, it wouldn't happen to you." Lars picked at dirt smudging his fingers. "I don't know if Damian can help you, but if he can't, we'll still figure out a way to get you out of this. And help Rose while we're at it."

Killian leaned against his shoulder and Lars nudged him back, wrapping an arm around him and ruffling the fur the wrong way as he released him. Killian growled in mock irritation as he shook it back in place.

"Get some rest, Killi." Lars pushed up to return to his pallet.

Killian grumbled the same sentiment, heart lifting a little at the smile Lars flashed his way.

It likely didn't take much to figure out what Killian meant in some circumstances, but seeing Lars and Rose respond brought some hope back.

He curled up more comfortably, one ear tracking as he located Felix's near-silent footfalls. All worry aside, they were safer at the moment than they had been the entire trip. He shut his eyes against the thoughts of tomorrow and slept.

Chapter 21

Noak never thought he'd be grateful to see the stifling greenery of Celedon Forest. The pale light of early dawn drew out the varied shades of green lurking in the clustered foliage. He ignored the sight, more concerned with finding their camp and a fire and a place to prop up his aching feet.

If I never see travel rations, deserted roads, or smell unwashed clothes again, it'll be too soon.

When he'd finished the task he set for himself years ago, he would focus his energy on finding somewhere to settle. Somewhere far away from plains and forests and hard travel bread. Somewhere to enjoy a world empty of faeries and their magic.

A world where humans like him might gain new respect without faeries constantly being held up as comparison.

Finn took the lead, taking faint trails scored through the scattered undergrowth to the camp they set up weeks ago. It took another hour of walking before he caught the tang of his magic and he pushed back the protective barrier to let them through.

Noak spent the next few minutes inspecting the wards. The shimmering threads of his magic would be visible only to a magic user's eyes. He ran his fingers over the rippling strands, testing the strength, and listening for any discordance in the thrumming of power. He circled the campsite, testing the wards on the ground, then reaching up to the bands that stretched above the campsite.

He finally nodded in satisfaction. The light blue glow was untouched. No other magic had attempted to meddle with them. *The faeries still have no idea where we are.* The faeries were also the reason he'd not sensed his wolf since early the previous evening.

"What's this?" Noak paused, indicating the red-haired figure hunched against a twisted pine.

"Caught him snooping around the wards a few days ago," one of his men replied. "Decided to wait and see what you wanted to do with him."

Noak's lip curled in disgust. The man wore the Ranger uniform. For the trouble the Rangers had caused, he might send the man back in pieces.

But, at the moment, he had other concerns.

He took a seat by the low fire despite the warmth of the summer morning. A pot of kaffe still simmered and he poured a mug. He still had six days until the solstice, but if the wolf didn't reappear by the end of the day, he would have to figure a way to draw them out.

Noak absentmindedly tapped the side of the mug, bringing the liquid to a more palatable temperature.

As if on cue, the tracking spell prodded his consciousness. He choked on his mouthful of kaffe and spread his hands to open the window that showed the wolf.

The creature paced the woods in the company of two humans. Their surroundings did nothing to help Noak. Every tree looked like the other to him. But if he concentrated, he could feel the wolf's presence some distance to the north. Another figure appeared, the faint glow of magic hovering around him.

Noak frowned. He didn't need the shorter stature or the glow to recognize a faery. There was a sort of pious arrogance to their walk. At least one faery to contend with, then. He focused on the area the spell drew his attention to. *They are heading toward us!*

"Finn!"

The man hurried over, a bit of jerky still hanging from his hand.

"The wolf is on the move. We strike tomorrow. I will distract the faery long enough to draw the others out. You are responsible for taking care of the young man."

"What about the girl?" Finn pointed to the laughing figure in the spell image.

"The prince is the real threat."

Finn smiled slowly. "I've never killed a prince before."

"Don't kill him." Noak scowled. "After this is over, I don't want to be hiding from a country out for revenge for killing their heir. Just make sure he can't interfere when we trap the wolf."

Finn reluctantly agreed. "How are you planning on drawing them out?"

Noak looked hard at the girl, then shifted his gaze to the meddlesome Ranger.

"I think we have something they might want." He pushed up to his feet and crossed to the man, nudging him with a toe. The Ranger raised his head to glare at Noak.

Noak crouched down to eye level. "You have a daughter? Red hair, freckles, looks like she wants to be just like you?"

Anger masked a deeper fear in the man's blue eyes. "What's it t' you?"

"She happens to be standing between me and something I need. I'll require your help to remedy that."

The man spat and looked away.

Noak wiped flecks of spittle from his face, then lunged and gripped the man's throat.

"You don't have a choice."

He murmured a brief spell, clenching his fingers against the man's skin. The Ranger's voice leapt to Noak's hand, and he pulled it away. He pulled a river stone, marked with flecks of gold, from his pocket and pressed his hand to its smooth surface. The gold absorbed the Ranger's voice and Noak handed it to Finn.

"I'll give her your regards." Noak watched as the man cursed and railed, but no sound escaped his lips. "Don't worry. It's not permanent. You'll have it back tomorrow when I have my wolf."

Chapter 22

"We have a fair idea of where the sorcerer is," Damian said as he led the way down a faint forest track. The golden sunlight of midmorning filtered through the treetops to brush the ground, dispelling the lurking shadows. Killian padded at the rear of the group with Felix, nose twitching at every scent.

"So why haven't you attacked yet?" Lars's hand hadn't moved from his sword in the hours since they'd left the oak.

"We knew he left the forest weeks ago. His camp is located near a part of the forest that houses the Nameless Ones—faeries that have fallen under the spell of dark magic. There are powerful wards set up just outside that feed off the power of the place. Adela has been trying to find a way around the warding, or at least see what lies on the other side. Noak returned to the forest last night, so we need to draw him away."

Killian darted another glance at a shadow among the trees. *I hate this. I'm jumpier than a pup on its first day out of the den.* He started. *Child. Not pup.*

"Think he'll take t' bait even if he knows we're here?" Rose effortlessly swiveled her glance from side to side, tracking their surroundings, red curls dancing with the movement.

"He went through a fair amount of trouble to curse Killian. I'd bet good steel he knows where you are." Felix spoke up from his place in the rear.

"Comforting." Killian lashed his tail.

His ears picked up a muffled chuckle from Damian.

"We won't go much further today. I don't want to risk exposing you for too long. We're close to the place Felix and I chose to trap him."

Four pines set in a wide square marked the next warded spot Adela had prepared for them.

Finally. I'd rather march a full day than spend another few hours jumping at shadows.

The knot in his stomach loosened, but Killian had resigned himself to permanent anxiety until he saw the sorcerer trapped.

I'd even stay a wolf forever if it means he's no longer a threat to anyone.

He padded over to Damian, catching his attention with a low-pitched growl. Damian had not said anything when he arrived that morning and Killian had avoided asking, but he could wait no longer.

"What do you know about my curse?"

Damian settled against one of the pines to come to eye level with Killian. *"Are you sure you want me to tell you now?"*

Killian flattened his ears. Damian spoke the language of wolves. Bad news, then.

"The sorcerer's spell bound itself to your family's original curse." Damian spoke gently, compassion in his gaze. *"It is such that I cannot do anything against it. The witch knew what she was about. Only she would be able to undo the curse. As such, I don't even know if the sorcerer could lift his spell on you."*

Killian glanced up at him with a whine. *"But the witch lived hundreds of years ago!"*

"If she had a descendent maybe, but even then..." Damian's shrug conveyed his doubt.

"Is – is there even a chance with the sorcerer?" Killian's head drooped.

"It's possible he might be able to lift the curse. That is, if we could persuade him. Say that or his death."

"That seems a lot of maybes."

Damian's smile didn't hold much mirth. *"I will keep searching for a way. But I understand if you wish to go your own way."*

He couldn't leave. Not with the sorcerer still a threat.

"No." Killian let out a long sigh. *"Noak needs to be stopped and I can help you. But if Lars asks, killing Noak will break the curse."* Killian cocked his head back to where Lars watched them.

"I can't lie," Damian said softly.

"You don't have to tell him the truth either. Not until we know for certain."

"And if nothing can be done? What then?" Damian lifted his eyebrows.

Killian couldn't find the will to lift his head to meet Damian's kind gaze. He looked away, staring out into the woods. Somewhere out there, the pack ran free.

"Then I leave. I can't stay with my family like this. Though maybe you could find a way to give me human speech."

Damian's touch ruffled his fur and comforted him. *"If all else fails, then I will. But let's not give up on those maybes just yet."*

Killian met Damian's eyes. *"All right. But you still won't tell Lars — or Rose?"*

"Not until we know for certain."

"Thank you."

"Whatever happens, the Creator has a plan for you, Prince Killian." Damian ruffled his fur one last time and stood.

Would I even keep the title if I stay a wolf? Family or not, it would be awkward to have a canine family member visit court. Better to just declare him dead or erase him from the annals.

His eyes stung and he swiped at his muzzle with an irritated paw.

"Killian?" Rose paused a few steps away. "We were going t' have an early dinner. Did you need t' hunt?"

The bits of dried meat he'd eaten that morning hadn't exactly been filling. Fresh meat would be good.

"Are you all right?" Rose touched his shoulder, frowning. "What were you and Damian talking about?"

Killian turned his nose into the wind and growled. Rose glanced at Lars and the brothers, who were deep in conversation planning the sorcerer's capture and demise.

"It all right if we go hunt?"

"Yes." Damian looked up and smiled. "The warding extends for a short distance. Just don't go beyond the outer ring of pines."

She strung her bow, nodding, and followed Killian out of the small clearing. Killian found the scent of deer and eagerly set them on the trail. Deer tracks took them parallel to tall pines that grew at random intervals. Killian paused only to test the wind before padding closer to the small pool where the deer grazed.

Rose freed an arrow from her quiver with a faint slither. The deer's ears twitched, but it continued to eat.

Killian crouched in the undergrowth, saliva beading his mouth as he waited. The creak of her bow sounded deafening in the quiet of the forest. The twang of the string startled the deer, but it had no chance to escape her aim.

Killian bolted forward to make sure it fell before it escaped the boundary, and Rose hurried over with a squeal of triumph. "Been too long since I've had fresh venison."

I heartily agree. If I have to eat any more rodents, I'll probably just starve myself.

"Do—do you want t' eat here and I'll take the rest back t' camp when you're done?"

He nodded gratefully, coming to nose at the handle of her sheathed knife.

"I should probably dress it first." She drew the knife.

Killian had only performed the process himself a handful of times, and watched, impressed, as she completed the task with smooth efficiency. He dug a hole to bury the entrails, helping her nudge them in.

Rose sliced healthy portions from the haunches and set them aside, indicating the rest was his. Killian attempted some decorum while feasting on the carcass, but it wasn't easy. She gave him privacy as she wiped her hands on the grass, splashing water from the pool to clean the residual blood away. She sharpened her knife as he began to slow down.

"Better?"

Killian shook himself, but she showed no signs of leaving.

"Are you all right?"

For once, he was grateful human speech was beyond his reach.

"Damian didn't have good news, did he?"

It wouldn't have been difficult to infer, especially to a person as intuitive as Rose. He tilted his head to the side.

"Well he, Lars, and Felix are coming up with a plan. And you already know Lars is going t' do whatever it takes."

Killian growled. *"That's what concerns me."*

"I'm a little worried about that, so I'm sure you are. I hope it's all right you two have become a bit like family. I know it might be stupid of me, you being princes and I'm no one really, but…"

"Rose." His growl interrupted her, and he came closer, placing a paw on her knee. *"I wouldn't mind having a sister."*

She flung an arm over him, squeezing with a smile. "Just wish I could do more for you."

He nudged her arm. *You have already. Just wish I could tell you myself.*

She stood and dusted off her clothes, frowning down at the carcass. "Suppose we could just leave this here. You could eat from it tomorrow."

Even if another predator found it, there would be more than enough to make another meal for him. Anything but the rations or small prey that were his only options without a pack.

Rose retrieved her portion of meat and they made their way back to the clearing, walking side-by-side through the whispering pines.

When they arrived, Adela had joined the others, a satchel rested over her shoulder. Killian raised his head, catching the whiff of the jumbled scents of herbs, and a sweeter scent of an ointment, similar to one used by the castle healers.

Hopefully, no one would need it.

Killian relaxed in the grass a short distance from the fire, his stomach comfortably full. He yawned and blinked lazily.

"Move over." Lars's boot nudged his side.

He bared his teeth but squirmed over enough to allow Lars to sit next to him. Adela knelt by the fire, helping Rose cobble together a stew, and the two faery brothers settled in on opposite sides of the fire.

Rose began to ask questions about the faery mountain and life, which the faeries patiently answered. Lars simply sat back, arms resting atop his knees, appearing to only half hear what was said.

Killian kicked Lars's leg with a hind paw and his brother jolted and frowned down at him. Killian grumbled low in his chest. Lars shook his head with a faint smile and nudged his side.

Lars engaged in the conversation after that, but Killian still saw shadows of worry cross his face. The same shadows lingered in the others' faces as they ate. He tucked into a ball.

Whatever happens tomorrow will happen. We have plan, and three faeries to help us. We'll be fine. He turned his face from the reaching heat of the fire. *But I wish it was over already.*

Chapter 23

The twinkling lights of Moss grew brighter in the fading light. The small company of knights spurred their mounts to a quicker pace, and the horses, sensing the town and the possibility of a night in a stable, didn't complain.

The company slowed as they came into the town, hooves clopping over a dirt road molded and dried in uneven ruts from the rain a few days previous. They halted under a swinging sign that marked *The Weary Wyvern*.

A stableboy dashed around to offer his services and Einar dismounted, instructing one of the knights to assist the boy with caring for all the steeds. Jonas still sat on his horse, staring up at the sign.

"They wanted to hunt one together."

"We'll find them, Jonas." It seemed poor comfort to give.

The king slid from his horse with a weary sigh, handing the reins off to a knight, and led the way into the inn.

The wide common room was nearly empty of customers and a low fire flickered on the hearth. Murmurs of conversation paused as the five armed men stepped in, breaking the peaceful quiet with the tread of heavy boots and the tell-tale clank of swords.

"Evening." Jonas's friendly greeting seemed to allay the uncertain looks sent their way.

"Evenin', sir." Most of the scattered customers returned his greeting before picking up their conversations again.

"Einar," the king spoke softly to him. "Let's see what the innkeeper might know."

Einar followed the king over to the worn oak bar, where the innkeeper and a young man who was a less weather-beaten version of him worked to tap a new barrel of ale.

"Just a minute, sirs," he called in a gruff voice.

Einar leaned comfortably against the bar. He didn't mind waiting, as long as it meant a mug of whatever they were tapping. He pulled his gloves off, flexing the fingers of his left hand that occasionally stiffened on him, courtesy of an old injury.

Jonas watched the men with interest—and a bit of giddy enthusiasm, to Einar's amusement, at being treated like a normal person.

"What can I do for you, sirs?" The innkeeper wiped his hands on a cloth.

"Dinner and rooms for at least a night," Einar spoke up before the king could begin the interrogation. Best to attend to basic needs first, in case Jonas pressed too hard and alienated their host.

"You two and those three?" The man jerked his chin to the soldiers.

"And one more who's out helping with the horses."

The man nodded. "We have plenty of space. Rooms'll be ready when you're done with dinner."

"One more question for you." Jonas stopped the man before he turned away. "We're looking for several people." He gave a rough description of Lars and the girl.

"Haven't seen anyone like that..." the man began but was interrupted as his son joined them.

"They came in two nights ago when you were gone. Stayed t' night and left t' next morning."

"They say where they were headed?" Jonas leaned over the bar.

"He said he and his sister were going t' visit some family in Myrnius. Didn't much look like siblings, though. Maybe more like a noble's son who ran off with a commoner he fancied."

"Jannik!" His father glared, but the young man just shrugged and retrieved six mugs from under the counter.

He's observant. "Anyone else with them?" Einar asked.

"Just a dog. Looked like a wolf. Stayed with them t' whole time."

"Inside?" The innkeeper raised suspicious eyebrows.

"It was well behaved. And it was raining." Jannik gave a helpless shrug.

His father shook his head with a sigh. "Just don't let it get t' be a habit."

Good thing the boy has a soft spot, since that "dog" is a prince of Calvyrn.

"Henri was here two nights ago." Jannik pointed to a stoop-shouldered man sipping his mug of ale by the fire. "I know he spoke with them. He might have some more information for you."

Jonas wasted no time crossing the room to take a seat by the man. Einar left him to it, ordering dinner for the company before joining them. Henri, it seemed, hadn't needed much coaxing to recall Rose, her brother Ivar, and that clever dog of theirs.

"Polite young 'uns." He took a generous swig of ale, swiping a few stray drops from his greying beard with a shirt sleeve. "What is it you wanted with 'em?" He squinted.

"They got mixed up in a bit of trouble. Family is worried." Jonas reassured him with a smile.

"Then 'ere's hoping you find 'em." Henri lifted his mug in salute.

"You see where they went?" Einar signaled for another mug to replace Henri's precariously low beaker.

"Saw 'em talking with someone a day or so ago. He comes in every now and again t' do some smithy work. Strong-looking fella, never 'ave caught his name. Thinking maybe they left with 'im."

No more definite information seemed forthcoming from Henri, so they left him with his new mug and moved to their table.

"Now to determine where they are in Myrnius." Jonas rubbed his eyes.

"If they're searching for a faery, they'll stay in Celedon." One of the knights leaned his elbows on the table. "I know that doesn't narrow it down much, but still."

"Could have already met one." Einar found it hard to believe Lars and Killian would have gone off with a stranger otherwise.

"I suppose we'll find out. I'll use the stone tomorrow to summon the help that river faery promised." Jonas touched the pocket that housed the faery's enchanted stone.

The table fell silent as the innkeeper and Jannik brought food and fresh ale, the weary knights more than content to focus on the thick venison stew over the worries of tomorrow.

Einar tipped the last of his ale down his throat and signaled Jannik, only see the young man staring at him. Einar stood and instead went up to the bar, where Jannik turned to the barrels and filled him another mug. Jannik lingered after exchanging it for Einar's empty mug.

"You need something, lad?" Einar kept his voice kind.

Jannik rubbed the back of his neck, casting a glance at the nearby patrons, before leaning half a step closer.

"No, sir. But it's just that there's been a story about town. Prince Killian turned t' a wolf and Prince Lars and a Ranger seeking a way to break t' curse." He fiddled with the empty mug and darted glances at the men at the table, his eyes lingering on Jonas.

Einar took a sip of his ale. "Seems a fanciful tale."

"Aye, sir. Don't know I would have believed it, but I know what I saw. The ones you're looking for aren't siblings, and that was a wolf if I've ever seen one."

Einar leaned forward, beckoning him to step out of the hearing of the few customers that lounged near the bar.

"You've got a good mind, lad. Now, I'm not saying if you're wrong or right, but I'd appreciate it if you didn't repeat that to anyone just yet."

Jannik bobbed his head, his eyes wide as he took in the company again. He retreated without a word, but Einar had a feeling the secret would stay that way. At least until they left Moss.

*

Bright beams of morning sunlight snuck through the narrow window, shining brighter in delight as Einar rubbed heavy eyes. Jonas's snores still rumbled from the pile of blankets on the opposite bed.

Einar picked grit from his eyes, laying still for a few more minutes, and wished he could forget he'd woken up. He was too old to be rushing across the countryside in search of faeries and run-away nephews.

"You awake?" Jonas grumbled.

"What if I said no?"

"Well, it's been awhile since I've slept until noon, but I wouldn't mind trying."

Einar pushed back his blanket with a chuckle and sat up. "You've gone soft, Jonas. A few nights on the road and you're completely worn out."

"Don't pretend you're not, Einar. How old will you be this wintertide?"

"Shut up." Einar bit his cheeks to stave off a groan as he slid from bed and reached for his tunic.

Jonas emerged from the blankets with a grumble reminiscent of the brown bears that inhabited the southern hills. He ran a hand through tousled brown hair, trying to comb it into some order.

Einar pulled his boots on, half-heartedly fiddling with the knotted laces before giving up. He'd deal with it later.

Two of the knights were already downstairs and breakfast was on the way, judging by the savory scent of bacon filtering from the kitchen. Jannik served the meal, studiously avoiding eye contact and responding to any request with alacrity.

Einar smothered a steaming biscuit with apple butter and shook his head. He shouldn't have said anything last night. The poor lad would work himself to exhaustion trying to take care of them.

After the breakfast dishes had been cleared, Einar and Jonas stepped out into the cobblestone courtyard separating the inn from the stables, which took up two sides of the square. A well graced the center of the courtyard.

"Standing water." Einar indicated it with a shrug.

Jonas pulled the stone from his tunic, turning it over in his hand, before crossing to the well with abrupt strides and flinging the stone into its depths.

Einar wasn't sure what he had expected, but a delayed splash and ensuing silence wasn't quite it. He waited a long minute before joining Jonas.

"Now what?"

"Pray it worked. And wait." Jonas's lips tilted down into a grim frown as he stared into the darkness, where their hope of finding the boys now rested.

A low bench rested against the back wall of the inn, the stones just beginning to warm under the caress of the morning sun. They could do nothing but sit and wait.

*

The sun paused overhead, sending down extra warmth with its noonday rays, when they received the first indication that the stone had worked. Einar closed his eyes against the sunlight, trying to doze and ignore the restlessness of Jonas's leg beside him and the echoing clatter as the knights sparred.

"Excuse me?"

His eyes flew open, blinking as he saw a young woman standing before them. She offered a tentative smile, pressing her hands into the folds of her skirt.

"Can we help you?" He instinctively stood.

Her simple blue gown contrasted with an air about her that hinted she was anything but what she seemed. The woman tilted her face up to meet his gaze.

"I think it's more what I can do for you." She studied Jonas, who had also pushed to his feet. "You released the message?"

"Yes!" Jonas's voice rose in eagerness.

The knights began to gather around, but the woman did not seem concerned. She dipped a curtsey to Einar and Jonas.

"My name is Adela. We received the message because we met your sons and Rose two days ago."

"How are they?" Jonas crossed his arms.

"They are well." She smiled. "They are under our protection."

Jonas's shoulders sloped in relief and Einar felt as if a load had been released from his heart.

Thank the Creator they're safe!

"Lars and Killian both wanted to let you know they were safe and perhaps apologize for running away. I don't think they know their father came too." She smiled at Jonas.

"Where are they? What of the curse? Is Killian…?"

Adela raised a hand to halt Jonas's questions.

"He is still a wolf. The curse laid upon him is a strong one, but my husband is doing all he can. They are helping us hunt the sorcerer—"

"What?" Einar raised his eyebrows. *What are those boys thinking?*

"That's too dangerous!" Jonas scowled and shifted a hand to his knife.

"It may be the only chance we have of capturing the sorcerer and ending the curse," Adela spoke gently, but with a dignified firmness that brooked no argument.

"I need to see them," Jonas said. "Can you take us to them?"

"Of course. That's why I've..." Her eyes widened in horror and she turned away towards the forest. She clapped a hand over her mouth but couldn't stifle a gasp.

"What's wrong?" Einar took a step forward, hesitant to touch her.

She stepped away, a pair of creamy wings tinged with blue exploding from her back.

"Stay here! I'll be back!"

Einar closed his eyes against a gust of wind that knocked him back on his heels. When he opened them again, the faery had vanished.

Chapter 24

Killian watched from a safe distance as Felix kindled a small fire. The forest had begun to echo with the merry chatter of the morning. He came to his paws with an extended stretch. The others had yet to wake.

Nervousness prickled along his fur as an image of the sorcerer shoved its way into his mind. *I knew I'd regret this.* He padded away from the small clearing, investigating the outer ring of pines before jumping to a run around its narrow confines.

He paused at the pool to drink, blinking at the wolf that stared back. The deer carcass still lay nearby, untouched. His gut twisted. He didn't know if he could stomach a meal.

Do wolves get nervous, or is this just the human part of me?

The murmur of voices brought his head up. The camp was stirring. He loped back to the clearing before anyone could worry.

He wasn't the only one lacking an appetite. Rose nibbled at cold jerky and Lars nursed a mug of kaffe kindly heated by Adela. The faery sifted through the contents of her satchel, the corner of her mouth pinched into a frown of concentration. Felix and Damian checked their weapons, swords and daggers of a quality that made Killian and Lars's fine steel look like playthings.

Killian crept closer, eager for a better look. Damian glanced at him.

"These are high quality, even for faeries." He held his sword out on both palms. "Felix is the best smith you'll ever find."

A snow leopard leaped across the blade, etched into the steel, flanked on either side by runes. The castle smith had once attempted something similar, but the blade had broken with one strike. But the handle was worn to Damian's hand, and a tell-tale nick in the crossguard indicated that Damian's sword had seen combat.

"That's beautiful."

Damian's smile shone with pride, as if he made it himself. "That's what I tell him, but he won't listen."

"Because next you'll make me take commissions and you know how much I hate doing that." Felix sheathed a knife.

"Because you'd have to play nice with someone?" Adela chimed in.

"You know the only reason I tolerate you is because he's still ridiculous about you?" Felix leveled a glare at her, but a smile lurked not too far beneath.

Adela's laugh cut short as a ripple swept through the forest. Killian made out a few words, but nothing was clear. Rose tilted her head, her brow puckering. The faeries rose to their feet.

"Well, it looks like someone is looking for you." Damian glanced at them. "A water faery gave them a message for us."

"Do you know who it is?" Lars frowned.

"Sir Einar and five knights."

Killian pricked up his ears at the mention of their uncle. "Where?"

"The town where Felix found you."

Lars set his mug aside and stood. "What should we do?"

"It would be helpful to have the humans on our side, especially since we don't know how many men the sorcerer has." Felix buckled on his sword.

Damian slowly nodded, but before he could speak, a thunderclap echoed and shocked the forest into stillness. Killian instinctively looked up at the cloudless sky.

"The sorcerer." Felix spat, staring away at the forest.

"What's he doing, releasing that kind of power?" Damian clenched his sword.

"Drawing us out?" Felix ran a hand over the metal rod tucked beside a knife.

"We can't ignore it. Or the faery's message."

"I'll go to Moss," Adela said. "You two investigate. The three of them will be safe within the warding."

Indecision warred over Damian's features.

"Go." Lars nodded. "We'll stay here."

I'll be more than happy to stay far away from Noak as possible. Killian whined as another echo flooded the forest.

Damian and Felix sped away, Adela vanishing in the opposite direction. The three companions stood in the sudden silence. The explosions of the sorcerer's power echoed a few more times before fading away. The noise of the forest gradually returned, and they settled in to wait.

I hate not knowing what I'm waiting for. Killian tucked his tail around his hind paws as he settled down.

Half an hour crept by. Lars paced, and Rose built a sizeable pile of shredded grass and leaves.

A new cry split the air.

It echoed again. Killian picked out a plea for help. Rose struggled to her feet, her freckles standing out against her pale face.

"That's — that's my father!"

Lars stared at her. "Are you sure?"

"I — I think—" She gained confidence as a whistle pierced the air. "That's his call. It's him!" She clapped a hand over her mouth as the scream rose, infused with panic.

Killian leapt to his paws. *What do we do? Noak is still out there.*

"Rose," Lars began gently. "We don't know if that's him or not."

She shook her head. "I know! I know t' sorcerer's out there. But what if it really is him? We don't know when Felix and Damian will be back." She clenched her hands with a strangled scream of frustration.

Killian exchanged a glance with Lars. He didn't need to know what Lars was thinking. He growled to let Lars know he agreed.

"Rose, it's your decision. It's a risk and we all know it, but it could be a chance to find your father. You know he was tracking the sorcerer. It *could* be him."

Rose bit her lip until it bled as another cry echoed. She grabbed her bow and strung it. "Let's go."

"Killian, stay here," Lars ordered.

Killian flattened his ears and glared up at Lars. *"Not on your life. You two might need help."*

"Killi, don't be stupid!"

Rose stepped through the warding, barely stopping to look back at them in impatience. Killian growled and darted after her. Lars swore and joined them.

Killian took the lead, able to pinpoint the exact location of the sound with his wolf's hearing. It had carried further than he anticipated, but he finally slowed.

We're here.

Another clearing appeared a few paces away. The last cry echoed around the watching trees, but nothing stirred.

The forest had gone silent. Not even a branch creaked as the breeze died. The faint ring of steel startled Killian until he saw Lars's sword in his hand.

Killian crept forward, Rose and Lars following with a faint rustle of footsteps. Unease tugged at his paws as they entered the empty clearing.

But something *had* happened there. He could almost smell the magic. He took a few tentative steps into the open space, searching for any scent or sound. Lars and Rose followed, step by cautious step.

Killian froze. Something lurked just beyond reach of his senses. A growl tickled his chest. As if in response, the wind picked up again, bringing the scent of unwashed human and danger. He whirled to warn the others. A click echoed, followed by a whining hiss, and then a pained grunt from Lars.

A crossbow bolt protruded from Lars's left side above his hip. Rose screamed as if from the end of a long corridor as Lars's left leg collapsed beneath him.

"Killi…" Lars's voice jerked him back to the present.

He ran toward Lars, but gruff shouts startled him as men swarmed into the clearing. A flash of yellow snagged his attention to a man holding a crossbow with a satisfied smirk.

That's the man who injured me!

Lars cried out as he struggled to rise. Rose drew her knife and dropped into a defensive crouch beside Lars as the strangers rushed in too close for her to use her bow. The tang of blood filled Killian's nose as fresh red stained Lars's tunic.

Killian bared his fangs with a feral growl. *You'll pay for that.*

He leapt at the nearest man, bringing him down with claws and teeth. Killian lunged to the man in the yellow jerkin, but men ran forward with spears. He recoiled from the shining tips, snarling to find himself cut off from Lars.

Killian snapped at the spears, surging forward, but the sharp points drove him back.

"*Lars!*" A man approached his brother, and Rose engaged him with a cry.

A spearman prodded at his side. Killian swiveled away, and his hind paw hit metal. Searing pain clamped around his leg, driving all the way to the bone. A howl of agony burst forth as his hindquarters collapsed beneath him.

"Killi!" Lars redoubled his efforts to rise, but his face twisted in agony as the arrow shifted in his side.

The man in the yellow jerkin planted a foot against Lars and shoved him to the ground. The steel trap sliced deeper into Killian's leg as he leapt forward. A rope snaked around his neck, cutting off further cries.

Shouts echoed as Killian gained a few lunging steps, but the soldiers dragged him backward. He choked against the rope, pain radiating up his leg as he lost ground. Lars feebly reached for his weapon.

Lars! He sprang again. Hands latched painfully into his scruff and another rope tightened around his muzzle, trapping his frantic howls. He tumbled backwards against the soldiers' pull. He dug his paws into the ground, collapsing again as the trap latched deeper into his leg.

Another rope circled Killian's neck, choking him. The might of three men overpowered him. He couldn't resist their pull any longer as they retreated from the clearing, but he tried to bark one last warning as men advanced on Rose.

Chapter 25

Rose fought a losing battle and both she and her opponent knew it. He towered over her, wielding a short sword, and she had only a hunting knife. She jabbed and parried like her father had taught, struggling to hold her ground, trying to ignore Killian's howls.

She drew her knife back for another pass, and someone grabbed her wrist with a vice-like grip. A man in a yellow jerkin held her prisoner, smiling as he twisted her arm behind her. Rose clamped down on a cry of pain as her knife dropped from a nerveless grasp.

The soldier she'd been fighting placed his sword at her throat and her gasp edged past the razor-sharp tip.

"Leave her. These two aren't a threat to anyone anymore. The faeries are taken care of, and we have our wolf. These two are just dead weight." Yellow Jerkin nodded down at Lars. He twisted Rose's arm again, throwing her to the ground with stunning force. "Move out!"

Rose strove to pull air back into her shocked lungs as the sorcerer's men disappeared, dragging a struggling Killian with them.

"Killian!" Lars's cry brought her to his side.

"Hold still." Her voice shook at the sight of the crossbow bolt puncturing his stomach just above his hip and angling toward his side. The last bits of her small breakfast threatened to come up at the glimmer of the bolt's tip protruding from his back.

She rolled him over, pressing her hands around the wound. His bloodied hands slipped against hers as he tried to push her away.

"You have to go after him." Color rapidly faded from his face.

"Lars, keep still!"

Little good that'll do. I don't know how to help you! She swallowed the fear.

"Rose, Noak will kill him."

"If I go, you'll die!" She pressed harder against the flow of blood.

He shuddered under her hands. "You have to find him. Please!"

She stared at the blood dribbling between her fingers. She could go after Killian, but what could she do against the sorcerer and all his men? And she couldn't just leave the heir to her country's throne to bleed out.

"I'm staying right here, Lars."

He screamed through clenched teeth as he tried to sit up and throw her hands away. "Then he'll die, and it will be your fault! Useless!"

She pinned him back down with an elbow. *This is my fault. Every bit of it.*

She reached for her fallen blade as footsteps pounded towards them, but Felix crashed to a halt beside her.

"What happened?" Blood streaked his face and bruises were beginning to form along his jaw.

She stopped herself before asking what stained his jerkin. *I don't want to know.*

"Ambush." Blood smeared across Rose's forehead as she pushed escaped hair from her eyes. "Can you help him?" Her voice caught. Lars wasn't struggling much anymore.

"Move." Felix slid his hands alongside her. She relinquished her hold on Lars.

"Damian!" Felix shouted.

Six painful heartbeats later, Damian rushed into the clearing, dropping words she hadn't expected the faery to use. He knelt by Lars, pressing a hand against his side and drawing another groan from Lars's half-conscious form. Rose backed away, a helpless scream locking in her throat.

The beat of wings drew her gaze upward. Adela landed, stumbling in her haste. She dumped the satchel beside Damian as he and Felix rolled Lars onto his uninjured side.

"Hold him." Damian took the shaft of the bolt and pushed.

The tip broke free with a shuddering cry from Lars, and Rose pressed the back of a hand to her mouth. Felix drew his knife and sliced the head from the shaft, and Damian pulled the bolt free. Lars's eyes slid closed as Damian pulled bandages from the bag.

Rose stood, frozen, unable to look away as Felix and Damian closed and bandaged the wound. When they were done, they lifted the unconscious prince from the blood-stained grass and laid him on the blankets Adela spread out.

She tucked another blanket over Lars as the men turned away.

"What happened?" Anger and worry warred on Damian's features. Like Felix, he was covered in more than just Lars's blood.

"Ambush," she choked out, and the tears started falling. She swiped at them, but they only came faster.

Felix took her arm and helped her to a sitting position, taking a cloth from Adela and wiping the drying blood from her hands. Her sobs hiccupped to a halt, stray tears still escaping as she tried to find her voice. It didn't take long to tell, even though the few horrifying minutes had seemed like hours.

"It's—it's my fault." She stared at the bits of blood still staining her hands. "I thought I heard my father—I should have known—I might have killed them both."

Saying the truth out loud only compounded the weight of her guilt.

Her gaze fell to Lars who lay on the makeshift bed, pale and listless.

"He's right," she murmured. "I'm completely useless. I couldn't do anything t' help."

Rough hands tugged a cloak about her shoulders. "It's not your fault." Felix gave her a small shake.

She pressed her face into the cloak to stop fresh tears. Saying it wouldn't make it so.

"Get some rest." Felix pressed a hand to her shoulder.

Her eyes drooped shut against her will. *Rest, and then find Killian. I'm going to make this right.*

Chapter 26

"Hold him still!"

Hands gripped Killian by the scruff, pinning him to the ground as they pried the trap off his leg. The rope tied around his muzzle suffocated the worst of his pained cries. The soldiers released him, and he tried to lunge away, but they yanked him back by the rope still about his neck.

"Come on!"

Killian choked against its pull as his captors dragged him further into the forest. His strength waned. They kicked him to the ground in a clearing and pulled the muzzle away.

He'd barely scrambled to his feet when something slammed into him, tumbling him over. Killian rolled and glimpsed a bulky mastiff charging again, its beady eyes fixed on his throat.

Instinct took over as the mastiff went for his throat. Killian swiveled on his uninured hind paw and hurled his body at the mastiff's shoulder. The mastiff crashed to the ground, and Killian sank his fangs into the soft flesh of the shoulder. The mastiff howled and twisted away, clawing at Killian's stomach with forepaws, forcing him to release his grip.

Killian lunged again, biting and clawing with a savagery he didn't know he possessed.

He snarled his own threats at the mastiff. The mastiff wanted his blood, but Killian swore he'd win the fight for his life.

"Get it off him!" The enraged voice barely rose above their battle.

Blood dripped from half a dozen more wounds by the time the mastiff was hauled off. Killian crouched, his right leg collapsing beneath him.

"Well, well, you don't know how good it is to see you again, Prince Killian."

Killian pulled his lips back from his fangs, flattening his ears. A furious growl thundered from his chest as Noak paused a few paces away, looking down at him.

"A little more intimidating than last time." The sorcerer smiled. "You seemed to have settled in."

Killian sprang forward, snapping his jaws at the hem of Noak's dirt-stained robe. The rope cutting into Killian's neck saved Noak immediate injury, but he took a few prudent and hasty steps back.

"Put him over by the Ranger. And keep that dog away from him. I need some of his blood left for the spell."

The mastiff growled, sulking as the soldiers tied it up across the clearing, securing Killian to a stake on the opposite side. He pulled his mangled limb closer and hesitantly licked it. The human part of him revolted, but he gamely persisted. He had no other way to clean the seeping wound.

When he'd done what he could, Killian curled into a protective ball and closed his eyes, only to once more see the bolt protruding from Lars's side.

I just want to see him again.

*

Killian opened his eyes to see the sun's patterns dancing over the leaves had changed. His whole body throbbed, the fur around his wounds stiff. His hind limb burned with a fiery persistency and Killian whined as he shifted it and pain shot up his leg.

Movement behind him turned his whine into a defensive snarl. He whipped his head around to see a man crouching beside him, his hands bound in front of his body. The man's red hair and blue eyes seemed familiar.

He's Rose's father!

The man opened his hands in a placating gesture.

"Easy, boy, I just want t' help." Killian recognized the rumble as the voice that had lured them into the sorcerer's trap.

Killian's growl deepened until he remembered he hadn't seen the man there. He focused again on the ropes pinning the man's hands.

So that's why he hasn't been seen in weeks.

He didn't move as the man edged closer.

"Let me see your leg, eh?"

Killian rested his nose on his paws and let his injured leg extend towards the Ranger. He stiffened and choked the reflexive growl as the man poked at the wound.

"It true what Noak called you?" The man kept his voice low, glancing around as if afraid to be caught questioning a wolf.

No one in camp paid any attention, so Killian met the man's gaze and growled. The Ranger caught his breath. "Your Highness." He inclined his head in a hurried bow. Killian tipped his head from side to side. He wasn't a prince anymore. He would most likely die a wolf.

"Noak, he—he mentioned my daughter. You know her?" Desperation showed in the man's face.

Killian nudged his arm.

"She safe?"

Killian froze. His only focus had been on Lars. *She can take care of herself. I'm sure she's fine. Well, reasonably sure. I hate Noak!*

A look of frenzied desperation showed on the Ranger's face, and he didn't have the heart to remain silent. He placed a paw on the man's arm and yipped.

The man released a sigh of pained relief. "Thank you."

Killian rested his nose back onto his paws. *You're welcome. Though it's not like I did anything to earn it. I'm about as helpful as I have been this whole stupid trip!*

"Now, I don't have anything t' bandage your leg with. Doubt they'll give me anything." The Ranger wiped his hands on the grass. "Keep it clean as you can. Anyone coming for you?"

Killian turned his head away. Lars was injured, maybe even—dead. Noak lured the faeries away.

If something had happened to them, Rose was on her own. Maybe no one would come for him. Maybe it was best they didn't come for him.

Chapter 27

Rose curled under her blanket and stared up at the early evening sky, barely remembering falling asleep. She rubbed her eyes, still crusted with the remnants of tears, and dared herself to sit up.

A small fire crackled near the center of the clearing. Rose shoved the cloak away and stumbled over to the fire in search of food to placate her complaining stomach. Her gaze fell on the figure laying on the other side of the fire, and her steps faltered.

Lars still lay unconscious, his brown hair dark against his pale face. The blanket covering him hid the wound from sight. She stared hard until she saw the rise and fall of his chest, then exhaled a relieved sigh.

She spun in alarm at the faint rustle behind her. Adela gave her a small smile, hiding any surprise at Rose's sudden movement.

"I was hoping you would wake up soon." She moved past Rose to rest a hand on Lars's forehead.

"How is he?" Rose's voice wavered, and she blinked back new tears. *Useless!* She couldn't even survive a fight without breaking down every five minutes.

"He'll be all right. The arrow didn't injure anything vital inside, we just have to worry about blood loss."

"Has he woken up yet?"

Adela rose up to her feet. "No. Truthfully, I'm keeping him asleep right now to protect the wound. And—until we have any news of Killian."

Rose glanced around the clearing, half hoping Killian would come loping back in.

"Damian and Felix?"

"Out scouting. They should be back soon. Here." She picked up Rose's hunting knife from the rocks piled around the fire. Rose accepted the knife, sheathing it again with murmured thanks.

A lot of good I did with it. Maybe I shouldn't carry it. Stupid.

Her father's solution would be more training, but—she didn't know what had become of him.

It had been his voice. She knew it as sure as breathing, but there had been no sign of him at the ambush.

Adela tapped her arm. "Sit down, Rose."

Rose complied and took the beaker Adela pressed into her hand. She blew away the faint wisps of steam curling from the dark liquid and took a cautious sip. A light bitterness coated her tongue, followed by the faint taste of blackberries.

"What is this?" She took a longer drink.

"A tea my mother always swore by. She said it would help her think after a long day." Adela smiled as she sipped at her own mug.

Rose had to agree. The tightness behind her eyes began to dissipate, ushering in a sense of clarity.

"Wish I had something of my mother's. I was barely old enough t' remember her before she died." Rose traced the rim of the mug.

"I was young enough to be counted as a child when my mother grew sick," Adela said. "Not even faery magic could save her, so she and my father left to take the path to the stars."

"And left you?" Rose's voice pitched higher, incredulous.

Adela gave a light laugh. "For a faery to die is a terrible thing. I never could really blame them. Better to take the path to the Creator's halls than wander forever in search of them after your six hundred years is up."

Rose stared into her tea, swirling it against the sculpted walls of the mug. "I think sometimes my father wanted t' die after my mother did. But no matter what, he'd always let me crawl into his arms and tell me we'd make it together. He looked after me, and when he disappeared, I suppose I thought I could do the same…"

"What happened here was not your fault," Adela gently insisted.

Rose's throat tightened, preventing a reply.

"She's right." Felix strode into the clearing. "You can't change what happened, so focus on the future it created."

Rose was a little taken aback by the gruffness in his abrupt statement. *But that's nothing out of the ordinary for him.*

"Where's Damian?" Adela's eyes widened in concern.

"He went to report to King Borys."

Adela's shoulders relaxed only a fraction. "When will he be back?"

"A few hours. Don't worry. I've already made him promise to be careful." Felix added a small branch to the fire.

Adela's smile returned, a tinge of worry still lingering. It would stay until Damian returned. Rose felt the same when her father was sent on a mission.

"What did you find?" Rose glanced at Felix.

"Not much. But we've alerted the forest. There's three days to the solstice and the sorcerer can't hide forever. We'll find him and Killian."

Felix said it like there was no other outcome. He didn't seem like the type to subscribe to false hope, that thought alone reassuring Rose more than any platitude.

"What happened t' you this morning?"

"Yours wasn't the only ambush. The sorcerer set a trap with a few of his men and some Nameless Ones who are always on the lookout to cause trouble."

"And?"

"And the Nameless Ones got what they deserved, but the sorcerer and his men escaped." Felix scowled and crushed a stray ember under his boot. "We broke free just in time for Damian to hear Killian's cry."

Rose shuddered and took another fortifying sip of tea. "Thank you — for helping Lars."

"Felix poured his magic into the wound while they treated it," Adela said. "A bit rash, perhaps, to release that much raw power, but it got Lars through the worst of it."

Felix ignored the other faery's words, busying himself with tending the fire.

"Thank you." Rose whispered.

Felix sent her a small, genuine smile that softened his hard features. "Just tired of seeing people get hurt by that sorcerer."

She sniffed away the last of the lurking tears. "Me too."

Felix tipped her a nod.

Dinner was a quiet affair. Rose offered to take a watch and Felix gave her the first turn. The hours passed quietly, Damian returning at the end of her shift. She retreated to her pallet, trying to overhear the brothers' murmured conversation. They quieted after a few minutes and she was left with her fears of what the next day might bring.

*

A stream chuckled alongside clusters of slender aspens not far from the clearing, and Rose took her spare clothes and went to wash away the last traces of the ambush.

She plunged her dirty shirt and trousers under the cold water, scrubbing furiously with bits of soap against the bloodstains and dirt. Dried blood flecked off to be carried away by the river, but a few stubborn patches remained, even after she attacked it with handfuls of moss.

She laid the wet clothes on the grassy bank to dry and settled down beside them, re-lacing her boots over her trousers and resting folded arms over knees.

The sun trickled through the foliage to tease at her face. She closed her eyes, soaking in the warmth after the crisp chill of the water. Birds chattered to one another and a small animal trundled by with a rustle in the undergrowth.

All that's missing is the smell of sweet forest sage, and I could be home. In our cabin. Not an entire country away where everything bad that could happen, has happened. She pressed her forehead against her arms.

"Rose." Adela's voice opened her eyes. "Lars is awake and asking about you."

Rose nodded, taking her time gathering her clothes. No telling what he would say to her. Not after the ambush. "Rose." Adela's expression softened with a small smile of understanding. "I think he wanted to know that you're all right."

Rose gave a poor attempt at a smile and followed Adela back to the clearing. She left her clothes in a piled mess by her pack and tip-toed over to Lars. She couldn't quite meet his blue eyes as she sank to one knee a cautious pace away.

"How are you feeling?" She blurted first.

"I'm all right. It doesn't hurt much right now. Rose, I—I don't remember much, but I need to apologize for what I said to you." He shifted, trying to catch her gaze.

She shook her head. "You can't apologize for the truth."

"No. Even if I wasn't wounded, the two of us couldn't have stopped them from—from taking Killian."

Rose could only imagine how much he hated saying those words aloud. But he wasn't the only one who needed to apologize.

"Lars, this wouldn't have happened, if not for me. I sent us right into that ambush. And you were right. If anything happens t' Killian, it'll be my fault."

"Rose." He interrupted in his prince voice—a tone she hadn't heard in weeks. "Killian and I both made the decision to go with you. You can't take responsibility for our choices. I can't blame you for wanting to find your father, and I know Killian wouldn't either..." His voice broke and faltered.

Tears pricked at Rose's eyes again and she rubbed her nose before her reddening face could betray her. "I'm sorry anyway."

A small smile tugged at the corner of his mouth. "Thank you for what you did for me."

Her answering smile felt shaky. "Not much besides panic."

"Maybe, but that's more than you would have done for me a few weeks ago." He winked, and a chuckle bubbled in her chest. "Admit it."

She bumped his shoulder with her fist. "Yes, lucky for you, you boys grew on me. A little like mold."

His laugh halted as his face tensed in pain, and he pressed a hand to his side.

"All right?" She scooted closer.

He opened his eyes and nodded.

"Sorry." She flinched.

He waved off her sympathy and extended a hand. "Help me sit up."

"Oh, I'm not sure that's a good idea." Rose looked over her shoulder for Adela.

"It's all right," the faery reassured as she joined them.

Rose took Lars's hand, sliding an arm behind him to help him sit upright. He hunched forward, his face losing the little color it had gained.

"Lars?" Rose clutched his shoulder.

"Just dizzy." His eyes remained closed. It took a long minute before he straightened.

Rose kept a hold on him for support as Adela folded his shirt back, still crusted with bloodstains, to check the bandage.

"How is it?" Lars asked.

"Healing," Adela said. "You're lucky there are faeries around to shorten the process."

Lars tugged at the bandage. "How long?"

"A few more days."

"How long until the solstice?"

"Two days," Rose said softly.

Lars bit his lip against a frustrated sigh.

"Felix and Damian are looking for him, Lars. They'll find him." She gave his shoulder a light shake.

He nodded. "I know. I just need to be ready for when they do. I need to be there..."

"You will." And so would she. They'd find Killian and her father, and make the sorcerer pay.

*

Felix and Damian did not return until late that evening, still empty-handed. Lars sat up for dinner and he ducked his head, clenching his fists. The telltale twitch along his jaw showed his disappointment at the faeries' report.

Felix's lips were drawn in frustration as he flipped a knife between his hands. Damian, in contrast, just looked tired as he rubbed his face along his scars.

What now, then? Rose gathered her courage to ask the question in the frozen silence, but Adela beat her to it.

"We need to tell the soldiers in Moss."

"What's that going to do?" Felix growled.

Adela ignored his tone. "The king is there."

"My father?" Lars's head jerked up. "Why didn't you say earlier?"

"We have been busy," Adela said. "And I thought it prudent to wait until we were sure of your condition and had any information on Killian."

Lars lifted one hand, forced to concede the point.

"We'll need their help anyway when the sorcerer resurfaces," Damian said. "We can fight him because of his magic, but can't harm his men."

"What if we're forced to fight them for our own safety?" Felix raised his eyebrows.

"Felix, you know the law." Damian sent him a pointed look.

"Aye." Felix sheathed his knife with a snap. "I'll go to Moss and bring them back."

"Wait until morning. We know the forest, but they don't. It will be easier to lead them here in the daylight."

Felix grumbled agreement and strode off into the trees. Rose half-hoped he would go to Moss immediately, no matter what Damian said. *I just want this to be over.*

Chapter 28

Einar drummed his fingers against the worn surface of the table. *I hate waiting.*

Moss had been in an uproar ever since the faery had disappeared. Townsfolk flocked to the inn as the sighting place, but Einar suspected it also served as the central information exchange. It didn't take long for a stablehand to identify Einar and the king as the ones who spoke to the woman, bringing far too much attention to them. Which hadn't done much for their attempts at discretion.

Rumors flew regarding their identity, and only out of respect for them as guests did the innkeeper lock his door against the gossiping town.

Jonas paced the empty common room, impatience shortening his steps. The faery had said she would be back two days ago. Einar's gut told him something bad had happened regarding the boys, and in the absence of news, his imagination was quite happy to run rampant.

The clunk of wood on wood announced the innkeeper's approach. His gaze fixed intently on Einar as he approached in his peculiar rolling gait. Jonas tracked his progress and edged closer to the table as Niklas halted. "My Jannik just told me an interesting thing." He crossed his arms. "Seems tales of t' Wolf Prince have been circulating again and he's not t' only one as remembers those two and their dog."

"Your point?" Einar leaned on the table.

"Faery sightings, rumors t' king is off on some mysterious journey himself..." Niklas shrugged. "Now, I mean no offense, but I served t' king in his army, lost part of my leg for it. And I'm no fool that I can't recognize you, Sir Einar. But I'd like t' know who's under my roof so I might have t' privilege of serving my king again."

Jonas regarded the man with the beginnings of respect. "And how was it you lost your leg, Niklas?"

"Wyvern, sir."

"I thank you then for your service in my name." Jonas addressed him in the formal cadence reserved for knights or nobles.

Niklas raised one eyebrow, apparently surprised to find his guess confirmed. He bowed low, mumbling a humble, "Your Majesty."

Jonas shook his head. "For the sake of retaining what little anonymity we have left, you have my permission to dispense with the formality, Niklas. 'Sir' will suffice."

Niklas's other eyebrow joined its partner. "Don't know that feels right, sir." The address rolled slowly off his tongue.

"Would it help if I told you I prefer to just be called 'sir' every now and again?" Jonas gave the man a wry smile.

Einar chuckled. It wouldn't be the first time Jonas had complained about missing the relative simplicity of his time as a knight before taking the crown.

Niklas offered the king his own smile, smoothing his weathered features to those of a much younger man. "Suppose it might, sir. Now can I get you anything?"

"I'm afraid you can't get us what we need." Einar worked his stiff hand.

"Waiting for that faery t' come back?" Niklas nodded. "Your son, isn't it, sir?"

Jonas leaned both hands on the chair's back with a heavy sigh. "Both, I'm afraid."

Niklas crossed both arms over his burly chest. "My sympathies, sir. Don't know what I'd do if something happened t' my Jannik."

"Hopefully nothing as reckless as practically abandoning your country to go after him." Jonas tilted the chair back and forth under his hands.

Niklas shook his head with a chuckle. "Not sure anyone could blame you, sir. But I think a tavern might fall t' chaos quicker than a country if t' ruler left." He tilted a wink as Einar and Jonas gave way to laughter. "I'll be in t' kitchen if you need anything, sirs."

He supplemented with a bow and limped away.

Jonas spun the chair around to sit backwards. "I'm going to go crazy, Einar." He rubbed his eyes with a groan. "Should we go after them?"

"Where?" Einar's fingers resumed their tapping. "We've no idea where she went or where they are. Best keep on waiting." He loathed the idea himself.

Jonas groaned again as he rested his forehead against the chair back. Einar gave his shoulder a sympathetic pat, which he begrudgingly tolerated.

"Sirs?"

Jannik edged closer, hesitating as they raised their heads.

"There's someone here t' see you."

"Who?" Einar straightened.

Jannik shrugged and gestured over his shoulder. A young man who barely matched Jannik for height, entered the room. His feet made no noise on the floorboards, yet he looked bulky enough to match most of the knights in strength.

Faery? Or worse?

"Who are you?" Einar slid a hand below the table to grab his knife.

"Felix. Adela sent me."

Einar and Jonas leapt to their feet in unison.

"What happened?" Jonas clutched the back of the chair.

"The sorcerer attacked, Lars was injured, and Killian taken."

Einar raised his eyebrows as Jonas sank back into his seat. This new faery — Felix — certainly cut right to the point.

"Are they all right?" Einar stared intently at Felix.

"Lars is recovering. But the sorcerer has disappeared with Killian." Anger and apology warred on Felix's face.

"What's — what's being done?" Jonas's face still had not regained any color.

"We haven't stopped looking. I was sent to bring you to our camp."

"Now?"

"As soon as you're ready."

Einar glanced to Jonas and nodded. "Give us fifteen minutes."

*

The rough bark of the aging pine tree scratched Lars's back through his tunic. The ache in his side had not abated for hours. He rubbed at the bandage, wincing. He should have taken some of Adela's medicine earlier.

Damian had gone out scouting again soon after Felix left. Rose and Adela both refused to let Lars do anything but sit and wait for the men to return. At this point, he was slowly going crazy.

Across the clearing, Rose sat with Adela, graciously mending his torn shirt, now scrubbed free of blood. Rose chuckled at their conversation and his heart lifted a little to see her smile. At least she wasn't blaming herself quite so adamantly. But that didn't mean he couldn't take the responsibility. He was supposed to look after them. Protect his brother.

You failed him again. The nagging voice gained strength. Lars rubbed his side again. *How am I going to explain this to Father? Along with everything else that has happened. What's he going to say? Will I get a chance to show him I'm glad to see him?*

There had been plenty of lectures over the last few years, and this whole misadventure had been undertaken with the same impulsiveness he'd been warned to temper.

"All right?"

He jerked his head up. Rose had approached unnoticed. Lars tipped a pensive nod.

"I think they'll just be happy t' see you." She offered a half smile.

He tried a reassuring smile, but she didn't seem fooled. "Maybe."

Hoofbeats sent another tug of nervousness at his gut. Figures flickered through the trees, his father's broad figure leading the way. Relief, and a little fear, flashed through him again.

He gripped Rose's proffered hand, pressing the other against his side as he slowly gained his feet.

"Lars!" His father slid off his horse and rushed to him, grabbing Lars in a fierce hug.

Lars returned it with all his strength, ignoring the pain pulsing in his wound. When he drew back, Einar shouldered his way in, offering a rare embrace.

His father gripped his arm. "You're hurt? What happened?"

Lars moved his hand from his side, not wanting his father to begin to worry when they had more important matters to focus on. "They say I'll be fine in another few days. Father, I'm sorry. Killian is..."

"It's all right, lad." Jonas held Lars tighter. "Felix told us."

Lars managed a nod and cleared his throat. Rose edged away, wide-eyed, but he gestured for her to stay.

"Father, this is Rose. Her father trained her as a Ranger. She's one reason we made it this far."

Her face flushed red, whether from his words or the presence of more royalty, he couldn't be sure.

"Your Majesty." Her voice squeaked, a sure sign she was pretending not to be nervous. Her hands fluttered by her sides and she seemed frozen, undecided between bowing or attempting a curtsey in trousers.

His father solved the problem by extending a hand. "Pleasure to meet you, Rose. Thank you for assisting my sons."

She hesitantly clasped his hand and nodded.

I'll tell her how many gaps she just bridged later just to see if her eyes can get any bigger.

Einar gave her the same courtesy. "I'm sorry to hear your father is missing. Any news?"

"No, sir. I'm hoping for something when we find Killian and t' sorcerer."

If they were surprised by her informal manner, they didn't show it.

Lars gave the details as he knew them, starting with the ambush. From the way Einar and his father nodded at some of the details, he guessed they had heard it from Felix.

Adela waited for him to finish before approaching to greet Einar and his father.

"I'm sorry for leaving so abruptly and not returning sooner," she said.

Jonas waved away the apology. "How is Lars's wound? How long will it take him to recover?"

I'm almost twenty-one years and standing right next to him. Is he going to ask if I've been eating three meals a day next?

Rose caught his eye roll and grinned.

"Now," Jonas declared when he was satisfied. "Could someone please tell me what happened? From the beginning, if you would."

Chapter 29

Killian couldn't stop shivering, the tremors intensifying the ache in his body. His licked at his wounded leg, grimacing at the rancid taste it left on his tongue. The Ranger watched him, frowning as Killian simply sniffed at the scraps thrown his way.

"You need t' at least drink." The Ranger cupped some water in his hands.

Killian half-heartedly licked at the fluid before returning to his miserable ball.

"What's wrong with 'im?" A boot prodded his side.

He didn't even care to show his teeth.

"He's sick. That wound's infected!" The Ranger glared at the soldiers, his eyes snapping. Rose came by it honestly. She'd always spoken up for him.

"Well, 'e's gonna have t' move." The first speaker tugged at the rope around Killian's neck. "We're moving out."

The rough fibers snagged deeper into his fur, rubbing against raw skin. They apparently didn't care that Killain choked as they pulled him to his feet. He staggered a few steps, halted by a familiar blue robe. Noak stared down at him, little compassion in his grey eyes.

"I'm sorry it's come to this, Prince Killian."

"Don't lie."

"But come tomorrow at noon, you will no longer have to suffer."

No fear lurked in Killian at the news of his impending death, just stoic acceptance. He stumbled along at the end of the rope, not even caring as the mastiff snapped and taunted at his heels.

He put one paw in front of the other as many times as he could before his legs gave way beneath him. Noak ordered the Ranger untied enough to carry him, and they continued.

"Hold on there, lad," the Ranger murmured comfortingly. "We'll get you taken care of when we stop, eh?"

*

Killian pried his eyes open and stared at the slivered moon. He didn't remember their arrival at the new campsite. The Ranger slept nearby, hands bound again.

I hope whatever happens, Rose will have a chance to reunite with her father. At least that way, some good will come of all this.

Movement from the corner of his eye brought his attention to two stakes driven into the ground, rough-hewn branches stacked in a pyre around them. No doubt for him.

Noak circled the pyre, arms moving in tight symmetry. The light breeze carried his murmured words and Killian shuddered. He couldn't understand the words, but his animal instinct recoiled from them.

The man in the yellow jerkin stood nearby, arms crossed. Killian bared his teeth in a snarl. If he had a chance to make the man pay for hurting Lars, he would take it, no matter what.

The man met Killian's glare and a smirk played across his features, as if he knew Killian's thoughts. A growl rumbled against Killian's chestbone.

"Now, now, don't blame Finn for what happened. He just happens to be effective at following orders." Noak approached.

"I have no problem taking a piece out of you too."

"I wish I could understand your new language," Noak said. "But I must say, the curse that witch placed on your family was a beautiful one. So intricate. I wonder if the faeries were going to be able to help you?"

He laughed at Killian's silence. "They couldn't, could they? You'd already be human again. Now you know the sad truth about the faeries."

Noak crouched before him, eyes glimmering with hate. "Everyone thinks they have the answers, but they don't. Or they just choose to help when it's convenient for them. My family was no one important, but still good people. During the war, the soldiers came to my village."

Killian pricked his ears, startled, and Noak chuckled.

"Oh, yes, I was alive then. Magic soothes the years away. The soldiers accused us of harboring magic users, even though they knew we hadn't. A faery was with them, and he said nothing as my village was burned and slaughtered around me. I buried my family and decided I'd have my vengeance." Noak leaned forward, anger casting a deeper grey in his eyes.

"I was told magic had no place in the world except in the faeries. But if we humans could harness it, then it's clear the faeries want it for themselves."

Killian recoiled, doubt edging his mind. *What if Damian wasn't telling the whole truth about my curse? What if he could break it?*

He shoved the thought aside. Judging from the manic look on Noak's face, the man's opinions weren't to be taken too seriously. He'd much rather trust the faery who hadn't hunted him with the intent to kill him.

"I'm going to stop them. Crush their magic so they know what it's like to be powerless before they die." Noak rested his hand between Killian's ears. "You will help me, and for that I will always remember you."

Killian ducked his head away with a growl. *"I'd rather you not remember me at all."*

Noak only smiled and ruffled Killian's ears, to his eternal disgust, before leaving him to his churning thoughts.

Chapter 30

"They're moving!" Damian ran into camp, sparking a flurry of activity as the entire party leapt to their feet.

Lars grabbed his sword. *Finally!*

"Where?" He and Felix spoke in unison.

"The base of Mount Gwiador."

Adela paled. "But that's where..."

Damian gave a grim nod. "He wants to destroy our magic. He can draw power from the Mount."

Lars exchanged a confused glance with Rose. *That doesn't sound good.*

"What is this?" Jonas frowned at the faeries.

Damian glanced at the king, then at the others assembled. "The sorcerer cursed Killian because he needs his blood for a spell to take our magic, which would kill us."

His expression grew even more grim. "Unless a faery dies, they follow a path to the Creator's halls in the stars. Mount Gwiador holds the key to this path. Intentionally or not, the sorcerer chose this place to perform his spell. The raw magic there is intense. He could destroy the place."

"And I thought we already had enough to worry about." Lars's father raised his eyebrows. "What do we do?"

"The solstice is tomorrow. My guess is he'll perform the sacrifice at noon when the sun and the world's magic are at their highest. We have until then to stop him."

Lars swallowed his dismay. *That only gives us hours to rescue Killian. What if something happens again and we can't find them?*

"He has ten men with him. Some had a touch of magic about them."

"What does that mean?" Einar crossed his arms.

Felix gave Einar a grim smile. "It means we can help you fight them."

"Your father was also their prisoner." Damian nodded to Rose, who swayed as if she might collapse.

Lars tightened his grip on his sword. One more to rescue. "How—how was he?"

"He looked fine." Damian touched her arm, likely to steady her more than reassure.

"And Killian?" Lars forced his voice to remain level.

Damian hesitated, and Lars forced his expression to remain neutral even as his heart stuttered in his chest.

"Injured from the ambush. But he was walking."

His father gripped Lars's shoulder painfully tight. "Can we attack tonight?"

"No. The sorcerer has warded their camp. It will take us some time to prepare a counter spell. We attack in the morning."

Jonas grudgingly murmured agreement, and Lars jerked an abrupt nod. Magic was one battle they would not win.

"Very well, Lars, you will—"

"I'm going." Lars left his father no other option.

"You're wounded."

"I'm fine. I'm going to get him."

"Lars." The king frowned.

I'm just as stubborn as you. Lars set his jaw. *I'm going.*

"I'm not going to sit back and watch the horses. There are enough knights to take the sorcerer's men. I don't have to fight, if that's what you want, but someone will need to help Killian get away."

He forced away the memory of Killian's pained howls as the soldiers dragged him away.

Jonas pushed his thumb against the bridge of his nose. "Very well," he finally said. "I know what I'd do for my brother."

He glanced at Rose. "And I suppose I have no grounds to refuse you either."

Rose bit her lip as she ducked her head. "No, your majesty. I can fight well enough t' get t' my father. I've come this far. I'm not staying behind now."

"Very well." But his father looked down at both of them with a slight smile, a tinge of pride lighting his eyes. "What's our plan?"

*

Lars's sword weighed heavy against his side as he followed Rose in the predawn darkness.

Killian would be impressed I'm even awake. His slight smirk died as fast as it came at the thought of his brother.

The rustle of footsteps marked the progress of the rest of the company. A bird had begun to test its song when Felix held up a hand and they came to an uneven halt. The faeries vanished to scout ahead.

Lars bit the inside of his cheek as he crouched down against a tree to rest. It would be easy to regret his decision, but any sign of complaint from him would change his father's mind. Rose sank to one knee beside him, raising one eyebrow in a silent question. He nodded once and moved his hand from against his side.

Felix returned in a matter of minutes, signaling them on. Rose helped him to his feet and they trudged on.

Dawn had just begun to filter through the trees when they halted again. Felix slid his metal rod from his belt and glided away. Damian disappeared in the opposite direction. The others began to spread out and advanced another twenty yards to wait for the signal.

A deep rumble shook the forest and the ground quaked beneath Lars's feet. He freed his sword, the knights on either side echoing his action. The harsh shriek of a hawk pierced the quiet and they dashed forward into a wide clearing, pandemonium erupting as the sorcerer's men leapt into battle.

A snow leopard drove one man to the ground, clearing the way for Rose to run to her father. The leopard shifted to reveal Damian as he locked blades with the man in the yellow jerkin. A red-tailed hawk shrieked again, diving and clawing at the man who dragged Killian, snapping and growling, over to a pyre.

Lars ran to his brother and severed the taut rope with one swing. The man reeled away, cursing, and the hawk swooped to the ground, shifting into Felix. He spun the metal rod between his fingers into a spear.

"Go!" Felix dropped into a fighting stance as the soldier regained his feet.

Lars didn't argue. "Come on, Killian!"

Killian barked, growling and yipping in mingled pain and excitement as he hobbled after him. Lars parried a blow from a soldier, shoving him backwards into Einar's waiting blade.

The ground fell out from beneath his feet and rushed past him. He crashed to the ground with a sickening thud. He rolled to see the sorcerer standing beside him, cold fury in his gaze.

Noak stabbed with a sword and Lars rolled again, coming up to his feet in time to parry another strike. Noak's form held little grace, but he hammered relentlessly at Lars, who stumbled back under the barrage.

Lars gripped his sword with both hands, catching Noak's blade and pushed the sorcerer back to gain a few feet. Noak disentangled his sword, snarling as Lars went on the offensive. It wouldn't take long to beat Noak now that Lars had his rhythm.

But a frantic wave and shouted word from Noak between strikes ripped his feet out from under him, slamming him to the ground. The impact drove his breath away and fresh pain lanced his wounded side.

Noak raised his sword.

Killian latched on to Noak's arm with an enraged growl. He dragged Noak, screaming, to the ground and tore with teeth and claws. Lars rolled over, dragging air into his abused lungs and fumbled for his sword. His heart lurched as Noak drew a knife from the folds of his cloak, slashing a scarlet wound deep along Killian's side.

Killian collapsed with a pained squeal. Lars shoved to his feet as Noak threw Killian against the pyre. Blood stained the wood and Killian tumbled in a twisted heap. Noak raised his arms and began a chant.

"No!" Lars charged ahead, skewing Noak through his gut.

Lars pulled the sword free as the sorcerer fell. The clearing had fallen silent. The battle over.

"Killi!" He ran to his brother.

Killian raised his head with a snarl, pain and fear clouding his eyes in feral rage. Lars slowed, dread threatening to swallow him. The creature before him looked nothing like his brother.

"Killian, it's me."

Killian whined softly, his head thudding back to the ground. Lars knelt beside him, panic welling up as fast as the red stain spreading across the grass.

"Killi…" He loosened the frayed rope about Killian's neck, pulling it free, and gathered his brother in his arms, pressing a hand against the wound.

"Killian!" Their father knelt beside them, eyes wide in horror.

Killian lifted a trembling paw to brush Jonas's arm.

"Don't move, Killi," Lars chided in a quivering voice.

Then Damian was there, pressing his jerkin against the wound.

"Help him." Lars met his hazel eyes. "Help him like you helped me. Please!"

Damian soothed Killian's fur as a pained whimper shook his body.

"I don't have the skill for his wounds. I'll take him to someone who does." Damian shifted Killian into his arms.

"Damian, is that wise?" Adela paused beside them.

"We have no choice." Damian stood. "Our care is for the forest and its creatures, is it not? This wolf needs care."

Adela smiled. "I'll go with you."

They stepped away from the gathering crowd and spread their wings. Lars stepped after them, but Felix held him back.

"No, I have to go with him." Lars's voice broke. "He's my brother. I have to stay with him."

"I know." Felix did not release his grip as Damian and Adela flew away with their precious cargo.

"Where are they taking him?" Jonas tore his gaze away.

"To our home," Felix said. "No mortal has ever set foot in the faery caverns, but if anyone can help him, our healers can."

Lars bent to retrieve his blood-stained blade, finally gazing at the carnage around him. The sorcerer's men all lay dead. His gut twisted at the sight, but he forced his gaze up to meet Rose.

She stood clutching the arm of an auburn-haired man who looked thin beneath the stubble coating his cheeks. She scrubbed a sleeve across her eyes and tipped a glance up at her father. He nodded and released his hold on her to allow her to join Lars.

"Will Killian be all right?"

He shrugged, not quite trusting his voice.

"They'll take care of him." She clearly forced the words, but he appreciated the effort.

"How's your father?"

"All right. Little worse for t' wear, but he'll recover." She winced, as if worried Lars would compare Killian's fate to her father's good fortune.

He gave her a genuine smile, if small. "Good. You going to introduce me?"

Her eyes widened, but she led him back to the auburn-haired man.

"Father, this is Lars." She flushed. "Prince Lars."

"Your highness." Her father bowed.

Lars extended a hand. "Sir."

"It's Kaspar, sire." The man hesitantly clasped Lars's hand.

"I owe Rose a great debt. We wouldn't have made it here without her."

Rose flushed and Kaspar looked down at her, pride shining in his eyes as he wrapped an arm around her shoulders again. Lars left them to their reunion, moving to help the knights gather the bodies. Felix shifted the earth for a grave, burying Noak separately, and cast a spell over the body before covering it with earth. They dismantled the pyre and scattered the wood before returning to their camp.

Lars went to the stream, dipping his hands under the cold waters and scrubbing at his hands. When the last flecks disappeared, he sat back on the bank.

It was done.

The sorcerer was no longer a threat. Killian was safe. He would just have to have faith that the faeries would do what they could.

"You all right, lad?" Einar knelt at the bank, plunging his grime-covered hands beneath the water.

Lars nodded, watching his uncle.

"Uncle Einar?"

Einar sat back on his heels, looking at him and waiting.

"I know I've disappointed you. I'm truly sorry. I'm going to try and do better."

Einar's face creased into a smile. "The last few days have shown me that you're already taking your responsibilities more seriously. You've always had a good heart, Lars."

Heat flashed across Lars's face and he forced himself to look at Einar. "Even if I've made a mess of everything?"

Einar dried his hands on his trousers. "The mistakes won't matter as much if you try to learn from them."

Lars rubbed the back of his neck and stared at the rippling reflections of the trees. *Good thing I have my entire life in front of me.*

"If you need help, for anything, you know where to find me," Einar said.

"Thanks," Lars murmured, and Einar smiled again, clapping him on the shoulder.

"I'm proud of you, Lars. I know your father is too."

Lars nodded as Einar stood and left him alone on the riverbank. As he stared at the ceaseless flow of water, his mind strayed back to the fight and the sorcerer.

The sorcerer! He straightened. Damian had said that the sorcerer's death would break the curse, but Killian had still been a wolf.

He'd forgotten about it in the aftermath with Killian bleeding to death in his arms. Lars bolted to his feet, rushing back to confront Felix.

"The curse. Was it broken?"

Felix paused his sketching, taking precious time to reply.

Lars's gut twisted. *Something's wrong. What happened to Killian?*

"Damian will know. He'll come back with news." Felix folded away his paper.

"No. He said killing the sorcerer would break the spell. I need to know!" He had to know. It all would be for nothing if Killian survived, only to remain a wolf.

"Damian will explain everything when he returns."

Lars scowled and stalked away when no other answer seemed forthcoming. If Damian didn't return soon, he'd find some way to get answers.

Chapter 31

Rose smoothed the fletching of one of her arrows between her fingers, over and over, studying the fine line of the feathers. The sight of Lars hunched over Killian's bleeding body still haunted her. *Please just let him be all right.*

"Told you that'd ruin 'em, didn't I?" Her father paused beside her.

She managed a smile and tucked the arrow back into the quiver at her side.

Kaspar groaned as he sat next to her. "What's wrong?"

"Just worried about Killian is all."

It'd been a full day since the battle, but Damian had not returned. Lars looked like he hadn't slept, and he kept touching his wounded side. He'd probably reinjured himself and not told anyone.

"I'd never seen a faery before yesterday, but I'd say he's in good hands."

She rested her head against her father's shoulder. "I know."

He wrapped an arm around her, as if she were still a little girl and they still sat in front of their cabin watching the deer in the twilight.

"I'm sorry," he said.

She looked up at him. "Why?"

"For disappearing on you. I don't want you t' worry."

"Too late for that." Rose shrugged. "I've always worried."

He squeezed her shoulders. "I'm proud of you, Rose."

"Really? I did run away just t' prove t' you and myself I could be a Ranger and—"

"Rose." Her father shook his head. "I am. Wouldn't have trained you if I didn't think you could do it."

She fumbled with the hem of her tunic. "Thanks."

"And you rubbing shoulders with royalty? Think of t' stories you can tell." He nudged her and she giggled.

"Aye, Kaspar's daughter, the one who shook t' king's hand."

"You know Magda will want t' kiss your hand. She does love our king."

Rose dissolved into laughter. *Oh, I miss home!*

Kaspar chuckled, patting her shoulder.

"That faery's coming back. You should hear what he has t' say."

Rose looked for Damian and saw nothing. "How do you know?"

"You're not a Ranger yet, girl. Can't be telling all t' secrets." He winked.

She rolled her eyes and went to alert Lars. A bit of disbelief clung to his face in a tiny frown, but he watched the forest with her. Seconds later, Damian stepped from the trees into the clearing. Lars's eyes widened in surprise and she shrugged her shoulders.

"How did he know they were coming?" Lars spoke to her under his breath. "Can you do that?"

"No." Rose smirked. "Not yet, anyway."

Lars and Rose joined Damian and the others who spoke earnestly with the king.

"The healer expects him to recover, however..."

"He's still a wolf, isn't he?" Jonas spoke quietly.

Damian nodded.

Lars scowled, pushing to the front. "But the sorcerer is dead. You said—"

"I said there was a chance," Damian gave Lars an even stare. "Killian didn't want me to tell you the other alternative."

"Of course he didn't."

"The original curse is strong and overtook the sorcerer's," Damian said, speaking once more to the king. "The only way to break it would be to find the witch."

Jonas blanched. "But she's long dead. So, you're saying—there's no chance."

Damian shook his head.

"No." Lars stumbled back a step and Rose grabbed his arm, holding him up. The king flinched at the faery's words as if he'd been punched in the gut.

"There's—there's nothing—?"

"I'm sorry. We'll do what we can, but..." Damian gave a shrug.

Rose let Lars go as he turned and stumbled away. *What do I say? There's nothing that will mean anything.* Angry tears pricked at her eyes.

Their journey to save Killian had been for nothing.

She made her way back to her father in a daze, sinking to the ground beside him.

"What happened?" He studied her face with concern.

She blurted the terrible news, new tears threatening to clog her throat. At the mention of the witch, a look of puzzled wonder came over her father's face.

"What?" She broke off. "What is it?"

"Something I haven't thought about in years. Something about your mother." Her father hesitated, gripping her hand. "Rose, there may be a way to help Killian."

*

"Lars?"

Rose found him just outside the camp, sitting atop a fallen oak, staring at something she couldn't see. Her heart twisted at the despair in his slouched shoulders.

"Lars?" She tried again, and he jerked his head up to see her.

"Sorry. It's just..." He lifted one hand in a helpless gesture.

She sat beside him. "I know."

"I just wish I could do something—*anything*..."

"Lars, I—my father just told me something that you need t' hear."

Rose paused, searching for the right words.

"My mother's ancestor was rumored t' be a witch. A witch that was summoned t' the castle one winter's night."

Lars's tapping hands stilled.

"As tales of t' royal curse spread, the family 'forgot' the truth t' distance themselves from t' witch. But t' tale was whispered through generations. Father says my mother had a saying: 'One day when t' king repays his debt'. She always used it t' predict some fanciful notion. When he asked her what it really meant, she only laughed and said it was a family legend."

Rose leaned forward to see her friend's face. "But—but I think we know better. Lars, I don't know if..." She paused to breathe and pray again her mad idea would be true. "I just wanted t' say that you and Killian have become a little like brothers t' me. You let me come along and looked out for me when you didn't have to. And Killian protected me against that Baedon."

She took Lars's arm, gripping it tightly, her heart pounding in her chest. "I hope it means something now when I say the debt has been repaid."

Lars doubled over, the breath rushing from him, leaving him gasping. Somewhere in the trackless forest, a wolf howled.

Chapter 32

Killian couldn't ignore the gentle persistence of the morning sun any longer, its warmth and light gradually teasing him awake. He stirred and rubbed his eyes. His hand froze in the midst of tousling his hair.

Am I – ?

He sat bolt upright, staring at his shaking hands. Bright pain in his side cut through the giddy shock, and he lay back down with a grimace. Killian pushed soft blankets away to reveal the bandages around his torso, pain running along his ribs to just above his left hip.

He remembered seeing Lars lying helpless, attacking the sorcerer, and being stabbed. The sorcerer was dead, but — he stared at his hands again.

Maybe Damian was wrong.

Killian sat up more cautiously and pulled the blanket away from his foot, which had been wrapped in a bandage up his calf. He glimpsed himself in a mirror leaning against the opposite wall—mussed brown hair, human features, and amber eyes.

I almost don't recognize myself.

His bed filled one corner of an unfamiliar room made of dark grey stone, swirls of lighter grey creating patterns across the walls and ceiling. Rich wood panels of varying widths covered the floor, and the table, chairs, and bed had been etched with carving along the edges. Through the rounded window, Killian looked down on the tops of trees which extended over the horizon line.

He lay back down, clutching the blankets against his chest.

Where am I?

He didn't remember much besides Lars holding him, and then—nothing until now.

Do they know? He ran a hand over his face, reminding himself it wasn't a dream.

The door clicked open and Felix stepped in. He took one look at Killian and stuck his head back out, calling for Damian.

"Finally awake then?" Felix took a seat by the bed.

Killian nodded, suddenly afraid his speech hadn't changed as well.

Don't be stupid.

He attempted a question.

"How long have I been—human again?" He needn't have worried. His voice came out croaky from disuse, but it worked. His heart lurched in relief.

"Almost two days," Felix said. "And you've been here for almost four, including the solstice."

Killian shuddered. Noak had come so close to fulfilling his plans. "Where am I?"

"Our home. You're the first, and most likely the last, human to set foot in the faeries' mountain."

Killian blinked. "Is that allowed?"

"Our king is a little more understanding than the last one." Felix smirked. "He didn't raise an objection when Damian took a literal interpretation of our law, since you were still a wolf when he brought you here."

Killian grinned. It sounded like something Lars would have done. *Lars!* "How are the others?"

"Anxious for you to return."

"When can I?"

Felix shrugged. "That's up to the healer. All I know is, you're not dying anymore."

Killian chuckled. It felt so good to be able to laugh again. "That's helpful."

Felix winked. "I know. Damian will let your family know you're awake. Though I'd pray the healer has good news before Lars goes crazy with waiting."

Killian laughed again. Lars had never been a patient person. "How is he? He was wounded during the ambush."

For a moment, Lars's shocked and pain-filled expression flashed in his mind. The scent of blood had been so strong. *I should have sensed the ambush sooner!*

"Damian and I were able to help him. He should be healed by now."

"Thank you."

I wouldn't have forgiven myself otherwise.

Someone knocked on the door and Damian entered, joining Felix at the bedside.

"How are you feeling?"

"Not terrible."

Damian's face twisted in a smile. "Healer's on her way to check on you."

"Damian, how am I—human?"

"Rose."

"What?"

That makes no sense. She said she didn't have magic. But what did those trolls say?

"I said the witch was the only one who could break the curse." Damian crossed his arms, smiling. "Rose is a descendent of the witch. She considered the stipulations of the curse fulfilled. The king had repaid his debt."

"The only time he's enjoyed being wrong about something," Felix cut in with a grin.

Damian shoved his shoulder, but Felix barely moved. "I just wish I had realized the truth sooner. We'll let you rest and go tell your family."

"Thank you, for all of your help. I'm just glad that you don't have to figure how to help a wolf talk," Killian said.

Damian chuckled. "Me too."

Killian looked to Felix. "And thanks for protecting us."

Felix tipped one eye in a wink. "It wasn't quite the chore I expected."

Killian braced a hand against his side as a laugh broke free.

"Get some rest, Killian." Damian touched Killian's side and some of the pain eased.

Killian nodded and settled back against the pillow as the faeries exited the room. He stared up at the ceiling, tracing the swirling patterns. He remembered the gruff voice of his father at the end. *If only there'd been a way to save Uncle Hugo, too.*

He sighed and tried to adjust more comfortably. Despite the novelty of staying in a faery castle, he was ready to go see his family and Rose.

*

To Killian and Lars's mutual dismay, two more days passed before the healer allowed the former out of bed. The faeries gave him new clothes of incomparable quality and gave him permission to roam the hall outside his room, though they were reluctant to let him wander the mountain.

Finally. He swung his legs over the edge of the bed. *I'm about to go crazy if I stay in here any longer.*

He took a step and nearly tripped. He stared down in horror. *I knew the trap had damaged my leg. But this...*

The toes of his left foot dragged against the ground as he stumbled to the opposite wall. Killian braced one hand against the stone and stared down at his rebellious foot, his mind refusing to accept the truth.

Crippled.

The word haunted him. Gritting his teeth, he pushed away from the wall, clenching hands into fists as he limped back to the bed. His lower leg already ached as he sat down.

"Give it some time." Felix stood in the doorway.

Killian hadn't even heard the door open.

"I don't think time will make this better." Killian fisted the blanket in his hands. He hadn't noticed the injury as much as a wolf when he used three paws to balance instead of just one foot.

"You will get stronger, adapt to it. If you give up now, you'll never finish healing."

"Know this from experience?" He couldn't keep the bitterness from his voice. Felix looked the picture of health.

Felix huffed a faint laugh and opened his wings. Killian's breath froze. It should have been a proud sight, but holes punctured the shining membrane near the tips, large enough to cause an unnatural fold along the edge. Other small rents had been slashed along the edges.

I've never seen him fly!

"What happened?"

Felix's face remained impassive, his jaw clenching slightly, but he folded the wings away, and he sighed.

"Years ago, probably counted around Lars's age as you'd see it, I'd been commissioned to make a sword for one of the king's guard. I was a good smith, even then." Felix half-smiled. "But I was stuck, didn't know how I wanted to design it. So, I went for a walk in the woods. Damian and I would go out all the time, wander wherever we wanted. I didn't think twice."

He shifted between his feet, rolling his shoulders before continuing.

"But that day, I got caught by a Nameless One nowhere near where they usually lurk. He pinned me to the ground by my wings." He paused again. Killian's blood ran cold. Felix recited the story so matter-of-factly.

I was almost sacrificed by an insane man. I can't imagine getting tortured too.

"There are more scars. He took most of my magic. It was a long time before it came back. So, I had to learn how to function without it, and believe me, for a faery to lose magic—it's worse than your leg."

"Can—can you fly?" Killian hesitated over the question.

"I can fly for short distances. But it took time to learn and become strong enough. So, yes, I know from experience." Felix raised one shoulder and offered a faint smile. "And it turned me into the grumpy, withdrawn faery you see today. So, take it from someone who knows."

Killian took in a breath and stood again, wobbling a little as his left foot reluctantly accepted his weight. He walked again under Felix's watchful eye, accepting occasional help from the faery. By the time he made it back to the bed the third time, his leg and side ached.

"What if it doesn't get any better?" Killian let his shoulders droop. "What if I can't run or fight or—just become useless?"

Yet another reason for people to whisper about him.

"You only become useless if you choose to be." Felix leaned on the chair. "You have a life to live, Killian. Don't waste time worrying what others think."

"Is that what you do?" He tilted his head.

"I won't say it's easy." A slight grin touched Felix's face. "Ready to try again?"

Killian pushed to his feet.

One day at a time. Although I'll settle for being able to walk in a straight line when I see Father and Lars.

*

Two days later, the healer removed the bandages for the last time. Killian ran a hand across the red scar that traced his side. Even if it hadn't killed him, without the faery magic it would have taken months to heal. Other scars marked his shoulders and chest, and small scars from the fight with the mastiff marred his face.

I'm never going to look at those animals the same again. He shuddered at the memory.

Adela had left clothes cut in the Calvyrnian fashion and he dressed. Killian pulled on his new boots, refusing to stare at the slight twist in his left foot that would never vanish. Killian shut the door behind him, meeting Damian in the hall. He followed Damian through corridors and down steps, catching glimpses of other faeries in rooms crafted with beautiful care. He tried not to stare, but he'd never seen the like. Damian paused before a carven oak door.

"I'm probably not supposed to show you, but..." He cracked the door open and Killian stared in shocked amazement.

The faeries' great hall was a cavern in which his home could, no doubt, fit comfortably. Gems inlaid into stone pillars winked in the light of lanterns suspended from the ceiling. Tiles of dizzying shapes and colors swirled together in spiraling patterns, leaping from pillar to pillar across the floor. Two empty thrones graced the dais at the far end.

"It's even more impressive when prepared for a feast." Damian shut the door with a quiet click. "Come."

Killian followed in awed silence.

And I'm the only human to have ever seen this!

Damian took him down one more staircase to another door, opening it and allowing a rush of fresh air into the mountain. Killian stepped outside, breathing easier in the wide space of the outdoors. He glanced up at the slope of the mountain, catching the glint of windows and terraces in the sunlight.

A few steps later, Killian glanced back again and saw only tall pines and tumbled rocks littering the mountain.

"The veil is covering your sight now." Damian said. "You won't be able to find your way back ever again."

Killian turned away with a strange resignation that dissipated the further he walked until he had to remind himself why he felt sad.

After a time, Damian stopped to let Killian rest. He sank gratefully onto a fallen trunk, rubbing his aching leg. Excited chattering from above made him jump. Two squirrels circled a tree trunk, clambering and leaping on every available limb.

"There goes a faery. Lovely folk!"

"Aye, aye, aye. Oh, brilliant looking nut!"

"Oh, lovely!"

"Did you know Alpin's family knew a faery?"

"Great, great, great, great, great, great, great grandfather or something, wasn't it?"

"Aye, aye, aye."

Killian stumbled away from the tree, staring at the squirrels as they darted away.

"I can—understand them!" he stammered.

Damian laughed. "Once you hear the language of the animals, you can't forget it. I think you might find the curse left you with a few gifts."

Killian shook his head, focusing on listening to the forest. He'd retained the hearing of a wolf, catching the many conversations of the woods.

Including the sounds of horses and men. Killian tensed, a sudden irrational fear gripping his chest.

"Come." Damian rested a hand on his shoulder.

Damian urged him onward, but Killian fell a step behind. Lars hurried to greet Damian, a question dying on his lips as Damian stepped aside to reveal Killian.

Both brothers froze, staring at one another, until Lars lunged forward to hug Killian.

Lars pounded Killian on the back and held him at arm's length. "I'm going to miss those cute ears."

Killian rolled his eyes. "You're an idiot."

"I know." Lars chuckled, pulling him into another hug, before releasing him into their father's hold.

Killian fought the sudden rebellious dampness in his eyes, swiping it away before his father pulled back. Jonas cleared his throat in a futile attempt to speak, only to be saved by Einar.

"I think you grew a little, lad."

Killian laughed, but glanced down at himself with fresh eyes. Even just three weeks ago, he hadn't been able to look his uncle in the eye.

He found Rose loitering a few paces away, respectfully staying clear of the reunions. She cleared her throat and sniffed, eyeing him with barely-shrouded curiosity.

"Hello, Rose." *I can finally greet her properly.*

"Hello, Killian." She gave him a nervous smile. "It's good to see you."

"Thank you." *I hope she knows I mean for everything.*

Her pale cheeks flushed, and she glanced down at her boots before meeting his gaze again.

"You're welcome." She gave a small nod.

He fought quick disappointment at the hesitation that marked her speech. *I suppose it is a little jarring. She's only ever seen me as a wolf.*

Killian reached a hand to her father, who stood behind Rose with a protective hand on her shoulder.

"Thank you for your help." The words hardly seemed sufficient, but they would have to do for now.

"Just sorry I couldn't do more for you, Prince Killian. Glad t' see you human again."

Killian moved to find a place to sit and rest his leg, flinching as he caught Lars's dismayed stare.

"Killian..." Lars caught his shoulder.

Killian fought the urge to flee at the look of horror on his brother's face. Killian forced a smile instead.

"It was too late for the healer to do much with it. But it won't slow me down."

I won't let it.

Lars nodded, respect showing in his quick smile. Killian accepted his brother's help to sit on the ground and resisted the urge to rub his aching calf.

"I'm all right," he reassured Lars before he could start hovering.

Lars didn't appear convinced, so Killian changed the subject.

"What's the plan for going home?"

Lars settled next to him on the grass. "Father wants to leave tomorrow if you're able to make the trip."

"Good. I'm ready to go back."

"Are you ready for the tales of the Wolf Prince?" Lars nudged his shoulder.

Killian tilted his head back against the tree with a groan.

"Well, anything will be better than what people said before. There's no more curse now."

"True." Lars sighed. "Killian, I—I'm sorry there were days I paid too much attention to the whispers."

"I know," Killian said softly. "But I won't blame you. I let it govern my life to the point that changing to a wolf was the first time I'd felt free."

"I had no idea," Lars murmured.

Killian smiled wryly. "Who was I supposed to tell that to?"

"You should have been able to tell me."

"Forget the past, Lars. We can't change it. I'm just grateful you won't have to sneak off to visit your wolf brother."

"Don't tell me you were planning on staying in the forest?" Lars raised an eyebrow.

Killian rolled his eyes. "It would have been more than a little awkward to have me wandering the castle as a wolf."

"But state and family dinners would be less boring."

Killian shoved his shoulder. "I thought you were being more responsible now. You can't call them that."

"No change of heart is going to make them interesting." Lars punched his arm.

Killian chuckled and settled back against a tree.

"Though, if things get too tedious, I'm sure there are plenty of Baedon sightings to investigate," Lars said.

Killian laughed. Although the next time he'd have weapons in hand, he'd be happy to never face one again. "Think Rose will go with us?"

"It's going to be quiet without her." Lars smiled. "But I had an idea."

Chapter 33

Killian sat back and watched everyone pack up camp with a certain degree of helplessness. He had nothing to pack. It was an odd feeling to have nothing but the clothes on his back.

The horses murmured to one another, speculating on the journey home. Killian made a pointed effort not to look their direction. He hadn't let anyone know yet about the residual effects of the curse.

His enhanced hearing picked up three different sets of whispering footsteps. He was familiar with the faeries' tread by now and pushed to his feet, debating on alerting his father until they were closer.

Kaspar beat him to the news. But he couldn't have heard the faeries yet.

"I don't know how he does it, either." Rose stepped up beside him, following his gaze to her father.

"How did...?"

Pink tinged her nose. "You tilt your head a bit t' the side when you're focused on something. You did it before, too." He raised his eyes to the sky. "Perfect. Now I'll have to figure out if I did that before the curse or if it's another charming residual trait."

She giggled. "Don't worry. I don't think anyone's noticed yet."

He raised an eyebrow. "Lars will eventually."

"Sorry?" She lifted one shoulder.

A smile teased Killian's lips. "No, you're not. You probably think it's hilarious."

She had the grace to add a hint of apology to her wide grin. "I won't tell anyone."

"Thank you."

"For what?" Lars paused beside them, rubbing his side. Their father had forbidden him from helping break camp at the first sign of a grimace.

"Agreeing that you are getting ridiculous about your tea drinking." Killian easily ducked Lars's swipe.

"What? No, I—he's not wrong." Rose took a step back as Lars turned on her. "You know my grandmother loved tea."

Lars shook his head with a rueful grin. "I don't know if it's a good idea you two can understand each other."

Killian and Rose shared a laugh.

"You tell her yet?" Killian tipped a nod in her direction.

Rose stiffened, glancing between them. "Tell me what?"

"You may or may not recall a conversation when we first met where you called me ignorant." Lars crossed his arms.

Killian bit the inside of his cheek to stop his laugh. True or not, it wouldn't do to ruin the surprise.

Rose opened and shut her mouth a few times, then squeaked, "Yes."

"I think we can all agree you were right. You also happened to mention Ranger law."

Her eyes began to widen, and she looked back and forth between them.

If he doesn't hurry up and tell her, she's going to burst.

"I spoke with your father last night to make sure there was nothing that would prevent someone, say a young woman, from joining." Lars struggled to contain his grin. Killian made no effort to hide his own smile as Rose searched for something to say.

"You mean...?"

"I mean that when I need a Ranger I can trust, I'd rather call on you."

She clapped a hand to her mouth. "Lars, I—"

"I'm also going to need some good Ranger captains one of these days," Lars said.

"Captain? Oh, I don't know if I'd make it that far." She shook her head. "I have t' make it through training first."

"Why not? I bet on you becoming commander." Killian smirked. "You've gotten enough practice bossing us around this trip."

Rose laughed as she flicked a hand over her eyes, surprising them both with quick hugs.

"You knew about this?" She glanced up at her father as he joined them.

"I've known your dream for a while now," Kaspar said. "But I was more than happy t' have Prince Lars help you out."

Her smile threatened to split her face. "I won't let any of you down."

"Hope not." Lars smirked.

"If you change your mind, we could use someone to hunt Baedons and Wyverns with," Killian said.

Rose shook her head. "No, thank you. You boys are on your own."

Kasper chuckled. "Those faeries are here."

Lars and Rose sent Kaspar a slightly exasperated look. *How could they possibly have missed the faeries' approach?*

Kasper sent him a knowing look and Killian ducked his head. *So, someone has noticed.*

The faeries entered the clearing, greeting Jonas first out of respect before seeking out the trio for a last farewell. Adela embraced them all, brushing her hand across their foreheads. Killian shivered from head to toe at the touch of her magic.

"I hope this isn't the last time we see each other." She stepped back with a smile.

Damian clasped each of their hands. "Remember what I said," he told Killian. "Gifts shouldn't be feared."

He moved to Rose, smiling gently. "Trust your instincts. A Ranger needs them to survive." Rose smiled and nodded as he turned to Lars. "I've no doubt you'll make a good ruler. Just don't forget what you've learned here."

"I won't." Lars clasped his hand.

Felix hung back, looking a bit uncomfortable as he pulled three knives from the bag at his side. Killian took the blade Felix handed him, rubbing a hand across the embossed sheath before pulling the knife free.

A small wolf, engraved hear the hilt, howled at an invisible moon. On the opposite side, Felix had etched two runes.

"It's beautiful." Rose turned her knife over in her hands. A wolf ran along her blade.

Lars tested the edge of his blade where a wolf leapt along its length.

For once, Felix seemed at a loss for words. "The — um — blade will never dull, and you won't ever lose them." He fidgeted with the bag's strap.

"Amazing." Killian tossed it high enough to catch, and it balanced perfectly in his hand as it landed. "Thank you."

A smile cracked Felix's frown as Lars echoed Killian. His smile vanished into wide-eyed shock as Rose surprised him with a quick hug. Even Damian looked stunned, but Felix patted her shoulder.

He finally shooed her away with a barely-suppressed smirk and eye roll. "Just be careful with those."

The faeries said one last farewell before vanishing back into the forest.

"Part of me still doesn't quite believe all this." Rose sheathed her knife.

Killian nodded. The last three weeks occasionally seemed like a strange dream. *Except for my new — abilities.*

They reached the edge of the forest by late afternoon, entering Moss to obtain four new horses for the trio and Kaspar. The townsfolk threw strange looks Killian's way and he ducked his head.

Odd one out again. They don't remember me with any of the others. I hope they don't put it together.

Lars took the news they could return to Sandnes for Jeppe with relief. But apprehension bubbled in Killian's stomach as his father gave permission. The village was the origin of the wolf prince tale. He wasn't sure he wanted to ride back and give fresh life to the story.

Three days after leaving Moss, they splashed across the ford and parted ways with their father and Einar, who, along with most of the knights, would return to the castle in order to placate his father's anxious council. Killian, Lars, and Rose remained with Kasper and two knights to fetch Jeppe.

Along the river, they found no sign of Kaja, but a mile up from the ford, Lars pointed at the heron that circled above them. Killian shielded his eyes against the sunlight and caught the whisper of a blessing in the wind before the heron dove towards the river, skimming the water and vanishing.

The closer they came to Sandnes, the more Rose and Lars appeared to share the same apprehension. Lars's hands remained tight on the reins, and Rose's laugh came too quick or loud.

There wasn't much to do when the thatched roofs came into view and villagers ran from the field to announce their arrival.

Killian tugged at the reins until he gradually fell to the rear of the small group.

Adam was the first to greet them with a low bow. "Prince Lars."

Lars dismounted and clasped his hand in greeting. Adam's eyes widened, but he returned the gesture.

"We couldn't believe t' tale Sir Einar brought, your highness," he said.

"I had trouble enough believing it myself. You seem to have done well since we left." Lars glanced around the town square.

Killian silently agreed. The stale scent of fear was gone, and the fields had an ordered look. Killian slid from his horse, catching a young girl staring at him with a frown of concentration. He offered a tentative smile. She frowned deeper and whirled away to whisper something in another child's ear.

"Ah, Rose! Good t' see you, lass!" Adam caught her hand as she joined Lars. "Now then, since you're back..." He looked over their troop and Killian resisted the urge to run. Instead he limped forward.

Can't put this off any longer. Here goes the rest of my life as just Killian.

"Good to see you again, Adam," he said.

Adam's eyes widened. "By t' Creator!" He bowed again. "Prince Killian! Glad t' see you alive and — human."

"Thank you." Killian nodded as a murmur of surprise ran through the onlookers, as if they hadn't really believed it was him.

Adam shook his head. "How long will you be here?"

"I'm afraid we can't stay long," Lars said. "We leave tomorrow."

"The inn is at your disposal," Adam offered. "We'd feast with you again, but knowing you're royals, it'll be poor fare t' you."

"We'd be honored," Lars assured him.

He means it. Killian watched his brother with a hint of pride. *Though I know I'd rather feast with these people than the nobles at the castle.*

A wide smile deepened the creases of Adam's face and he sent a stableboy to care for their horses. Marten pushed past Adam to bow to Lars.

"Will you want t' see your stallion, sire?"

"Yes!" Lars grinned. "How is he?"

"Recovering well. I took 'im out for some easy rides t' last few days. Hope you don't mind?" Marten winced.

"Not at all. He's in the stables?" Lars strode towards the building.

Marten nodded, and Killian fell into step beside him, adopting a more dignified pace. *Who knows what Jeppe will do once he sees Lars?*

The stable shook with Jeppe's thunderous neighs as they entered.

"You came back! All in one piece? Don't tell me that was what you were riding?"

"Jeppe!" Lars caught the stallion's halter, rubbing his broad white blaze.

"You're not leaving me this time." Jeppe bumped Lars's chest with his nose. "Marten says I'm recovered, as if I was injured before!"

Killian bit back a snicker. Lars stepped into the stall to run his hand over the silver scars streaking across Jeppe's hindquarters.

"How do they look?" Killian stepped up to lean on the stall. Jeppe wrenched his head around as he caught Killian's scent. He received Jeppe's nose in his face.

"Killian! You're back on two legs! Leifr will be pleased."

Killian scratched under the stallion's jaw and tried to focus on Lars's one-sided mutterings.

"They closed well. Doesn't look like he lost too much muscle. Probably shouldn't ride him back, though."

"The other side could use a scratch." Jeppe butted his hand.

Killian nodded and switched sides. Jeppe's nose immediately shoved back into his face.

"You can still understand me! Can't you? Can't you?"

Killian tried to move away, but Jeppe wouldn't allow him to dodge his whiskered muzzle.

"Yes, fine, I can!" Killian glared at the contrary animal and shoved its nose away.

"Can what?" Lars looked over in confusion.

Jeppe nickered smugly and Killian's face warmed.

"Killi, can what?" Lars's eyes narrowed.

"Nothing."

Jeppe nickered again.

"Oh, just shut up," he muttered.

"You can…?" Lars pointed between him and Jeppe, his eyes wide with alarm.

Killian leaned on the stall in defeat, nodding. "Damian said because I'd heard the language of the animals, I'd never forget it. He also said I'd have some other 'gifts' from the curse."

"Like what?"

Killian shrugged, letting his head slump to rest on his arms.

"All things considered, it's not a bad thing to be able to do." Lars nudged his shoulder.

"Maybe I just wanted to be normal." It was a petty statement, but it slipped out anyway.

"So, don't tell anyone?"

"It's not something you mention in everyday conversation, is it?"

Lars chuckled, giving Jeppe a last pat and stepping out of the stall.

"He threatened to buck you off next time you got on, by the way." Killian hooked a hand into his belt and returned Jeppe's satisfied expression.

Lars whirled on Jeppe, who backed up a step, tilting his nose up in smug aloofness.

"I'll just leave you here then." Lars glared at the stallion.

"Don't you dare!" Jeppe leaned over the stall barricade to nip at Lars's arm.

"Do I want to know?"

"No." Killian pushed off the stall.

Lars chuckled, giving Jeppe a loving slap on the nose and earning a placated rumble.

*

"It'll be t' pride of this village for generations t' come that we hosted royalty. Twice!" Adam beamed at Lars and Killian over beakers of the town's finest.

Now that Killian could more easily partake in the celebration, it seemed like everyone wanted to make sure he tried everything he had missed last time. By contrast, Lars kept hold of the same beaker, making the contents last for an impressive time length of time.

Killian avoided a second helping of pie from the baker's wife, stepping away from the bonfire to find a moment of peace. But a small tug on his tunic shattered the illusion. The girl from that afternoon peered up at him. Two other children loitered nearby.

She glanced at them for support before blurting, "Were you really a wolf?"

Killian crouched down to eye level with her. "I was. Birte, isn't it?"

She clasped her hands in delight. "You remember me! I knew it was you!"

Killian was forced to smile as she dashed off to tell the others, but she ran back just as quick. "Did you like being a wolf?"

"Sometimes," he admitted.

"Did a sorcerer really turn you into a wolf?"

"He did."

"Was 'e scary?"

Killian nodded. He'd rather not think about Noak.

"Did you eat 'im?"

"What?" He supposed it was a somewhat logical question, if rather bloodthirsty. "No, actually Lars beat him."

Birte turned to stare at Lars, who was standing across the square with the innkeeper, engaged in a serious conversation.

"Did Rose help?"

"She did, just like when we fought the Baedons."

Birte nodded. "We wanted t' know for when we play t' Wolf Prince."

Questions answered, she ran off with the others, stopping to steal sweets before vanishing with a war cry.

He stood with a shake of his head. He never thought he'd inspire a tale grand enough to warrant retellings by children. He and Lars had re-enacted tales of heroes as children. *But I don't fit into that category.*

"There you are!" Rose found him as the fiddles struck up a new tune. "How about a real dance this time?"

Killian set his empty beaker down and accepted her hand. "You'll have to re-teach me."

"Don't worry, I'm better at teaching partners with two feet." She winked.

"Hilarious." He rolled his eyes as she laughed.

Rose had apparently spent her time convincing the young women of the village that the wolf prince wouldn't bite, judging by the abundance of dance partners as the celebration continued.

Lars also allowed himself to be dragged into the dancing throughout the night. Killian escaped another partner to join him by the drink tables.

"This is testing my resolve not to drink any more tonight." Lars said as he turned away another hopeful dance partner.

"But she had green eyes." Killian barely repressed a snicker. Lars grabbed him in a headlock. Killian elbowed him in the stomach. Lars released him with a last tousle to his hair.

"But really? Think Pauline will be glad to see you?" Killian gave up trying to fix his hair. *I'd bet good money she will. You're finally taking every piece of advice she's ever given.*

Lars sighed, his shoulders slumping. "Maybe. I probably ruined everything—again—by running off. You know me."

Killian nudged his shoulder. "Need me to give her the sad dog eyes?"

Lars snorted a laugh and shook his head. "Can't let you jump in on all my fights, can I?"

"I'm your brother, idiot. What else do you think I'm here for?"

Lars chuckled and tapped his arm in a light punch. "I know."

Adam stumbled over, beaming at the two of them. "You boys need anything? Another drink?" He raised an eyebrow at Killian.

"No, thanks," Killian said. "It's getting late."

"Late?" Adam frowned. "It's barely midnight!"

Two hours ago. Though I think this is the longest I've ever stayed at a party.

Adam gave an unsteady bow and linked arms with his wife and returned to the dancing.

"What have you and Adam been talking about?" Killian asked.

"I asked him what I could do to help the village, and others around here. Turns out there's a lot that can be improved now that I've stopped to ask." Lars rubbed the back of his neck.

"Lars, you can't take responsibility for that. I hate to say it, but Father hasn't done anything to help either. But now you know and can do something about it."

Lars took a breath and squared his shoulders. "You really think I can?"

Killian met his gaze. "I've always known you can. But now I believe it."

Lars tilted a smile. "Thanks."

"You going to start crying on my shoulder?"

Lars rolled his eyes and shoved him a step away. "Go play the part of the dashing prince for once and go rescue Rose. She's under attack from her awestruck admirers again."

Chapter 34

Killian stared at the fried bread and chunk of cooked gazelle on his plate. His stomach rebelled at the thought of eating the cooked meat. He shook his head and the feeling passed.

Is it always going to be like this? I hope that one of the 'gifts' isn't a taste for raw meat. He suppressed a shudder. But the food looked more appetizing now in the fading light of evening.

"Need anything, your highness?" One of the knights had noticed his hesitation.

Killian jerked his gaze up to meet the man's. "No. Thanks."

"You all right?" Lars asked, brow furrowed in concern as he and Rose settled in on either side of him with their own plates.

"I'm fine." Killian forced a smile.

"Sure?" Rose prodded his foot with the toe of her boot.

Killian rolled his shoulders back and tore a chunk of meat away. "You're annoyingly observant."

She flashed a pleased smile and crunched a bite of bread. "Well?" Lars pushed.

"Just—you know—still trying to get used to human food again," Killian admitted.

"At least she washed her hands before cooking this time." Lars smirked.

Rose widened her eyes in mock outrage and flicked bread crumbs at Lars.

"No respect, this one." Lars shook his head.

Killian cut another bite away. His stomach settled and called greedily for more. Jeppe wandered over and nosed at Lars's hand.

Sandnes lay a day's journey behind them, but the stallion had gamely trotted alongside them the entire way, having assured Killian he would only go with Lars. Even at camp, he remained unhobbled like the other horses. Though from the way he eyed Lars's bread, Killian suspected he had ulterior motives for promising good behavior.

"You'll make 'im fat!" Rose protested as Lars gave Jeppe the lion's share of his bread.

"He will not." Jeppe lipped at Lars's arm.

"He was wounded. He's still recovering," Lars protested, reaching up to scratch Jeppe's chest. Jeppe lipped fondly at his hair in return.

Rose rolled her eyes. "He has. In a nice comfy stable."

Killian laughed as he stretched his leg out. Spending the day crammed into a stirrup had brought the ache back.

Rose and Lars continued their friendly bickering, and Killian tilted his head back to glance at the first stars that began to appear. He found the white wolf curled around the waning moon.

I'll miss this. Maybe even miss the wolf a little. The realization came as a light shock.

Rose's clear laugh brought a smile to his face. *And I'll miss her and that refreshing honesty. She might even be one of the first real friends we've ever had.*

"Killian! Convince her to come along on our first wyvern hunt." Lars interrupted his thoughts.

Killian glanced at Rose, who shook her head with pursed lips.

"You get first pick from the treasure trove," Killian said.

She tilted her head back, considering. "What's my share?"

"Definitely the smaller one."

She swatted at his shoulder with a laugh. "Knowing you boys, I'll end up doing most of t' work."

"What if I promise we'll just go after *one* wyvern at a time?" Lars asked with a grin.

"Famous last words."

"Credit for the kill?" Killian offered, holding up a hand to forestall Lars's protest.

She sat back, crossing her arms. "You have my interest."

"Your name first," Lars said.

She tapped her chin. "Perhaps I can be persuaded. And when are you planning this grand adventure?"

"Well." Lars sighed. "I don't think our respective parents will be letting us out of their sight anytime soon."

"Not a chance, sir," Kaspar called from his place by the fire.

Rose giggled and licked her fingers. "Though it wouldn't be t' first time I've snuck out. I'm sure it wouldn't be too hard t' come rescue you two damsels in distress."

"Lars, maybe." Killian tossed a smirk, righting himself from Lars's shove as Rose snickered.

"So, is that a 'yes' to hunting with us?" Lars asked.

"It's a maybe."

"So a 'yes'," Killian said.

Rose rolled her eyes. "Let's get home without running into any other creatures, and I'll consider it."

Lars and Killian exchanged a triumphant glance. *It's a yes.*

*

Lagarah Forest came into view when they halted at a crossroads. Killian and Lars would continue north into the forest to Roskalde Castle, but Rose and her father would travel east to the Ranger headquarters hidden in the eastern section of the woods.

They stood in silence, staring at each other without words, before Rose moved first, hugging Lars.

"Thank you for tolerating an aspiring apprentice Ranger."

Lars chuckled and released her. "Thank you for tolerating a rather ignorant prince."

Rose smiled. "Not sure which of us had it worse."

"Probably you," Lars admitted.

They shared a laugh and Killian accepted her hug.

"We wouldn't have made it without you." He smiled at her.

A blush tinged her nose and she struggled for words.

"If you need anything, don't hesitate to ask us," Lars broke in.

"You boys know if you need a Ranger, or even just a friend, for anything, I'll be there?"

"Same here," Killian said, speaking for both of them.

Rose nodded, sniffing as she mounted and joined her father down the road. She gave one last wave before disappearing into the dust.

Killian and Lars spurred their mounts into the woods, taking the road that led them directly to the castle. They arrived at the lake as the sun touched the western sky. The castle gleamed in the light, framed on the hill by a sky of pinks, blues, and oranges.

They had not even made it to the path that twisted up the hill when horns began to sound their arrival. Killian and Lars exchanged a grin and urged the horses up the road as fast as safety would allow.

Grooms hastened to take their horses in the gathering commotion of the courtyard. Everyone wanted a glimpse of the returned princes, but Killian only cared about the figures waiting for them at the head of the keep's stairs.

Queen Aina crushed Killian in her embrace and he even suffered her kiss. Jonas dragged him in for a hug even though it had been less than a week since they'd last seen each other.

The rest of the castle was destined to wait for the tale as the royal family withdrew for a private meal. It was late by the time the story had been told to Aina's satisfaction and she was willing to let her sons out of her sight.

Killian let out an exhausted sigh as he stepped out onto the walls to breathe the clean night air. A wolf's howl echoed across the lake. He leaned against the battlement and listened to the exuberant calls of the pack to one another. *The grey wolf's pack.* It took on a new feeling now that he could understand their calls. Part of him would always regret not joining them. But only a very small part. Boots scuffed the walkway as Lars joined him. "I keep telling myself they sound different now." He crossed his arms on the battlement and rested his chin atop them.

"Me too." Killian stared at the rippling reflection of the moon in the lake.

"It's a full moon tonight." Lars's voice was suspiciously calm.

It only took Killian a moment to catch on. "Hilarious."

"I just thought I'd point it out, in case you felt you needed to express yourself."

"I'm not a wolf anymore, idiot. And wolves howl all the time."

"Well, you would know."

Killian shoved him away, and Lars regained his balance with a laugh.

"I noticed a certain someone was very happy to see you." Killian shot his older brother a sly glance. "There might even have been tears."

Lars reached over and tousled his hair before Killian could duck away.

"Good night, Killian." Lars retreated from the walls.

Killian shook his head and lingered a few minutes longer. One last call filled the night and Killian smiled as the wolves welcomed their human brother back to the forest.

Epilogue

"And that's the true story of the Wolf Prince."

Killian paused outside the family solar, leaning against the doorframe to watch the occupants. A green-eyed lady leaned towards the two small children sitting cross-legged on the rug before her.

"And Muvver became a captain!" The auburn-haired boy declared triumphantly.

The woman smiled. "That she did. And she should be back with your uncle and father soon." She tapped the other boy's nose.

"Or she would if your father wasn't trying to convince her to stay longer."

"Uncle Killian!"

Both boys leapt to their feet and darted over. Killian laughed and crouched to give them hugs.

"Did you get the wyvern?" The green-eyed boy asked eagerly.

"We did." Killian reached into the pocket of his travel-stained tunic and pulled out two glittering blue scales.

The boys took them reverently, cradling them in small hands.

"Do I want to hear the story?" Pauline rested a hand on her son's head, leveling a pointed stare at the bandage peeking out from under his left sleeve.

"We're all in one piece."

She shook her head. "You three will be the death of me one day."

"We're perfectly fine!" Lars strode into the solar, pulling her in for a kiss. She pursed her lips and swatted at his chest.

"Rose, I want the real story later."

Rose swept up her son and planted a kiss in his red curls. "Of course." She grinned.

"Uncle Killian." His nephew tugged on his tunic. "Can you really change back into a wolf if you want like everyone says?"

Killian hesitated, glancing at the adults. No one outside the room knew the truth for certain. Lars lifted one shoulder in a shrug.

"That would be something, wouldn't it?" Killian said instead.

"I know you can talk t' animals." The red-haired boy announced gleefully from Rose's arms.

Killian crossed his arms. "You do, eh?"

"I saw you talking t' Leifr before you left. What did he say?"

"That he expects you to bring him more carrots next time you visit." Killian reached over and tweaked his nose. The boy grinned and twisted away.

"Are we staying?" He looked up to Rose, his eyes wide in pleading.

"We need to get back home. Your father should be back from his patrol by now," Rose said.

"Muvver, I want t' be a knight!"

"And I want to be a Ranger!"

Their parents laughed.

"Being a knight will be up t' your Uncle Lars." Rose ruffled the boy's hair.

"I'm always on the lookout for new knights. But you have to train hard first." Lars frowned mock seriously.

"I will!" his adoptive nephew promised earnestly.

"Aunt Rose, will you train me?" Lars's son asked.

"Of course! As if I'd let any other Ranger train you." Rose smiled down at him, keeping hold of her son as he attempted to squirm down from her arms to go play at his intended profession.

Pauline gave her a quick hug and kissed the boy's head. "We'll see you soon."

"Did you do all t' work again?" Her son asked as she left the solar.

She tossed a grin back at Killian and Lars. "Of course."

They laughed, and Killian took his leave, allowing a smile as the old grey wolf howled in the distance. The stories surrounding him had taken on a slightly more positive note over the years, and there were many tavern bets as to whether he truly could shift back to wolf's form at will or talk to animals.

No one will ever know.

*

Rose's oldest son became a knight, serving in the Brigade that had been brought to new distinction under King Lars. Her second son became a Ranger like his parents. Lars and Pauline's three children were trained by Rose in the tradition of the king's line.

When Killian married, he took a holding in the southwest of Calvyrn, where Celedon Forest spread across the borders. Rumor held that some of his strange abilities passed to his children. Long after the castle was abandoned, wolves remained to guard the ruins.

All three companions lived long beyond normal age, having been touched by faery magic. Felix's knives were passed down the generations, keeping their descendants linked. There were even those who spoke of the Myrnian faery who blessed their children, but perhaps that is a story for another time.

The End

Winterspell

The Faeries of Myrnius Book 3
Coming Soon!

Acknowledgments

As always, to my family, who never fails to support me in my writing endeavors. I wouldn't have made it this far without each and every one of you.

To my brilliant editor, Katie Philips, who helped me transform this story into something amazing. You knew how to push me to level up this story in so many ways.

To my brilliant beta readers. Thanks for believing in this story and giving me awesome feedback. You keep inspiring me to write.

To all the people who kept asking when my next book was coming out. I hope this doesn't disappoint.

And to Rachael and LoriAnn, who produced the formatting and cover designs to make this book epic. I would be completely lost without you

More books by Claire M. Banschbach

Book One of The Faeries of Myrnius Series

THE FAERIES OF MYRNIUS
BOOK I

ADELA'S CURSE

CLAIRE M. BANSCHBACH

𝓐 curse. A murderous scheme. A choice.

A witch and her master capture a young faery and command her to kill their enemy. Adela has no choice but to obey. If she does not, they will force the location of her people's mountain home from her and kill her. To make matters even worse, the person she is to kill is only a man struggling to save his dying land and mend a broken heart.

Count Stefan is a man simply trying to forget the woman he loves and save a land crippled by drought. When a mysterious woman arrives at his castle claiming to be a seamstress, he knows she is more than she seems.

Adela enlists the help of Damian, another faery, to try and delay the inevitable. He insists she has a choice. But with the witch controlling her every move, does she?

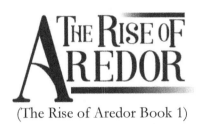

(The Rise of Aredor Book 1)

Lost in a foreign land and separated from his family, Corin does his best to survive as a slave in the household of a Calorin lord. With newfound friends he fights for survival in ambushes and wars. For one act of bravery, he is awarded his freedom and returns to a home that has been invaded and ravaged by the Calorin armies. When Corin sets foot on Aredor's shores, he has one goal in mind: find his family. He is driven into the forest, where he is reunited with childhood friends. From the shelter of the woods, they begin a spirited rebellion against Corin's former cruel master, who now holds sway over Aredor. Follow Corin's path in his quest to free his imprisoned brother, find a father who has vanished, and ultimately free his country in The Rise of Aredor.

THE WILDCAT OF BRAETON

(The Rise of Aredor Book 2)

His term of service to Lord Rishdah now complete, Aiden returns to his home in Braeton. As he travels he hears rumors that trouble plagues Braeton. Clan Canich is being attacked from within. He arrives, determined to save his father, his brothers, and his Clan from the treachery of one man.

A year has passed since the Calorins were driven from Aredor and Corin is struggling to rebuild his country. Despite the peace, a fear haunts him that the Calorins aren't far away. The Hawk Flight takes to the forest again to defend the borders against a possible attack from the neighboring country of Durna and its Calorin ally.

As Aiden and Corin struggle to adapt to their new lives they know one thing for certain - war is coming to the North!

About the Author

CLAIRE M. BANSCHBACH is a native West Texan. She discovered a deep and abiding love for fantasy and science fiction at a young age, prompting her to begin exploring worlds as a teen armed only with an overactive imagination and a pen. She's an overall dork, pizza addict, and fangirl. She enjoys meshing stories of family and faith with healthy doses of action and adventure. She talks to fictional characters more than she should while trying to find time for all their stories. She currently resides in Arlington, TX where she works as a Pediatric Physical Therapist.

You can find out more about her and discover short stories, writing updates, and a fun mailing list on her blog clairembanschbach.wordpress.com.

She loves to connect with readers on Facebook and Twitter where you can find dorky life and writing updates.

Twitter: twitter.com/cmbanschbach
Facebook: facebook.com/clairembanschbach/
Instagram: instagram.com/cmbanschbach/